Fox Tale

by

Karen Hulene Bartell

Sacred Emblems Series

Dedication

To Peter Bartell, my travel partner through Japan and life.

Prologue—Kyoto, Japan

Sunday Afternoon

Why risk my neck? Knees shaking, I willed one foot in front of the other as I fought my fear of heights. *Because if I want this assignment, I have no choice.*

Ignoring any survival instincts, I pried my gaze from the rocky path to Mount Inari's sheer granite wall, and the view took away my breath. Inches ahead, the clouds hung vertically—an immense, lacy veil shrouding the mountain. I stepped closer, reaching out as if in a 3D theater.

Suddenly, loose stones gave way, rolling underfoot like ball bearings. Thrown off-balance, I lurched forward, grasping for a bush or tree—anything to break my fall.

With nothing in reach, I wobbled sideways on the ledge, balancing my arms like a tightrope walker, then teetered as my toes tipped over the edge. Adrenaline spiked when more pebbles slipped beneath my shoes, ricocheting off stony outcrops far below. I stumbled, and time braked to a slow-motion video. As I lost my footing, I shrieked, the sound cutting through the mountain's hush.

Birds took flight, their cries and flapping wings resonating against the hollow echo.

Are these the last sounds I'll hear?

"Hold on!" An arm reached through the swirling mists and yanked me back to solid ground.

I breathed a silent prayer as I regained my footing. *That was close, too close.* Hands trembling, I wiped the perspiration from my forehead.

My rescuer's shoulder and torso emerged from the haze first, then his face—strong jawline, tanned complexion, and a silver shock of thick hair.

Piercing blue eyes met mine—haunting, violet-blue eyes—the exact shade as the Siamese kitten's…

"Are you all right?" His brow puckered.

"Yes, I didn't realize how close I was to the edge." Still gulping air, I smiled my gratitude. "Thank you for catching me."

"Glad I was in the right place at the right time." He shrugged, downplaying his role.

"The fog's so thick near the ground, it hid the drop-off."

"Fog." The corners of his almond-shaped eyes crinkled. "What is it but low-lying clouds? Climbing this mountain, you're literally walking in the clouds."

The description seemed poetic until I glanced about. Visibility was inches, maybe a foot in any direction. I reached into the thick vapor, and my fingertips vanished in wisps of saturated air. *On a mountain, hidden from view…with someone I just met.* Whimsy fled while I traded my fear of heights for fear of strangers. *Can I trust him?*

Though he'd probably saved my neck, I was wary as I appraised his sharply creased trousers and crisp, buttoned-down shirt. Impeccably groomed, he looked fortyish, had an athletic build, and stood several inches above me. I craned my neck to better see his face: A finely chiseled chin, upturned nose, and pointed, foxlike ears. Only his hooded eyes with their slight angle gave away his Asian heritage, and a phrase came to mind: *silver fox.*

The mist billowed, enfolding me in its moist embrace. As its dewy tendrils wrapped me in an airy cocoon, I listened to my senses. *Yes, I can trust him.*

His cheekbones rose in a subtle smile. "I'm Ichiro Sato, but call me Chase."

"Ichiro..." I rolled the word over my tongue. "What's it mean?"

"Firstborn son. It's a popular Japanese name."

"My name's Ava West—"

"Notice the path on your left to *Shimosha Shinseki.*" A guide's microphoned spiel signaled an advancing tour. "*Inariyama* is a mountain shrine, where deities coexist with nature." Footsteps pounding, the group descended like a flock of chittering crows in a cacophony of conversations.

I eyed the narrow trail as I stifled a groan. *Nowhere to pass. I'll get stuck behind this slow-moving crowd.* "Thanks again for saving me from a bad spill." I grimaced an apology. "Sorry to rush off, but I'm on a hard deadline."

"For what?" His eyes widened.

"After touring the shrine, I have to dash back to my hotel to write an article."

He tilted his head. "For a newspaper feature?"

"Online magazine. I'm the new food and travel correspondent." Still reeling at my luck in landing the job, I tried to keep the excitement from my voice. "It's my first international assignment, 'Kickin' Around Kyoto.' "

"Then be sure to include tonight's lantern festival—*Yoimiya*." His eyes flickered like blue flames. "Between the thousands of red, glowing lanterns and the pounding *taiko* drums, this sacred mountain's heart seems to beat."

How poetic. "That's *exactly* the kind of story the magazine wants." Resenting my tight schedule, I swallowed a sigh. "Wish I had time."

"The festival doesn't start until six. You've got plenty of time."

"Not really." I glanced at my phone's app. "Based on my pedometer, I'm only a quarter of the way up the shrine's twelve thousand steps."

"*Make* time." A nod emphasized his words. "Grab opportunities when you find them."

"Wish I could…" Shrill laughter drew my attention as the tour group closed in.

"How would you like to see the shrine *and* join tonight's festival?"

I checked my watch. Squinting, I debated. *Grab opportunities when you find them…*

The approaching crowd's din increased the sense of urgency.

"I know a shortcut." His chin high, he challenged me with an impudent smile, then pointed to a vertical path behind a minor shrine.

Should I follow him? Conventional wisdom shook its head *no*, while instinct whispered *go*.

"It's steep but faster than the main trail." His eyes danced. "And we'll avoid the tour groups…"

His offer tempting, I gauged the stairs' sharp angle of ascent. "But heights make me dizzy."

"Don't worry. I'll catch you if you stumble." He gestured to the narrow stairway, palm up. "Ladies first."

4

I sucked in my breath, gathering courage, then started the climb. Each step a test of will, I became lightheaded from hyperventilating.

"Did you know *Fushimi Inari* was established in 711 AD?"

"That long ago?" Hiking single file, I spoke over my shoulder, focusing on his voice rather than the rising elevation.

His conversation engaged me as I mounted the seemingly endless series of steps, and my panic gradually subsided.

When the path finally merged with the main route, I glanced behind at the distance we had covered and staggered. Then steadying myself against a boulder, I shot him a grateful smile. *He kept me so distracted during the climb, I forgot my fears.*

He pointed to the double rows of pillars flanking the trail. "Those are *torii*—traditional Japanese gates."

"Gates?" I searched the immense columns for swinging doors or turnstiles but saw nothing that resembled hinged gates.

"See the crosspieces at the tops, connecting the posts? These gates separate the secular from the sacred."

I nodded as I studied the sunlight and shadows' interplay on the scarlet-red pillars. "They're such a vivid shade."

"It's called *shuiro,* the color of the sun."

"Of course, Japan's the Land of the Rising Sun." Thumping my palm against my forehead, I studied the statues beside the pillars. "And why are these stone foxes here?"

"Ah…" He peered into my face as if assessing me. "They're *kitsune,* messengers of the Shinto god *Inari.*"

"Foxes? Why?"

"In nature, foxes are cunning animals, but building on the idea that *kitsune* are envoys, they assist in all areas of life—health, happiness, love…and especially wealth."

The effect unnerving, his relentless gaze invaded my space, my senses.

"Wouldn't *you* want a clever fox on your side in the precarious world of business?"

I squinted at his *non sequitur*. "What do foxes have to do with business?"

"Rice was the original measure of wealth, and *Inari* was the goddess of rice harvests. Since foxes kept away the field mice, they protected the crops. But over time, *Inari* became the deity of prosperity, whether from rice or any other source, and foxes evolved into agents and guardians."

Hiding a smile, I turned toward the nearest statue and ran my fingers over its weathered surface.

Perched on a pedestal, the fox sculpture stared back, blindly watching, and mutely listening.

"Farmers and merchants have revered *Inari* for centuries, but now, even multinational companies pay tribute." He nodded toward the closely spaced red pillars. "Not just individual contributions, but corporate gifts built this shrine's ten thousand *torii*. Each was donated in appreciation of an answered prayer."

I stared at the immense gates rising above the trail like an arch of swords. So compactly constructed, the columns formed a meandering tunnel.

I slid my fingers along a pillar's smooth surface. "Interesting how the ancient and modern coexist here."

A gray mist gradually enclosed us, hiding the midafternoon sun. The sky became so dark that, as we navigated the densely erected gates, we seemed to enter an underpass.

Outside the path, a twilight hush came over the birds, and the underbrush rustled.

I jerked. "What was that?"

"Cats. Hundreds of stray cats inhabit these woods." His eyes glimmered in an otherwise expressionless face.

His reaction piqued my interest. "Are you fond of cats?"

"Some say they're *Inari's* liaisons"—he shrugged—"fox spirits in disguise."

A smile tickling my lips, I waited for his joke's punch line.

But except for a subtle curl to his lip, his expression remained impassive. "The Japanese believe cats are lucky. Think of the *maneki-neko*—"

"The what?"

"You've seen those cat statues in restaurants." He lifted his hand, demonstrating.

"Yes." I nodded. "But sometimes they raise their left paw, and other times their right. Does it matter which?"

"The left paw attracts customers, while the right invites good luck." He paused, seeming to scrutinize me. "But seeing a cat at a shrine—especially if it approaches you—*that's* auspicious."

"Are you serious?" I recalled the stray kitten earlier that morning but doubted any mystical connection.

"You don't believe me?"

"I can accept the foxes' symbolism as tradition, but cats being auspicious?" I dismissed the idea with a laugh. "That's just superstition."

He gave a knowing grin as if he were right but chose

not to argue. Then turning wordlessly, he resumed the steep trail.

Breathless from the ascent, I welcomed the conversational lull as I struggled to keep up with his pace. I studied the back of his head, contrasting his silver hair with his speed and agility. *What is he, part goat— the legendary Pan?*

The higher we climbed, the fewer the *torii,* letting more of the mountain's natural beauty show through. A fresh breeze sighed through the trees, providing background music, while birds called and twittered from the boughs, adding countermelodies.

Instead of painted wooden *torii,* ancient stone columns rose as we approached the mountaintop.

At the summit, Chase swept his arm across the vista. "This is *Ichinomine*, the highest peak of *Inariyama*. People have worshipped here for thirteen hundred years."

His husky voice grabbed my attention.

He stared over the cliff's steep slope as if peering into the past. Then turning, he locked his gaze onto mine. "You could be her twin…"

"Whose?" I tried to look away, but his piercing stare held me captive.

"With your pixie smile and jade-green eyes, you remind me of someone I once knew. No! More than remind, you could be her double…her reincarnation."

Is that why he stares?

"This was *Yua's* favorite place…" His voice broke. Clearing his throat, he started again. "Happiness is fleeting. Like the tides' ebb and flow, it comes and goes. *People* come and go." Looking past me, he snickered. "Their paths cross briefly, each pausing on their separate ways, but too soon they…leave." He spoke in a ragged whisper. "Only the mountain remains."

Then as if he pulled on a mask, he assumed his earlier composure, speaking with a tour guide's detachment. "In a Shinto shrine, the connection between landscape and religion is powerful. A sacred mountain—"

"Wait…wait." Puzzled by his abrupt shifts, I waved my hands to stop him. Then I shielded my eyes, squinting against the sun's diffused glare. "What happened here that upset you?"

His shoulders hunching, he seemed old, worn out. He glanced over the escarpment, his chest rising and falling in a silent sigh. "This is where my fiancée…left me."

Jilted. Ditched. He knows what it is to be discarded. Inhaling his sense of abandonment, I remembered rejection's sting. "Sorry. I've been there myself." A derisive snort escaped. "Someone once broke up with me on my birthday."

He slowly shook his head while he stared, his eyes glazing.

What's he thinking? As the pause lengthened, I became uneasy. "You said this mountain is sacred…?"

"Yes." He blinked. Then like straightening his tie or cuffs, he assumed an inscrutable expression before pointing to an inscribed rock. "This boulder is the main shrine's holy of holies. People worshipped here long before they built *toriis* to *Inari*. Times change, yet believers still make pilgrimages to this mountain peak to be spiritually revitalized."

I stared at the massive stone, sensing a connection. Gradually, an indefinable energy infused me. "Is this what attracts pilgrims?"

"It's a power spot—a place to recharge with the earth's energy. Constant and permanent, mountains are a spiritual focus—a universal symbol for approaching the heavens." He tilted his head, as if considering me. "For many, climbing Mount *Inari* represents overcoming challenges."

Challenges…I swallowed hard, as my fear of heights rose in my throat like acid reflux, burning and sour.

"But you know this already." He stared into my eyes. "Height has always frightened you."

"Not always—only since I was three…" *When my aunt dangled me over a balcony, threatening to drop me.* My childhood memory was so vivid, I took a deep breath to dispel it.

"But the thought of being dropped scared you—scarred you."

About to agree, I woke from my reverie. "How'd you know that? How could you possibly have known that?" *Can he see what I'm thinking?* I felt violated, as if he'd eavesdropped and fingered through my unguarded thoughts.

Then common sense took hold. *He can't read my mind. He's just guessing.*

"Your fear was so palpable" —he sniffed—"I could smell it."

Are my thoughts so transparent? "Sure, when I nearly fell—"

"No, before you started up the mountain, when you petted the cat this morning." His stare penetrated.

How did he know? Was he following me? His words unsettling, I recalled the feral kitten as it rubbed against my legs…

****

Unable to resist the Siamese kitten's crossed blue eyes and silver-gray coat, I'd knelt to stroke its silky fur, but the chatter of an advancing tour group was my cue to move on.

"Sorry, kitty. Got to go." I began the climb despite my fear of heights, rushing along the paths because of the tight schedule and only glimpsing the *torii* or fox statues.

The labyrinth of trails deviated and intertwined through lesser shrines and wooded areas. Other times, it teetered along steep cliffs with dizzying drop-offs.

But unable to read Japanese *kanji* signs, I missed turns and wasted time by having to backtrack. Then to make up for lost time, I'd scrambled over the uneven stones and rushed through the fog until I lost my balance and…

****

Chase caught me…or was he stalking *me?* Alarmed by the idea, I about-faced, and started back solo.

"What was that meme I saw?" His voice loud, he called after me. "Foxes are just cat software running on dog hardware, or was it the other way around? Dog software running on cat hardware? Either way, like I said, cats are messengers."

"You said cats were auspicious." Leery, I spun around. "Foxes were messengers."

"But cats can be foxes in disguise." Arms clasped behind his back, he casually joined me, apparently unaware of any tension. "Like I said, Mount *Inari* symbolizes rising to a challenge…" He shrugged. "*Ichigo ichi-e.*"

"Which means?"

"One time, one meeting." His face relaxing, he gave a slight bow. "A chance encounter can alter your life's path."

Curious, I tried to read his impassive eyes. "How?"

"Because of its branching power, an unplanned meeting can trigger a chain of events that shifts the course of your life…if you allow it."

"You mean destiny, fate." The idea captured my imagination. *Is it possible?*

Chapter 1—Kyoto

Monday Night

My cell phone rang as I reached the hotel room.

"When do you get into Tokyo?" My old college roommate's voice needed no identification.

"I'm taking the early bullet train, so just past noon."

"Great, we'll catch up over lunch." Mia paused. "How long has it been?"

"Two years." I laughed. "Should be a long lunch."

"Incidentally…" The smile left her voice. "Rafe's in town."

My mind drifted to the last time I'd seen him—just after he returned from Vegas.

"Did you hear about his wife's freak acci—"

"Sorry, don't mean to interrupt, but I've got a hard deadline tonight." Uncomfortable discussing Rafe, I begged off. "Talk tomorrow?"

****

I emailed the Kyoto article as the clock ticked eleven. *Made the deadline.* Exhausted, I turned off the laptop, leaned back, and eyed the bed's inviting pillows. Though tempted to sleep first and pack in the morning, I shook my head. *Don't put off...*

I packed, showered, set the alarm, and as a backup, dialed the front desk for a wake-up call. At midnight, I nestled between the bamboo sheets, closed my eyes, and waited for sleep. Instead, memories haunted me…

Three days after my birthday, Rafe appeared at my door, haggard, hung over, and unshaven. His eyes bloodshot, he reeked of alcohol.

I cracked the door but left the chain bolted.

"Hey." He wore a penitent smile and held up his hand in a friendly wave.

"What do you want?" Arms crossed, I dug my nails into my biceps.

"I…uhm"—he chewed his lip—"guess I owe you an apology."

"Yeah, guess you do."

He glanced at his shoes. Twice he opened his mouth to speak but instead cleared his throat.

"If you have something to say, spit it out." I was in no mood for games. "If not, get out."

He stiffened. "Sorry about your birthday. Something came up—"

"Something *always* comes up." I took a deep breath. "You always have some justification, some excuse, but the truth is, you don't care about anyone but yourself. Everything's always about you—"

"I got married."

"So, don't expect me to—*What?*"

****

Tokyo

Tuesday

Though early afternoon when my cab stopped in front of Mia's high-rise, a forest of vertical neon signs already blazed in *Kabukicho's* shady canyons. A-frame sandwich boards lined the sidewalk, displaying colorful graphics and Japanese *kanji* fonts.

But except for numbers and an occasional English word, I couldn't read the signage. I double-checked the address on the business card, comparing it to the building's number, then rolled my suitcase to the vestibule door and rang Mia's intercom.

"You made good time. Take the elevator—unless you want to walk up four flights."

As the outer door buzzed open, I entered the foyer, stepped inside the elevator, and paused before the button panel: 1, 2, 3, 5… *Where's four?* I glanced at Mia's business card a second time—5F—and pressed five.

She met me at the elevator with a warm hug. "Hey, Girl, good to see you."

"Thought you said four flights up. There's no fourth floor."

Mia chuckled. "Yeah, like our 'lucky' thirteenth floor, Japanese buildings usually skip from the third to the fifth floor."

"Why?"

"Because four sounds like the word for death. Worse, my apartment number is 59, actually 49—*shijuuku*, which means *suffer to death*—and that's why I got a break on the lease." She snickered. "Neighbors said this place was empty for years because it was unlucky. Only a *kureijīamerikan*—crazy American—would live here." Grabbing the suitcase, Mia ushered me inside. "Welcome to my 2LDK—two bedrooms, living, dining, and kitchen areas—home sweet home."

I took in what would be an efficiency apartment in Manhattan.

A queen bed took center stage with a narrow nightstand on one side. On the other, a small table stood in front of a window wall in a breakfast niche, while a large television angled toward the bed from the nook's opposite end.

An adjoining alcove contained a single bed, desk, and built-in drawers, while a breakfast bar with three stools divided the kitchenette from the living space. The bathroom was petite but ultra-modern with a porcelain tiled shower, frosted glass sink, and a gadget-ridden toilet and bidet. Though compact, the apartment was bright, chic, and immaculate.

"Looks contemporary and…cozy."

"Codeword for cramped." Mia laughed. "Believe it or not, this place is luxurious by Tokyo standards. Like I said, if it weren't for the superstition surrounding it, I never could've afforded it." She opened the closet's sliding door. "Unpack, then let's get lunch."

Ten minutes later, we walked along *Kabukicho's* streets, rubbing shoulders amid colliding streams of humanity.

"I knew Tokyo was crowded, but I wasn't prepared for this crush." As the traffic light changed, I squeezed through the nearly solid wall of pedestrians. "It's like playing football—our team versus theirs as we cross the street to the 'end zone.' "

"You get used to it." Mia shrugged. "*Kabukicho* is part of *Shinjuku,* which claims boasting rights of the world's busiest train station. Three and a half million people funnel through these streets every day. And *Shinjuku* is just one of the city's twenty-three wards. With over thirty-seven million people, Tokyo's the largest city in the world."

"And I thought New York was overcrowded at eight million." I gave a low whistle before glancing at the *kanji* signs' smattering of English: Club Private, Secret, Joysound, and Feel Tokyo. Then one sandwich board caught my eye. "Gorilla?"

"Look at the end of the street." Grinning, Mia pointed.

An animatronic Godzilla head peered over a building, its huge neon teeth, enormous claws, and red eyes glowing brightly, even in the afternoon.

"I had no idea Godzilla was real."

"Thought you'd get a chuckle *and*"—Mia gritted her teeth while she opened a restaurant's door—"a surprise. Hope you like it."

"Sure, Godzilla's a hoot." As I entered the dimly lit eatery, my eyes took a moment to adjust.

Then a familiar figure emerged from the shadows.

The air went out of me like a slashed tire. "What's *he* doing here?"

The two years since last seeing Rafe melted like shaved ice on a July sidewalk. My first impulse was to turn tail, but a morbid fascination froze me in place. Unable to keep from staring, I compared the man before me to the mental image I carried.

A touch of gray at his temples, he sported a shorter haircut. His cheeks fuller, he had lost his youthful lankiness to a brawnier frame, but his hazel eyes were riveting. Neither arrogant, nor cynical, they shone with a gentle sincerity I did not recall.

I blinked, and when I opened my eyes, a more mature Rafe reached for my hand.

"How good to see you again." Even the tone of his voice was warm and genuine. "Has it really been two years?"

"Rafe?" I questioned my memory as he took my

fingertips in his.

"I hope you don't mind, but when Mia mentioned you were visiting, I invited myself along and asked her to keep it a surprise."

I shot my hostess a dirty look.

"Don't blame Mia." He let go of my hand. "It was entirely my fault."

He's accepting responsibility…? I did a double take. "I couldn't have heard right. You're taking the blame?"

"I can understand your skepticism." His smile faded as his shoulders slumped. "But so much has changed since—"

"*Kochira e dōzo.*" A waiter motioned toward a table.

"After you." Rafe politely stepped aside.

I exchanged a look with Mia.

After the waiter took our orders, Rafe turned toward me. "I suppose you've heard"—he swallowed—"my wife died in a freak fall."

"Mia mentioned an accident involving your wi…." I swallowed the word, unable to voice it, then kicked myself. *Grow up.* "I'm sorry for your loss."

"Thanks." His voice shaky, he glanced at the table as he cleared his throat. When he raised his head, his eyes glistened.

Crocodile tears? Teetering between pity and doubt, I busied myself with the table's tiny flower vase rather than meet his gaze. "How did you end up in Tokyo?"

"I needed a change, so I sold my car, put everything in storage, and accepted a position here."

"Doing what?" I glanced up.

"Missionary work—"

"You're a *missionary?*"

"And I teach ESL, which is where Mia and I

reconnected." The two shared a smile. "I was glad to see a familiar face so far from home."

Mia nodded. "We taught at the same language school before I took the hostess job."

"Despite my best arguments, I might add." Rafe made a humming sound in his throat.

"Counting gifts and tips, hostessing nearly triples what I made teaching, and it leaves time for research." Mia shrugged. "Besides, it's easy money."

"But dangerous, especially with the *Yakuza...*" As the pause lengthened, he pressed his lips together as if wanting to say more but deciding against it.

I shook my head. "Somehow, I can't picture *you* a man of God."

"God chooses those who're weak." His smile faded into a nostalgic gaze. "Experience changes us—if we recognize the need to change."

"By leaving everything behind, you've certainly changed your way of life." *And your image—but could a person's character change in two years?*

Rather than meet his direct stare, I instead assessed him from nose to toes, looking for the self-centered chameleon I recalled. His clothes lacked starched collars, sharp creases, and name brands. Instead, he seemed to dress for comfort—a stretched polo shirt over loose-fitting, khaki pants.

"I couldn't change the situation, so I changed myself."

What angle is he playing now? I studied his face. *Are these his true colors or just another camouflage?*

Mia's phone rang, and she glanced at the number before answering. "*Moshi-moshi.*" *Sorry*, she mouthed, turning away as if for privacy. "*Hai.*" After a few moments of listening, she nodded. "*Hai*, five o'clock. See you then." She made a note in her phone's app, then turned back. "Sorry, a client."

"Doing *dohan*?" Rafe arched his brow. "Meeting men is dangerous."

"Atsuki's a sweetie. Don't worry about him—or me." Mia stiffened.

"Don't forget the British hostess who was abducted and killed—"

"Rafe, that happened twenty years ago." She gave a weary sigh. "Let it go."

"What does 'doing *dohan*' mean?" Though curious, I was more interested in ending their battle of wills.

"Accepting dinner dates is part of my job—"

"You mean accepting *paid* dinner dates."

"Quit being such a purist, Rafe." Mia rolled her eyes. "It's strictly business, plus I eat at the best restaurants every night." She chuckled. "Frankly, I consider it a perk."

"And what do these 'gentlemen' expect for their high-end dinners?" His narrowed eyes were critical.

"Nothing but a charming dinner partner while they practice their English." Crossing her arms, she tapped her foot.

"So, Rafe"—I leaned in front of her, running interference—"what does your job entail?"

"Also teaching English, but to language students"— his lip curled as he glanced at Mia—"not *Yakuza* hitmen."

"Why do you insist Atsuki's *Yakuza*?" She peered around me to meet Rafe's gaze.

"Have you seen his tattoos when he loosens his tie, and his shirt falls open?"

"What's that prove?" Mia huffed.

"Red koi fish and dragons?" Shaking his head, Rafe sniffed. "He's *Yakuza*. Be careful."

"He's not—"

"What's *Yakuza*?" I looked from face to face.

"The Japanese mafia." Rafe's nose wrinkled. "Their tattoos identify them."

"All kinds of people get tats"—Mia scowled—"and for just as many reasons."

The waiter brought their food, interrupting the discussion.

"Shall we pray?" Rafe folded his hands as he bowed his head.

Incredulous, I caught Mia's gaze. *What?*

****

As we left the restaurant, a metallic screech like a thousand fingernails on a chalkboard halted all conversation.

Looking about for a car wreck, I finally glanced up.

High atop a building was Godzilla, peering over Tokyo like a low-budget, fifties' sci-fi monster.

Despite the kitsch, the image tickled my imagination as I compared its comic-book glowing eyes and claws to the surrounding ultra-sleek, uber-modern architecture. Disbelief suspended, I thought of Chase's stories of half-human, half-fox *kitsune* and chuckled at the notion. *If shapeshifters or ancient behemoths exist, Tokyo is where I'd picture them.*

"Inventive, isn't it?" Rafe leaned close as he nodded toward the reptile.

"What? Oh!" His words brought back the present. "Godzilla definitely opens the mind to flights of fancy."

"That animatronic head is forty feet tall—life-size

for the original hundred and sixty-five-foot sea monster—roughly sixteen-stories high."

"Quirky is the word"—I glanced at the monster again—"especially his metallic roar." When I looked back, Rafe was studying my face.

"What are you doing while Mia's on her dinner date?"

Is he asking me out? I straightened my shoulders. *He's got some nerve.* "I…I don't know." Caught off guard, I looked to my hostess for an alibi. "Mia…?"

"To be honest, I hadn't thought about it." Wincing, she oozed an apology.

"Why don't I show you *Shinjuku's* sights?" He didn't miss a beat. "Maybe start at the Tokyo Metropolitan Government Building? Its observation deck on the forty-fifth floor has the best views—"

"A skyscraper?" The thought of peering from forty-five stories above suddenly made me queasy, and I breathed deeply, trying not to lose my lunch.

"Yup, one of the tallest in Tokyo…" Stopping mid-sentence, he smacked his forehead. "Sorry, I forgot about your acrophobia."

"Actually, it's a good idea." *Forcing myself to look down might desensitize me.* "That's why I'm here—to see Tokyo for the travel article." *Not that I want to go out with him, but maybe he can walk me through my fears—like Chase helped me hike Kyoto.*

"Are you sure?" A deep crease forming between his eyes, he looked as concerned as he sounded.

"Yes." Surprised by his genuineness, I did a double take. Has *he changed?*

Chapter 2—Kyoto

Sunday

"*That's* what I like about you." Chase's face brightened.

"What?"

"Your zest for life, your eagerness"—his eyes flashed—"despite your fears."

"I hiked a mountain." *Big deal.* His flattery was getting on my nerves.

"No, it's much more. Don't you see? All this is unfamiliar to you." His movements fluid, he gestured to the view. "The shrine, the traditions—yet you approach them with such raw enthusiasm. You make the stale fresh and the ordinary extraordinary."

Unsure how to respond, I tried to read him, but I couldn't see past his polished façade. *Guess I'll have to take him at face value.*

"I've made pilgrimages here for so many years that..." He spoke slowly, choosing his words as if making a confession. "I've become jaded." His eyes blazed. "*But* interpreted through your lens, *Fushimi Inari* is new to me again. Seen through your eyes, it's as if *I'm* experiencing the shrine for the first time."

"Glad you think I contribute something."

"Of course, you do! Why would you think

23

otherwise?"

I hunched my shoulders. "With you either talking me through my fears or introducing me to your culture, I thought our conversation was one-sided."

"Not at all. Your perspective's refreshing."

"Don't get me wrong. I enjoy our conversation, but you're the interesting one—the instructor—while I'm just the student, listening and learning." *And taking notes for my article.*

His gaze met mine and lingered.

A warm tingling tugged at my chest, as if drawing me toward him. *Am I imagining this sensation, or is he silently communicating?*

The sun slipped behind a cloud, casting us in shadows, and I glanced about the deserted walkway, once again uneasy about being alone with a stranger.

"Don't worry. In a few minutes, we'll rejoin the main trail in *Gozen-dani*."

He can *read my mind!* I caught my breath as I reached a decision. "Thanks for acting as my tour guide, but at the next turnoff, it's best if we go our own ways."

"Suit yourself." He shrugged without looking.

At *Gozen-dani*, he followed the main trail, passing a stairway that led to a lower route.

I made a half-hearted attempt at courtesy. "Enjoy your day…"

"You're not taking that path, are you?" He spun toward me. "I'd advise against it."

He's giving me orders? "Appreciate your concern, but that trail's already beginning its descent." I forced a smile.

"My only goal is to help you."

Help or manipulate? I wiggled my fingers in a

toodle-oo and took the stairs. "Bye."

Despite my bluster, my fear of heights returned with a vengeance, drenching me in perspiration before I reached the bottom step. Weak-kneed and wobbly, I struggled to keep going.

A steady stream of pilgrims navigated the main path overhead, but the trail I chose was deserted. *Is this a shortcut or a mistake?* Panicking, I considered reclimbing the stairs. *Or would that be like changing checkout lanes?*

Then yowling cats drew my attention. A striped, red cat pounced at a silver-gray kitten, overpowering it and knocking it off a high stone wall.

The kitten landed with a thud. Mewing pitifully, it hunkered beneath an azalea shrub and watched me with luminous blue eyes.

You can't be the same one I saw earlier, can you? "Kitty?"

Whimpering, it limped toward me.

I picked it up, cuddling it against my chest. Then I noticed the cat's hind right paw dangling. When I touched it, the kitten cried and pulled back.

"Now what?" *I doubt the hotel allows pets, but I can't leave it here, either.* "Don't worry, kitty. I'll backtrack to the main path—probably the fastest way to the exit—catch a cab and get you to a vet."

Supporting the kitten with one hand, I hugged it with the other as I took the stairs two at a time. But at the top, I looked back and lost my balance. Lurching, I grabbed the nearest support—a cement signpost.

The kitten leapt from my arms and dashed into the crowd.

No! Breathing deeply to regain my equilibrium, I

tried to follow, but the moment I let go of the post, I teetered.

"Are you all right?"

The familiar voice jolted me. Turning, I gasped. "Mr. Sato—"

"Chase, please." Stiff-backed, he gave a slight bow.

"I thought you'd gone on."

"Just after you left, I tripped on a tree root, wrenched my ankle, and was resting on a bench."

"Are *you* all right?"

"I'm fine." Lifting his hand loosely, he waved away my concerns. "I saw you stumble, but this time, regrettably, I couldn't catch you."

I stifled another sigh, frustrated I had veered off the main path in the first place. "It was my own fault..." My words drifting, I peered up and down the trail, looking for the kitten.

"Your fear of heights again?"

His tone drew my attention. "I was carrying a hurt kitten, and when I lost my balance, it got away."

"Don't worry." The corners of his eyes relaxed. "The kitten took off like a bullet train."

"It didn't limp?"

"It was fine." Though a smile played at his lips, his narrowed eyes lent his face a shrewdness. "Kittens are resilient—like foxes."

"That's the second time you've compared cats to foxes."

"It's splitting hairs, but what I'd said was, cats could be fox spirits in disguise." Again, he stared as if assessing me. "Ready to push on?"

Do I want to walk with him? I finger-combed my hair as I weighed my options. *The exit can't be far.*

"Sure."

We joined the crowd, but as people began passing us, I noticed his limp. "You're hobbling."

"Just a sprain." He casually flicked his shoulder.

He's favoring his right leg...like the kitten's right hind paw. I swallowed a groan. *Wish I could've taken it to a veterinarian.*

"Still worried about the cat?" His forehead wrinkling, he turned toward me.

"Why do you ask?"

"Your mind seems elsewhere, but I'm sure the kitten's fine. Cats are irrepressible"—his eyes glimmered as if amused—"like foxes."

"Okay, that's the third time you've compared cats to foxes." I studied his face, trying to read him. "Why? Are you trying to tell me something?"

"You have to admit they share similarities." Pokerfaced, he shrugged.

"Like what?"

"For one thing, retractable claws. Foxes are the only canines with partially retractable front claws. They can even climb trees."

"No…"

"It's true. They have the same sensitive whiskers, sleek physiques, and 'cat eyes' with elliptical pupils. Like felines, they're solitary hunters that first stalk, and then ambush their prey in a burst of speed. Dogs, on the other hand, hunt in packs, wearing down their prey with relay teams."

I glanced at the steeply sloping, uneven path, surprised to take the gradient in stride. Instead of being weak-kneed, I felt empowered. *He distracts me from my fears. No, it's more. When I'm with him, I don't* feel *afraid.* A smile tickled my lips as I considered the silver-haired stranger. "How else are foxes like cats?"

His blue eyes twinkled as if he knew I knew he knew, but he continued in a lilting voice.

"Their kits hiss and spit like kittens, while the adult foxes purr, mew, and caterwaul like alley cats in heat." The corners of his eyes crinkled. "When frightened, foxes arch their backs and puff out their fur, just like Halloween scaredy-cats."

His imagery made me chuckle. "Why the similar behavior?"

"Cats and foxes stalk the same prey. Since they've adapted to similar situations, they've developed parallel strategies—like birds and bats. Though bats are mammals, they occupy the same ecological niche as birds, so they've developed comparable habits."

"I never thought of the connections." I gave him a once-over. "But you've gone on and on about foxes' similarities to cats. Why? *Are* you trying to tell me something?"

For an instant, his lips rose in a smirk. His eyes as cold as blue ice, he stared down his nose. Then as if he pulled on a mask, his face resumed its impenetrable façade. "The only thing I'm telling you is a story to pass the time."

"And take my mind off my fears." I dismissed my suspicions with an embarrassed laugh. "I appreciate your walking—and *talking*—me through the climb and now the descent." Repentant, I hunched my shoulders. "Do you have any more stories to get me down this mountain?"

"One." He flashed a toothy grin, showing strong, white teeth. "A boy once trained to be a monk. He sat in lotus position each day, chanting with his teacher until his knees and back ached. If he dozed, the priest whacked his head with a wooden spoon. If the priest left him alone, he took out pen and ink and sketched pictures of..." His tone changing from casual conversation to a pointed question, he paused.

"Foxes?"

He shook his head.

I snickered. "Cats?"

"*Cats*, every kind of cat: Long-haired, short-haired, brindle, calico, striped, ginger, red"—he eyed me—"and even silver-gray cats. The priest was patient at first, but after a while, he lost hope. 'Maybe you'll be an artist one day, my son, but you'll never be a monk. However, I'll leave you with this advice. Always sleep in a tiny space.'

"The boy took his pen and ink and left. After walking all day, he came upon a large, deserted temple filled with plain screens, which gave him an idea. 'To pay for my lodging, I'll decorate these panels with...' "

Stopping in his tracks, Chase turned toward me.

"Cats." I rolled my eyes.

"Sketching cats onto each, he left no screen untouched. Then that night, he remembered the priest's advice and found a tiny closet for a bedroom. At midnight, something began howling and screeching. At the sounds of furniture being overturned and pottery shattering, he huddled in a corner, hoping it was a nightmare.

"In the morning, he slunk from his nook into the temple, deserted except for a dead rat the size of a water buffalo. 'This must be what frightened away the monks.' He lifted the overturned screens, but they were all bare. His drawings were gone. Then he looked about. The temple was overrun with cats—cats he recognized from his imagination."

Secure as we reached the foot of Mount *Inari*, I joked. "And the moral is…?"

"Things aren't always what they seem." His eyes were so wide, the whites showed around his pupils like a Kabuki actor.

His stare was intimidating until I dismissed his expression as a dramatic flourish to his tale. "Your stories made me forget my fear of heights." Comparing my inexperience to his worldliness, I felt naïve as I glanced from him to the mountain. "I doubt I could've made this climb without you." Then as my deadline came to mind, I glanced at my watch. "But I do have to say good—"

"The lantern festival is starting soon. Won't you join me?"

"Better not." I shook my head. "I have to budget my time."

"For your article?" Rocking back on his heels, he crossed his arms.

I nodded. "I have this evening and tomorrow in Kyoto, a travel day, and then two days in Tokyo before I head home."

"You can't see Kyoto in a day and a half." He scoffed. "Or Tokyo in two. It's ludicrous to think you can author articles about Japan's ancient and modern capitals without experiencing them. Your articles can't do them justice."

"I know, but I'll research what I don't have time to see." The truth made me wince. "This is my first international assignment, and I—"

"Want to impress your editor into assigning you

more exotic locations, right?" His eyes seemed to glow.

Does he have X-ray insight?

"Let me be your guide." Though low and intense, his tone coaxed as if encouraging a child. "I know Kyoto like I know my own name. In the time you'd fumble your way to a tourist trap or two, I'd introduce you to this ancient city's soul."

He's persuasive. Debating whether to believe him, I locked my gaze on his.

"Trust me. Join me." His cheekbones rose in a subtle smile. "I'll escort you around a Kyoto few foreigners see. You'll feel its heartbeat—its pulse. I'll initiate you in its customs and traditions, and by the end of tonight, you'll have more knowledge than you can pack into any one article." Chin high, he held my gaze. "What do you say?"

His charm struck a deep chord, appealing not only to my ambition, but to my Achilles' heel—the urge to travel. *This is my first trip outside the USA. Who knows when—if—I'll get another chance?* And if I'm honest, he arouses more than my sense of adventure.

As if he pulled invisible strings, he had me dancing to his music like a wooden puppet. My mannequin's limbs that had dangled randomly for two years, now stirred with latent yearnings at the hands of this master marionettist...

"Okay, I'm on a deadline to churn out an article. I need an interesting angle, *and* I have to sound like an authority." I snickered. "That's the hard part."

"Don't worry. You'll have enough insight and information for two articles." His smile reassuring, his gaze held mine.

"I *am* writing a second piece about Tokyo..." Caught up in his enthusiasm, I considered the possibilities. Then I pressed my lips together as a question gnawed at me. "But what do *you* expect from this arrangement?"

"Me?" He assumed a surprised, wide-eyed smile. "Merely the privilege of escorting a lovely woman around *Fushimi Inari*."

"Seriously."

"It isn't often I meet…" His shoulders slouching, he dropped his persona like a middle-aged man, who'd been sucking in his belly and suddenly let go. Then his gaze homed in on mine. "It's been a long time since I've met someone daring enough to explore foreign ideas, despite her fears."

Is this a Japanese come-on?

As if a reaction to my thoughts, he let out a frustrated sigh. Then steepling his hands, he seemed to search for the right words. "Each time you see new sights or conquer new heights, it's *my* 'first time,' too." The light in his eyes blazed before dimming. "I've seen it all, done it all many times. Life's become dreary and…" He lowered his voice as if sharing a confidence. "Lonely…apparently, it has been for some time. I just didn't realize how much until I saw this shrine through your lens."

He sounds *sincere, but…?* His smooth, unlined face and clear eyes were at odds with his silver-gray hair. "Except for your hair, you don't look old at all. Yet to hear you talk, you've been around for centuries."

"Seems that way." He straightened his spine.

"Why? How old are you, anyway?"

"Seven hundred and seventy-two next winter." His eyes leveled with mine.

Swallowing hard, I blinked, then chuckled at my

naïveté. "Okay, I get it. You're sensitive about your age. Point taken." I ran my fingers through my chin-length hair, frustrated at my inability to read him. "So, we're back to where this conversation began. What do you expect from our arrangement?"

"Nothing but the pleasure of your company."

"Seriously."

"I am serious." He spread his hands, palms up. "Everything I've told you is the truth—with several half-truths interspersed." The corners of his eyes creased in a quasi-smile. "You decide which is true and which isn't."

How can I trust him when he speaks in riddles?

"Remember, I'm here for you." He stared without blinking.

The setting sun broke through the clouds in a dazzling burst of light. The trance broken, I put on my sunglasses. "Wow. Who turned on the lights?"

"You did it again." Chuckling, he cupped my elbow.

"Did *what?*" I jerked away, then chided myself. *Quit reading more into a simple gesture.*

"Made the mundane imaginative. You're not only the spitting image of *Yua*, but you have her sense of humor, too." He gave a melancholy sigh before homing in on my face. "I've seen this shrine hundreds of times, but you make it unique again."

Uncomfortable, I looked away, glimpsing the stone shrine ablaze in the late afternoon sunlight. "*Fushimi Inari* is unlike anything I've ever seen."

"Ah, but you haven't experienced half of it." His face took on an inscrutable expression, not exactly a smile, but more a sphinxlike trace of amusement. "Just wait until dusk."

Within minutes, we reached the shrine's front

gates—and the street vendors.

"Have you ever tried *taiyaki*?"

****

Tokyo

Tuesday Late Afternoon

Rafe rang the downstairs' doorbell at five o'clock sharp.

Buzzing him into the lobby, I spoke through the intercom. "Be down in a minute." Then I glanced at Mia. "When will you be home?"

"Late. I'll go directly to work after dinner, so don't wait up. Just make yourself at home." Winking, she handed me a keycard. "And enjoy your date."

"It's not a date." I tossed my chin in denial.

"Right…"

"Rafe's the one person I never wanted to see again." Like monthly cramps, a sinking feeling gripped my core. "I never should've agreed to meet him."

"Don't second guess yourself. You said *yes*. Now, see what happens." Mia unlatched the apartment door. "Besides, Rafe isn't the same guy we knew in school. He's changed—matured."

"How can you be sure?"

"I've seen how he acts with the students. He's an entirely different person." Mia hugged me. "Now, go!"

Groaning, I dragged my feet across the hall and pressed the elevator button.

"It's only for an hour or two. Have fun." With a smile and a wave, Mia closed the door.

*What am I doing? This is the guy that dumped me. I can't pretend nothing happened…*As I stepped in the elevator, I began gulping air. By the second floor, I was hyperventilating when an idea hatched.

After the elevator stops, I'll press five, *go back upstairs, and simply 'give my regrets' over the intercom. Ha! Give him as good as he gave.* The moment the doors opened, I pressed the *close* button. My fingers were poised over *five*, when a familiar voice hijacked my plan.

"I'm so glad you came."

No need to look. *His voice's every inflection was tattooed on my brain—but this time it rang with a humility I didn't recall.*

Now what? My adrenaline racing between fight and flight, I wavered so long, the doors began to close.

He blocked them with his arm. "Ava, are you all right?"

"Yes…" His anxious eyes cleared my mind like fog lights cutting through mist. "I *am* all right." Tossing my chin, I took a deep, cleansing breath. "No thanks to you."

"I deserve that." His chin dropped on his chest.

"That and so much more." This time, anger rose in my throat like bile.

After the breakup, I couldn't mention the bastard's name for a year. Always questioning what I'd done wrong, I finally realized his leaving was *his* flaw—not mine. Then I fantasized telling him off, rehearsing what I'd say and how I'd say it. I'd make him suffer…

But now, face to face, the bluster left me.

Worry lines radiated from his glistening eyes. Deep creases wrinkled his brow.

Mute testament to what? Grief? Remorse? Like drops of water eroding stone, what thoughts etched those furrows? His face was gaunt, haggard. *His looks have changed, but has he?*

"Your behavior two years ago was unconscionable."
I pressed *five*, and the doors started to close. "I shouldn't
have come."

He intercepted, and the doors reopened. "Please
stay…"

I took a deep breath, debating as the seconds ticked
by. Then rather than hold up the car again, I stepped into
the vestibule.

"Can you forgive me?" A deep V showed between
his red-rimmed eyes.

"No. Standing me up on my birthday was bad
enough, but then eloping…That was unforgiveable—
and crocodile tears won't help."

"Yet here you are…" A light flickered in his moist
eyes.

"I know." I glared at my nemesis in a silent standoff,
annoyed as I stifled a sigh. "What I don't know is why."

The elevator doors opened, and Mia stepped out,
wearing a slinky black dress and stiletto, three-inch
heels. "You're still here?"

"We were just"—my mouth dry, I swallowed—
"leaving."

"Are you okay?" She gave me a once-over.

"Yeah." I winced.

"You look flushed." Her eyes narrow slits, she spun
toward Rafe. With her heels' additional height, her eyes
were level with his. "Watch your step, you hear?"

"Isn't that what I always tell you?" He gave her a
wry smile.

Mia paused as a slow smile warmed her face. Then
linking arms with us, one on each side, she escorted us
from the building. "Come on, you two. Try to get along."

A stretch limousine waited curbside. The chauffeur

bowed the moment he spotted Mia and opened the passenger compartment door.

"Don't wait up." Then she stepped inside the sleek black car with limo-tinted windows so dark that light did not penetrate.

As the chauffeur closed the door, it seemed a great beast had swallowed her. *Like she was cast with a cloaking spell. Now you see her. Now you don't.* I blinked, and when I opened my eyes, an odd sensation of loss engulfed me as the low-slung limo pulled into traffic.

"Do you?"

Rafe's voice pulled me from my musings.

"What?" Turning toward him, I noted his left hand. *No ring.* Irritated, I flinched. *Why did I notice that? I'm just worried about Mia. That's all.*

"I'm as nervous as a chain smoker on a no-smoking flight." He wore a sheepish grin as he ran his left hand through his hair. "I feel like we're on a blind date. Do you?"

"No"—I growled—"because we're not on a date."

"Then what are we?" His tone was penitent.

What are *we?* "We're…two characters in a movie we saw or a book we read…people we knew once upon a time."

"In that case, may I introduce myself?" A smile ghosted his face.

Glimpsing his younger self, I did a double take.

"Hello, I'm Rafe Armstrong." He grinned. "Since we're virtually strangers, maybe we should visit a public place—perhaps the Tokyo Metropolitan Government Building?"

"Fine." Playing along, I stifled a sigh.

"And a truce?" His somber eyes searched my face.

Two truces in two days with two men? Maybe it's me…Groaning inwardly, I nodded. "Deal."

"Thank you." His face brightened as if the lights switched on or the sun peeked out. The glow seemed to fill in the wrinkles and erase the tension.

For an instant, the boyish face I'd loved tugged at my heart. *Let it go.*

"*Tochō's* only a few blocks away—"

"*Tochō?*"

"The government building's nickname. Instead of a taxi, would you like to walk?"

"Absolutely. Walking's the quickest way to 'own' a city—absorb its atmosphere."

"To 'feel its beat' "—his tone was tongue in cheek—"so you can write about it from experience?"

"Something like that." I hurried to keep up as he crossed the street.

"What's the title of your article?" He gazed straight ahead as he spoke, his focus on the swarming pedestrians.

" 'Toolin' Around Tokyo.' "

"Do you have an itinerary"—he slid me a sidelong peek—"or are you playing it by ear?"

"A little of both. I want to cover *Kabukicho's* nightlife since I'm here, and Chase gave me several ideas for touring *Shinjuku*—"

"Chase?" He slowed his stride, his interest apparently redirected. "Who's Chase?"

"Someone I met in Kyoto." The hackles rising on the back of my neck, I stiffened. "Why?"

"Nothing." Shrugging, he picked up the pace. Several silent steps later, he glanced my way. "If you'd like, after seeing *Tochō*, we could grab some pub grub for dinner, then barhop in *Kabukicho*…as background for your article."

"You're actually interested in helping me?" My words dripped with sarcasm. "Where was this consideration two years ago?"

"Look"—he stopped in his tracks—"I admit there were mistakes—"

" 'There were mistakes'? Passive voice. Just listen to yourself." My pitch rose with my temper. "Why not 'mistakes were made…by someone'? Could you be any more evasive?"

He chewed his lip while people surged past us.

"You haven't changed—not one bit." Blood pressure rising, I shook my head. "You're still the narcissist, and you'll never learn because you never own up to your mistakes."

"Okay! I screwed up!" Sucking air between his teeth, he squeezed his eyes shut and pressed his fingers into his temples. A moment later, he grimaced and began again. "It's taken me two years to realize my mistakes— and admitting them still isn't easy. My behavior was inexcusable, and I'm honestly sorry."

Huh. Inexplicably dissatisfied, I sniffed. *Those are the words I've waited to hear, but his apology's a hollow victory. Too little, too late?*

He gave me a tentative, half-smile. "Do we still have a truce?"

Chapter 3—Kyoto

Sunday Dusk

I breathed in the sweet aroma as we neared the outdoor food stall. Behind the counter, a baker ladled batter into row after row of waffle molds, each in the shape of a fish.

"This is *taiyaki*." Chase handed me a steaming pastry wrapped in waxed paper.

I sniffed the confection. "It doesn't smell fishy."

"Nothing is fishy but its shape." He chuckled. "It's a dessert."

I cautiously bit into its crispy tail.

"Try its filling."

Not trusting him, I spread the waffle apart, eyeing its contents. "What's this lumpy red stuff?"

"Azuki beans."

"*Beans* for dessert?" I wrinkled my nose at the idea.

"Try it." The corner of his mouth lifted in a patient, long-suffering expression, like a mother urging her fussy toddler to eat. "You'll like it."

I half-heartedly nibbled the stuffed pastry, tasting the warm goo. When the flavor was sweet, neither bitter nor salty, I took a larger bite. "Not bad—a nutty flavor and mealy texture."

Though he said nothing, his fish-eating grin conveyed an I-told-you-so smugness.

"Don't look so self-satisfied."

"I could eat sweet red azuki three times a day, every day."

Skeptical, I pouted. "Nothing tastes that good."

"It's comfort food to many, although…" He cocked a brow, studying me. "Supposedly, it's irresistible to people possessed by fox spirits."

I couldn't hold back a dubious chuckle. "What?"

"Until a century ago, the go-to explanation for mental illness was fox possession, and because Azuki beans are *kitsunes'* favorite food, a fondness for this snack was considered proof of *kitsunetsuki or* fox possession."

"You make *kitsunes* sound like a demographic group—like soccer moms or dentists."

"Who says they aren't?" His gaze probed.

Uncomfortable beneath his stare, I wolfed down the pastry to break the connection.

He glanced at the sun's low angle. "We have roughly a half hour until sunset when the lantern festival begins. Want to see a Zen garden?"

"Definitely." *Another tidbit for my article.*

Chase hailed a cab, and a five-minute ride later, we wandered along a path flanked by two rows of weathered stone lanterns. Their moss-covered roofs a testament to their age, they rested on cracked stone pedestals.

I gave them a wide berth as I sidestepped them. "Shouldn't these safety hazards be replaced before they topple over?"

"An earthquake caused the damage recently, but rather than exchange these ancient lanterns for new, their *wabi-sabi* beauty remains."

"Wobbly what?" I glanced at Chase, thinking I'd

misheard.

"*Wabi sabi.* Roughly translated, it means finding beauty despite imperfections—accepting the cycle of growth and decay. It's a Zen concept about accepting transience."

"Like their discoloration from time and exposure?" I studied the fuzzy, green lanterns. *How many centuries has it taken the moss to cover them?*

"Everything's flawed. Everything's in transition." As he spoke, his eyes became misty. "Water falls as rain, then rises as evaporation. Tree leaves bud, mature, turn color, and fall, revealing the beauty of the bare branches. Nothing's flawless, and nothing lasts forever."

His words sparked my imagination, and I tried to visualize a sped-up cycle of nature.

"You should be here in winter, when this garden's covered with freshly fallen snow." His face lighting up with a smile, he lightly touched my elbow. "It's a silvery wonderland."

"I bet it's lovely." His burst of enthusiasm made me laugh.

"It is." His hand dropped, and his eyes took on a dreamy, faraway expression as he glanced at the garden's treetops. "The trees are cloaked with an ethereal shawl. The hush of the snow blankets the raked gravel." He closed his eyes as if imagining its wintry attire.

"You make the garden sound like a frosted fairyland." I stared across the shimmering shades of green. "But I can't believe that stark beauty competes with this lush, leafy woodland."

"*That's* wabi sabi." His eyes opening wide, he gave a short laugh. "You're present in the moment, looking at the current beauty, while I was dwelling in the past, missing all this splendor." After staring at the wooded area, he turned back, nodding slowly, like a teacher pleased with his student's progress. "Well done. Once again, you've taught an old dog a new trick."

As we continued along the paths, I gazed at the symmetrical rows of white sand and raked gravel. "Not a stone or grain of sand out of place, its uniformity has a certain serenity."

"That's its 'white space'—not necessarily empty or blank—but negative space."

"Like magazine layouts with wide margins and gutters between the columns." I nodded, applying his reasoning to my journalism background. "The white space helps readers ignore the chatter and dwell on the message."

"Exactly. The void focuses your attention." He pointed at the meditation gardens. "The vacuum invites contemplation, like recalling the past year's events at New Year's or on your birthday."

Birthday. I drew a raspy breath. Even after two years, the recollection was raw…

****

I applied my makeup with an artist's hand, blending three shades of eyeshadow and going heavy on the mascara. Then I slipped into the black cocktail dress I'd bought for the occasion—a fusion of chic and slutty.

Wish I knew what Rafe planned for my birthday. Dinner at an upscale restaurant? Pub food at a sports bar?

"A surprise," was all he'd said.

What's the fine line between dressed to kill and overdressed? Glancing at the mirror, I glimpsed the exposed décolletage, then examined my naked left hand.

More importantly, is tonight the *night?* After dating for three years, the conversation had finally turned to rings and weddings, and with graduation a month away, I was eager to take the next step.

At six o'clock sharp, I sat by the door, butterflies fluttering in my belly.

Ten minutes passed. Fifteen. Worried he'd had a last-minute meeting, heavy traffic—or an accident, I texted him. An hour later, I called. When he didn't pick up, I left a voicemail.

At eight o'clock, I checked my email. No messages, no texts, no callback—radio silence.

At nine o'clock, I removed my makeup, the black, smoky taupe, mauve, and greige streaks on the cotton pad mirroring my mood. After showering, I picked at soggy leftovers as I studied my bare left hand. *Leftovers...*

When the phone dinged, I flinched. *Rafe?*

Mia—*Guess who's at Tootsie's? And Rafe's not alone. What's going on?*—

I sat back, stunned. *He wouldn't break up with me on my birthday—without even the courtesy of telling me—would he?*

****

"Ava? Ava!"

"What?" Blinking, I emerged from my reverie.

"You were a million miles away." Chase wore an impatient smile. "Where were you?"

Not a happy place. I took a cleansing breath, dispelling the memory. "Remember how I'd mentioned someone broke up with me on my birthday?"

"What a fool." His tone bitter, he spat out the words.

"Why do you say that?" Puzzled by his reaction, I

turned toward him.

"Because only a fool would let you go. You deserve a man who appreciates you, who'd never leave you. He must've been..." Shaking his head, he muttered under his breath.

"Did you say...possessed?" I leaned closer to hear.

"Enough contemplation." He waved his hand, dismissing the question. "Too much is as toxic as too little."

Despite my curiosity, I didn't pursue the subject. *The last person I want to talk about is Rafe.*

He checked his watch. "We'd better catch a cab back if we want to see the *Taiko* drummers."

****

Tokyo

Tuesday Evening

"You deserve an explanation." Hangdog, Rafe stooped as if shouldering a great weight. "And I still owe you a belated birthday dinner."

Birthday dinner. Reminded how he had humiliated me, I resented him, but his tail-between-his-legs body language invited sympathy. Assessing him, I teetered between pity and repulsion.

Rafe's just three years older than me, but he acts old. Chase talked of being so ancient, yet except for his silver hair, he looks and acts like a young man. Of the two, Chase seems the younger.

"There's the *Tochō*." Rafe pointed toward skyscraper's twin towers rising above the surrounding buildings' roofs.

Discussing the observation towers was disturbing

enough but seeing them loom above the city was terrifying. Panicking, I took slow, deep breaths trying to regain control.

Acrophobia's irrational. I simply won't look up.

He turned toward me. "You're white as a sheet. Do you feel all right?"

"Just a little high anxiety…" My attempted laugh fell flat.

"Maybe you'd rather skip *Tochō* and just grab a bite to eat."

"No, I want to see Tokyo's points of interest—and while I'm viewing them, I'd like to desensitize my fear of heights."

"Why not ease into the idea?"

"What do you mean?"

He pointed to a restaurant's glass front. "Who said you can't confront your fears at your own pace? Why not view the towers from a window seat, over a beer? Then when—*if*—you're ready, we'll visit the observation deck."

A shudder slid down my spine as I eyed the twin buildings. His evasive tactics appealed to the coward in me, and I managed a feeble smile. "Sure, let's get a drink first."

"Hey, if I order a double, maybe you can coax me into telling you what happened two years ago."

His words had a sobering effect. "So, as I delay confronting my fears"—I met his gaze—"you tackle yours?"

"Something like that." He wore an ironic smile as he held the door. Then he snagged a table by the window wall, where the *Tochō* filled the view.

Uneasy, I glanced away while the waiter took our

order.

"And *yakitori*," added Rafe.

"Which is?"

"Grilled chicken on skewers"—he dimpled—"pub grub."

Again, I caught sight of his younger self. "Thanks for helping me ease into the idea of visiting the high-rise."

He glimpsed the *Tochō* before meeting my gaze. "No need to force anything. Get used to the view first—used to the idea—and if you want, we'll visit it. No pressure."

"That *laissez faire* approach helps." As I studied the enemy at close range, my curiosity overcame hostility. "What happened two years ago?"

"I haven't had a double yet." His sniff passed for a laugh.

"Are your memories so painful you need a drink first?"

"Nothing's strong enough to erase memories, but alcohol numbs the pain." He sighed. "On the other hand, alcohol caused it, too…"

His doubletalk confused me. "What do you mean?"

"I tried to tell you once, but—"

"*Kore ga anata no bīrudesu.*" Our waiter delivered the beer. "*Yakitori wa mōsugu junbi ga dekite imasu.*"

Frustrated by the interruption, I stifled a sigh.

As the waiter bowed and left, Rafe translated. "The chicken will be up in a minute."

I flashed a tight-lipped smile. "You were saying…"

"Ah, yes. Alcohol dulls the ache it triggers." He stared at his tall, frosty glass, grimaced, then raised it in a toast. "To sober days and abstinent nights."

"A double *entendre*?" I narrowed my eyes, squinting to read between the lines.

"You always could see through me." He gave me a crooked smile.

"Not always…"

"Then to truth." Again, he raised his glass.

"To truth." *Do I want to hear this?* I steeled myself as I clinked my beer against his.

He took a long draught before setting down his glass and meeting my eyes. "The last month we dated, I felt trapped."

I flinched. "Why?"

"Most of our friends had tied the knot…jumped the broom…gotten hitched. You hinted at marriage every time we passed a jewelry store or bridal shop."

"We went together all through college." Patience stretched thin, I snapped. "Wasn't it the logical next step?"

"In retrospect, yes"—he grimaced—"but I wasn't mature enough to realize it." He stared into his glass, apparently lost in thought.

After several silent moments, I couldn't contain my frustration. "So, what's your big revelation?"

"Okay, I'd—"

"*Soshite kore ga anata no yakitoridesu.*" The waiter set down small saucers and a platter of sizzling chicken skewers, then left with a quick bow.

I stifled an aggravated sigh as I counted to three.

"Sorry." Rafe grimaced. "I didn't mean to keep you in suspense. I just…" His words faded as he shook his head. "Poor timing…then and now."

Closing my eyes, I pressed my fingers into the bridge of my nose. "Defecate or abdicate."

"What?" He smiled. "Oh." He took another long draught. "Long story short, I started dating one of the undergrads."

"Which one?" My spine straightened.

"Ashley." He bunched his lips.

I remembered the wisp of a girl. Thin, short blonde hair, one of his idolaters when he had quoted poetry over pitchers of beer at Tootsie's. I wiped the foam from my lips. "Give me the condensed version."

"It was your birthday. As I left my apartment, she waylaid me. She was in tears—barely coherent. She told me she was pregnant, and—"

"You got her pregnant?" I slammed my glass on the table, foam sloshing over its sides.

His Adam's apple moved up and down as he swallowed. "No, n-not really—"

"You did, or you didn't. That's a yes or no question."

"She *told* me she was pregnant—"

"Did you, or didn't you?"

"I couldn't remember." He breathed shallowly. "We fooled around one night, but I didn't—"

"Didn't *what?*"

"Recall whether we did the deed." He took a deep breath. "She said she'd just come from the clinic, where she'd tested positive for pregnancy, and I was the father. She was crying, telling me her life was over, and it was all my fault—"

"This is the condensed version…?" I let out a frustrated sigh.

"Long story short, we eloped to Vegas and a few months later found out it was pseudocyesis—"

"What?"

"A phantom pregnancy—a false pregnancy, where her mind tricked her body into believing she was pregnant."

I slumped back against my chair. "You're telling me you married her because you believed you'd impregnated her and then learned she'd lied?"

"She was convinced—or at least convincing. Up 'til the last month, she swore the pregnancy was real…"

"What happened then?"

He finished his beer and signaled the waiter for another. "Told you I'd need a double." He attempted a smile, but it came out a twisted grimace.

"So, what happened?"

"The marriage was a sham from the start. Then when not one, but two doctors told her the pregnancy was imaginary—possibly a symptom of a more serious psychological condition—she became paranoid. She convinced herself I'd poisoned her, and she'd miscarried. She locked herself in the bathroom, only coming out when I was asleep or at work. I—"

The waiter brought him another beer and bowed.

"*Arigatō.*" He took a sip, pausing until the server was out of hearing. "I begged her to get help, but she went on a hunger strike. When I left food by the locked door, she screamed I was trying to poison her. I suggested marriage counseling, but she accused me of wanting her committed." He ran his hand through his thinning hair. "I was at my wit's end."

No wonder he's aged. "Mia mentioned that your wi—*she* had been in an accident…"

"Yes…Another long story short." He gave a sickly smile. "During her last weeks, Ashley came to terms with the false pregnancy. She seemed to get over her depression, even leaving the apartment to go food shopping. Until then, she'd barely left the bathroom, and she hadn't left the apartment for over a year—not even to get the mail."

He took a long draught. "Then one morning, just after I arrived at work, the police called." He lifted his gaze from the table. "According to eyewitnesses, Ashley walked to a pedestrian bridge during rush hour, climbed over its railing, and jumped onto three northbound lanes of traffic. She was pronounced dead at the scene."

What a nightmare. I blinked to shut out the image. "How awful for your"—I couldn't bring myself to say *wife*—"you. I'm so sorry." Elbows on the table, I folded my hands as if praying and pressed my fingers to my lips.

After several silent minutes, Rafe picked up a chicken skewer. "It isn't sizzling anymore." He bit off a piece. "In fact, it's barely warm."

Still envisioning the girl's death, I barely nodded.

"Have some." He pushed the platter closer.

I chose a skewer and nibbled, but the chicken was tasteless. Thinking of the misery Ashley had caused us all, I caught Rafe's gaze. "What a shame. What a wasted two years."

"Not entirely..." He glanced away as if lost in thought.

"What do you mean?"

He blinked and turned toward me. "During that time, I was so anxious about Ashley's mental health, I felt I was losing my own mind."

"That's good?" I gave a skeptical laugh.

"No, but it forced me to reevaluate my life."

"Go ahead." I gave him a grudging smile. "Tell me the whole story."

"One rainy night after work, instead of going home, I walked for miles just trying to make sense of everything." His bunched eyes relaxed. "At dusk, I came to a chapel. The stained-glass windows glimmered through the mist like a beacon."

His mouth twitched. "On impulse, I wandered inside and sat at a back pew. As it happened, a healing service had just begun."

"I've heard of those, but I've never been to one. What was it like?"

"Like any church service"—he shrugged—"music, prayer, and a sermon." He raised his index finger. "*Except* the theme was healing…physical, spiritual, and emotional healing."

I glanced out the window at the *Tochō. Somehow my fear of heights doesn't seem so overwhelming.* Then taking a deep breath, I turned back. "Did it help?"

"Yes." His lips relaxed into a weak smile, and his face took on a calmness. "For the first time in months, I was at peace. When the service ended, the celebrant invited anyone who needed prayer to join one of the small groups at the back of the chapel. He said the prayers could be for our own healing or intercessory prayers for another."

"You went?"

His eyes lit up as he nodded. "I asked them to pray for my wife."

"And it worked?"

"It seemed to." He shrugged. "When I went home that night, she opened the bathroom door and spoke to me. That was the breakthrough. Over the next few weeks, she gradually began to emerge from her depression."

"That's when she started leaving the apartment?"

"Gradual at first, she made steady progress…" Nodding, he licked his lips. "I joined the church and went to the monthly healing services. I had hope for the first time since w…" He ran his hand across his mouth.

Since…we? Does he mean we, *as in he and Ashley or* we, *as in he and I?* Suspicious, I leaned across the table. "Since what?"

He shook his head and took a long draught.

I leaned back in my chair. "So how long did it take from 'making steady progress' to committing suicide?"

He took a deep breath. "One night as I returned from a healing service, I heard her screaming. Calling her name as I searched the apartment, I found her in the bathtub." He drained his glass and motioned for another. "Do you want another?"

Still nursing my drink, I shook my head. "What was wrong?"

"She sat naked in the water, crying, rocking back and forth, and cradling her arms against her breast, while…" His voice breaking, he stared out the window as if to gather his thoughts.

Not wanting to intrude, I sipped my beer.

"She kept singing a lullaby—over and over." He spoke in a sing-song tone. "Rock-a-bye baby, in the treetop. When the wind blows, the cradle will rock. When the bough breaks, the cradle will fall. And down will come baby, cradle and all."

The waiter set another glass before him, cleared away the empties, bowed, and left.

"*Arigatō.*" Rafe called after him, took a sip, and turned toward me. "Ashley never took her gaze from her arms, while she asked, 'Do you want to hold it?' 'Hold what?' I asked. She held out her arms as if handing me something. 'Why, your baby.' "

I choked and took a quick sip of beer to cover. "She—"

"She'd snapped. I didn't know whether to pretend to take the 'baby' or make her face the truth." He took a long draught of beer. "I helped her from the tub, wrapped her in a towel, and put her to bed. Neither of us slept that night. Every hour on the hour, she turned on the lights to breastfeed. She'd hold the imaginary baby to her nipple and either make suckling sounds or hum Rock-a-bye Baby."

I chewed my lip, sorry for the resentment I'd harbored.

"I begged Ashley to see a psychologist, even though we couldn't afford one, figuring somehow, we'd manage. She refused, insisting nothing was wrong. 'I have everything I've ever wanted.' She'd kiss imaginary lips. 'My little kit,' she'd say, poking a make-believe nose. 'What a cute, pointy nose you have.'

" 'Kit? You mean kid?' Ashley shook her head. 'Kit.' Then wearing a sly smile, she looked at me. 'Aren't I your little vixen? This is our kit, our foxy little kit.' "

TMI. I inhaled sharply. "Did she get help?"

He shook his head. "She kept cooing and singing to her invented baby. After a week of pleading, I'd had enough. I thought maybe the truth would shock her— *shake her* from her obsession—so I was blunt. 'You have no kit, no kid, no baby. What you're holding in your arms is nothing but air.' " He took another draught of beer. "She looked at me like I was crazy. Then she lifted her shirt and pretended to guide a baby's lips to her nipple, all the while singing Rock-a-bye Baby."

He leaned his forehead against his palm. When he looked up, his eyes glistened. "I'm not proud of what I did next."

I took a draught of beer, preparing myself. "What happened?"

"Half crazed with fear, I thought honesty would be the best policy, so I went through the motions of pulling the imaginary baby from her breast. She bared her teeth, screaming a high-pitched howl like a wounded animal. Then she lunged at me, clawing my face and biting my ear."

He turned his head, showing his notched earlobe. "My face, neck, and shirt were covered in blood. Still, I pretended to hold the imaginary baby out of reach."

"Did you call an ambulance?" My hand flew to my chest. "Call the police?"

He shook his head. "I turned the tables, locking myself in the bathroom. Then I showered as she screeched and pounded on the door. Not until the shrieking subsided did I crack the door. Ashley was slumped in a corner, tears running down her cheeks."

Poor tormented soul. Instead of resenting the woman who had bungled our lives, I began pitying her. My contempt dissolving into empathy, I stared at the pawn in her sick fantasy. "Then what did she do?"

"Ashley glared from hollow, haunted eyes. 'You killed my baby, didn't you?' 'It drowned in the shower,' I told her. She stumbled to bed and lay awake, eyes wide open, staring wordlessly at the ceiling. I tried to comfort her, but she seemed miles—lightyears—away and nearly comatose."

"Did she snap out of it?"

"Not really." He pressed his lips together. "All night, whenever I woke, she lay awake, singing the words to Rock-a-bye Baby in a hoarse whisper. The next morning, I tried to rouse her, but she was nonresponsive—except for one lucid moment, when her eyes focused on mine, and she half sang, half spoke. 'And down will come baby, cradle and all…' "

He took a long draught of beer and wiped his mouth with the back of his hand. "I should've called in sick that morning, but the branch manager was visiting, and I had a proposal to present."

"Was that when she"—I took an uneasy breath—"had the accident?"

He nodded. "I'd just walked into the office when the police called. A pedestrian bridge crossed the freeway near our apartment. Somehow, she managed to climb over a six-foot railing and jump." His sniff passing for a bleak laugh, he stared out the window while resting his cheek in his palm. "I blame myself for her death. I shouldn't have left her alone. I shouldn't have 'drowned' her 'baby'—her 'kit.' "

What a living hell. "I had no idea. I thought…"

"You thought I'd walked out on you." Shaking his head, he turned toward me. "Nothing could have been further from the truth."

I stared past his face at the *Tochō* in the distance. *And I thought I had problems.* Nibbling at the chicken kebob, I expected white meat but instead bit into congealed, fatty skin. My stomach suddenly queasy, I washed out the taste and texture with a long draught.

"Want another?"

I shook my head. "I've had enough." The words came out wrong, sounding as if I'd heard enough. "I meant beer."

"Sorry to be such a killjoy. Tonight was supposed to be lighthearted." His lopsided smile morphed into a grimace.

"I'm just glad to know what happened—finally." I fumbled for the right words. "You can't imagine how I've despised you these past years."

"I can guess." His eyes heavy, he met my gaze. "And now?"

"I'm beginning to understand the nightmare you've lived."

He opened his mouth as if to ask a question. Hesitating, he gestured to the kebobs. "Want any more?"

I answered without thinking. "You kill it." Then hearing my words, I flinched and gazed out the window at the skyscraper. "I'm...not hungry." *Compared to Rafe confronting his past, facing my phobia is child's play.*

Frowning, he pulled the crispy chicken bits from the skewers and drained his beer. "Are you ready to face *Tochō*?"

Chapter 4—Kyoto

Sunday Evening

"Déjà vu." Recognizing the entrance of *Fushimi Inari* as the crowds streamed around us, I turned toward Chase. "Was that only hours ago we met here? Seems longer."

"Much longer. Seems I've known you for centuries." Wearing a warm smile, he held my gaze a beat too long before he turned and gestured to the main shrine. "Look. They're already lighting the lanterns. The sun sets early in the mountains."

As lamps began to illuminate the darkening sky, I whispered my impressions into my phone.

He spun toward me. "Did you say something?"

Busted. Warmth creeping up my cheeks, I was relieved the dusk hid my embarrassment. "I'm making voice memos to transcribe later into text for my article."

"Good idea." He nodded, apparently satisfied with the explanation.

Again, I clicked the app's button, held the phone to my lips, and began recording. "Thousands of suspended, red paper lanterns glimmer in the dusk. Their orange-red glow like flickering flames, the lamps bathe the shrine in a garish blush but plunge the people below into a shadowy twilight. On the mountainside, another shrine's immense *torii* light up in a neon, fire-engine red."

After tucking away my phone, I turned slowly, taking in the sights. "It's like Halloween on steroids."

Beginning as an ironic twist to his lips, he chuckled, building in volume until he threw back his head and belly laughed.

"What?" I stared, unsure if he was laughing at or with me.

"I love your perspective." He dipped his head in a slight bow. "Who else would compare *Inari's* Shinto festival to a Christian All Hallows Eve?"

Let me guess—Yua? I wrinkled my nose. *Being his lost love's doppelganger is unsettling.*

Then the rhythmic thunder of drums cut through my thoughts. "What's that?"

"*Taiko* drums. Want to watch?"

"Definitely." My body already responding to the drums' steady beat, I turned and all but marched in time to the commanding cadence. A sidelong glance confirmed that Chase kept pace.

In step with me...no, in touch *with me.*

As the thought gripped me, I took a deep breath, inhaling the idea. *With him beside me, I find my stride— my purpose. I'm a woman with a mission. Being Yua's proxy also has its rewards. When he's with me, heights don't frighten me. Deadlines don't intimidate me. Why is that? How does he do that?*

My mind working as fast as my legs, I sprinted, and we arrived ahead of the crowd to stand ringside. *Even the article seems to write itself.* I pulled out my phone to log my thoughts.

"As the percussionists strike their *taiko* drums in syncopated rhythm, their choreographed arm movements combine raw strength with grace. Their body language is aggressive—combative—but the drummers' intense actions harmonize with the fast-paced beat.

"The throbbing sound and raw energy electrify the atmosphere. Charged with its power, the spectators stand galvanized, apparently at one with the resonant beat, their eyes and ears riveted to the musicians dressed as fierce warriors." Transfixed, I put away my phone. *Is this driving pulse what rouses soldiers to war?* As if answering some ancient call to arms, my body itched to do battle…scale heights…overcome obstacles.

"It's easy to see the relationship between war and commerce, isn't it?"

"What?" Startled from my reverie, I flinched.

"Think of *The Art of War*, Sun Tzu's guide to military strategy written over two thousand years ago."

"What are you talking about?"

"The way generals once applied Sun Tzu's principles to war, today's business leaders apply them to trade. War and commerce have the same objective— victory, whether winning battles or winning bids." Then scanning the crowd, he nodded toward the drummers. "Do you sense the synergy between them?"

"Between whom?" Perplexed, I squinted.

"The interface between the drummers and the audience. The drums motivate the onlookers to act— whether it's to march into battle or drum up business." His gaze met mine. "Whether inciting military strikes or stimulating quarterly sales, *taiko* drum performances are appropriate at *Inari's* shrine—"

"Because…?" I scratched my head, trying to follow.

"Success is the goal of both war and business, and *Inari* is the goddess of success. Where better to invoke success than at her shrine?"

"Business and war." Nodding slowly, I turned back to the fifteen percussionists, each pounding the drums with precision rhythm. Marveling at their dynamic choreography, I glanced sidelong at Chase. "*Taiko* drumming is more than a performance. It's an extreme sport."

"Exactly."

"Just look at their toned biceps."

"No teacher arms there." His cheekbones lifted in a subtle smile.

"Teacher arms?" Thinking I'd misunderstood, I turned toward him.

"You know, jiggling upper arms when teachers write on the blackboard." He lifted his arm, pretending to write on a chalk board.

I laughed, comparing the mental image to the sleek drummers. "Not an ounce—or bounce—of fat between them."

"Drumming's a workout. I took lessons one year. Each beat resonates through your body like an earthquake's aftershocks. Your bones act like a sounding board, amplifying your heartbeat. You feel like you're beating on your chest instead of a drum."

"What upper body strength drumming must demand—and what stamina. They don't stop for a moment. My arms ache just watching." I took a deep breath. "They're not only musicians. They're athletes."

His laugh was dry. "I'm surprised no one's marketed *taiko* drumming as the latest boutique fitness trend—"

Frenzied yapping interrupted as a puppy strained at its leash, growling and snapping at Chase's heels.

"I'm sorry." A young man stooped to quiet the squirming pup. "The drums excited her. Now she thinks she's a fox."

Chuckling, I crouched to pet the puppy's bristling red and white coat. "What a cutie. She looks just like a fox—even to her pointy nose and bushy tail."

"She's a *Shiba Inu*," said the man. "Originally bred to hunt fox and other small game, the breed's ancient."

"Chase, would you like to pet her?" I glimpsed him as the puppy licked my hand with a velvety tongue. "She's a sweetie."

"That's all right." He stood ramrod straight, a curt smile barely flitting across his face.

"Oh, come on. She's a little love."

Lips compressed, he drew a deep breath through his nostrils. Then he tentatively reached down to stroke the dog.

The puppy bared its teeth, growling deep in its throat. Then as the hackles rose on its neck, it lunged at Chase, nipping his hand.

"I'm so sorry." The young man pulled back his pup, ticking its nose to scold it. "She's never snapped at anyone before. All this drumming must have upset her." He turned to Chase. "Are you all right?"

"I'm fine." Chase's chest rose in a silent sigh.

"Again, I'm so sorry." His shoulders curling over his chest, the man gathered the rigid dog in his arms and rushed away.

"That was weird." I frowned at the disconnect. "She seemed so sweet."

"I'm not fond of dogs." His voice shaky, Chase reached into his pocket for a folded linen handkerchief and mopped his brow.

"Apparently, they're not fond of you, either..." The words came out snippy and, caught in a bitter brew of guilt and gratitude, I stifled a groan. *He's the only reason I'm here.* "Maybe we should call it a night."

"No." Coming to attention, he put away the handkerchief. "The annual lantern festival is tonight only—and the sight's unforgettable. You've got to experience the lantern-lit *torii* for your article." Wearing an enigmatic smile, he beckoned with a flick of his head. "This way."

I followed him through the crowds, past the main shrine and immense fox statues, and up the steps to the thousands of *torii*. Marveling at the gates' otherworldly atmosphere at night, I spoke into my phone, composing the article on the fly.

"A stark contrast to the afternoon's backlit mist, the lanterns cast an eerie red glow, saturating the darkness with a mystical yearning, an expectation that something magical is about to take place.

"It's a fairyland." Thinking aloud as I tucked away the phone, my voice seemed to echo through the deserted, crimson-red tunnels. *Anything could happen here...*

****

For an instant, I was seven years old again, vacationing at a lakeside cabin. In the early mornings, wispy fingers of mist drifted off the water and reached into our wooded backyard, where I discovered a ring of mushrooms.

"A fairy ring," my mother said.

Thunderstruck, I imagined pixies beneath each toadstool and spent the entire vacation watching for sprites to show themselves.

****

What prompted that memory? I shook off the eerie

feeling.

Our footsteps resonated in the silent *torii* passageways. Without the crowd's background noise, every sound was magnified.

I grabbed Chase's arm, stiffening at a rustling sound just beyond the columns. "What was that?"

"Mice." His smile reassured me. "Nothing to worry about."

Tiny feet scampered over dry leaves, then high-pitched squeaks pierced the hush.

Where's the kitten now?

"I hope you don't mind not talking, but I enjoy night walks' contemplation."

A nervous laugh was my answer.

The lamplight filtering through the *torii* gaps formed crisscrossed shadow patterns along the dimly lit path.

After several minutes, a faint snoring broke the stillness, the sound growing louder with each step. All the signs I'd seen along the trail came to mind. Though I couldn't read the *kanji*, I recognized the pictures of monkeys, boars, and bears. *Do bears snore?* The hair prickled on the back of my neck.

"Are you cold?"

His voice slit the night like a samurai sword.

I yelped. Then embarrassed, I tried to laugh it off—until I glanced about. The path was empty except for us, and the tunnels were deserted. "I thought more people would be out and about."

"They will be. We're just ahead of the crowd."

"It's spooky at night." A chill slid down my spine. The lanterns' flickering shadows made me uneasy, and not just because I was alone on a mountaintop with a man I barely knew. A sporadic rumbling filled the air. "Is it my imagination, or do you hear snoring? Listen."

The sound of breathing filled the air, as if the passageways were the night's lungs, breathing in and out—contracting and expanding.

"Don't you hear it?"

"Imagination makes any sound take on a life of its own, especially in the dark."

"You're probably right." Recalling the mice's scrambling feet, I sighed and took several steps, but the sound became louder, closer—like the labored breathing of a hibernating bear or fire-breathing dragon. I stopped. "Don't tell me you don't hear *that*."

He cocked his head, listening. Then finger to his lips, he signaled to be quiet as he peered between two *torii*. He jerked back, motioning to follow, and sprinted along the path.

"What did you see?" My heart thumping like the taiko drums, my words came out a whispered hiss.

He stopped fifty feet away. "A wild boar."

"What!" Muffling my scream, I covered my mouth with my hands. "Why didn't we go back? Now, we're trapped."

He shook his head. "The crowds will scare it away."

"What crowds?" Tucking in my chin, I looked behind at the empty path and wiped the trickle of sweat from my temple. "Let's go back."

"I thought you liked to beat the crowds."

"In the daylight, yes—not in the dark." I groaned as I peered at the deserted path.

"Relax." He bent his head closer. "The people you saw at the entrance are just minutes behind us."

I took an uneasy breath. Prudence told me to turn back. *But I'd have to navigate past the boar and down the mountain...alone.*

"Wait 'til you see the crossroads overlook with its night view of Kyoto." His lips lifted in a reassuring smile. "The sight's worth the trek."

"I suppose"—I rubbed my chin—"as long as we've come this far..."

"Trust me. I'd never lead you astray." Nodding to follow, he started walking.

After another fifteen minutes, the *torii* looked familiar. *Are we going in circles?* "Didn't we pass through this 'tunnel' before?"

Eyes wide, he gasped. "We did..." Then he grinned. "This afternoon."

"Ha ha..." I took a deep breath to settle my nerves. "Seriously, I don't want—"

"Seriously"—he mimicked my tone—"we're almost there."

Ten minutes later, with still no sign of any scenic lookout, I broke out in a cold sweat as my imagination kicked into overdrive. *How far are we hiking? What if he's a schizo or serial killer? No one knows I'm here. No one would miss me except my editor...who's seven thousand miles away.* "It didn't take this long to reach the peak this morning, let alone some overlook. Are we lost?"

"Everything looks different at night."

"Then why does the trail seem so long?"

"Darkness makes the path more challenging. Rocks and roots are harder to negotiate, although..." He gave a dry laugh as he turned toward me.

His tone signaling a topic I did not want to hear, I braced myself. *What if he's a psychopath or escaped lunatic?*

"Locals tell of hikers that never reach the mountaintop. No matter how far they walk, they never reach the trail's end."

"Why not?" I jerked back, ready to turn tail.

"They swear the path transforms in front of them, stretching as they walk."

"What happens to them?"

He laughed. "They turn around and go back."

"Exactly what we should do." Relieved, I chuckled. "I thought you'd say they were shanghaied or teleported to another dimension."

A smile drifted past his lips while he gazed into the distance. "College students often test their courage here, and their stories are always the same. A student disappears, as if spirited away. Then after the group spends hours searching, the student returns, insisting he or she has been absent only moments." His voice was hollow, otherworldly.

"Are you talking about a time shift?"

"Interesting choice of words…" He raised his brow.

"Why?"

"For centuries, folktales have linked this shrine to time shifts *and* shapeshifters." His gaze never wavering, his cobalt blue eyes homed in on mine.

"Really?" The downy hairs on my arms stood on end. Wishing I'd brought a sweater, I chafed my arms.

"You're sure you're not cold?"

"Maybe a little." I snickered. "But mostly your stories give me chills."

"Perhaps this sight will warm your heart." As we rounded a corner, he gestured to the shimmering valley below. "You saw Kyoto in the daylight. What do you think of its night view?"

Catching my breath, I pulled out my phone to describe the scene.

"Red lights from radio towers blink in the distance like the pulse of the ancient city. Threads of moving red and white lights twist along tangled lines, defining Kyoto's streets. Light is its lifeblood as vehicles move along its arteries in a magnificent web of illumination. Sodium-vapor streetlamps lend the cityscape a warm, orange glow, while traffic lights blink red, yellow, and green, and the *Nishiki* Market's neon signs ignite the sky."

"Is the overlook worth the trek?" A smile came through his voice.

"Yeah." My voice barely a whisper, I nodded as I tucked away the phone. "Oh, yeah."

"Do you want to hike beyond the lookout, or are you ready to turn back?"

I looked up and down the deserted path. Behind us, the light from red paper lanterns amplified the overhead lights. But ahead was only the glare and shadows of the sparsely placed streetlamps, and the areas to the path's left and right dissolved into black oblivion. *Looks dicey.* My skin crawled. "Why don't—"

"Let's head down."

"Good idea." I drew a deep breath. "Besides, I really do have to get back to the hotel."

"So early?"

"I've been gone since"—with an incredulous laugh, I checked the time—"six this morning. That's fourteen hours. Plus, I need to transcribe my voice memos. The article's due tomorrow night." I stifled a groan at the deadline *and* the idea of trekking down the mountain in the dark. "Why don't you tell me more about this place's folklore? Keep my mind off the boar while we walk back?"

"Remember, you asked." Side glancing, he gave me a wry smile as he retraced our steps. "This shrine is so steeped in ancient myths about time shifts and shapeshifters, I suggest you take its oral traditions with several grains of salt."

"Point taken." I swallowed a smile.

"I'd already mentioned the *kitsune* is a supernatural fox that can disguise itself as a cat."

I nodded.

"Some believe the *kitsune* can take the form of rocks, trees, buildings—anything—including humans."

"Humans?" I spun toward him. "Men or women?"

"Either." His back stiffened. "Although most stories are about foxes disguised as women."

"Shapeshifters…?" I paused searching for an analogy. "Are these fox tales anything like the Western stories of werewolves?"

"Yes and no." He spoke with his hands, as if delineating the points of view. "They're similar in that wolves and foxes are canines that supposedly shapeshift, but the *kitsune* can also be tricksters."

"That sounds like Native Americans' coyote beliefs." Images of the roadrunner and wily-coyote cartoons zipped past my mind's eye.

"The fox myths resemble the coyote and wolf tales in some ways, but not all." He lifted his index finger. "The *kitsune* can also be *Inari's* messenger."

"So would angels be the *kitsune*'s Western equivalent?"

"They share a remote resemblance." His head tilting, he paused. "*Kitsune* can be further divided into the *zenko*—*Inari's* messengers—or the *nogitsune*, the field foxes that are at best mischievous and at worst wicked."

"Sort of angels versus demons, right?"

"In an oversimplified comparison, I suppose that's true." His forehead wrinkled into a skeptical expression, wavering between agreement and dissent. "But the resemblance isn't that clear-cut. You're contrasting Christian and Shinto philosophies when the two aren't parallel."

"I'm looking for points of reference, finding similarities to help make sense of *kitsunes*." I stifled a sigh. "Connecting the dots between Japanese fables and Western beliefs isn't easy."

"Comparison is complicated even more because fox legends don't always agree. Some contend a *kitsune* never takes on other forms. Instead, he only deceives people into believing he does. Others maintain he causes people to see, hear, or imagine anything he wants. Others say he makes it possible to see beyond time or space, to either recall the distant past, or peer into the future."

"*Kitsunes* sound powerful." I blinked, digesting the idea, then spun toward him. "But you keep saying *he*. I thought you said the foxes disguised themselves as women."

"*Usually* is the operative word." Squaring his shoulders, he peered into my face. "*Kitsune* usually shapeshift as women—that is, if they assume human form—but not always."

Caught in his gaze, I stumbled over an uneven tile. With only the red lanterns' diffused light, walking was risky unless I kept my eyes glued to the dimly lit path. "Are these *kitsune* stories relics of ancient beliefs, or do people still believe them today?" When he did not answer, I raised my voice. "Are these—"

"I heard you." A corner of his mouth curled. "I was debating how to answer. The belief in *kitsunes* began in simpler times when most people were farmers, who lived close to nature."

"And now?" I glanced at his face, his eyes lustrous in the dim light.

"Most Japanese live in concrete canyons, and rational university educations replace superstition. Still, fox stories persist through theater, festivals, language, and literature…"

"Despite a waning belief?" I leaned closer.

"Even today, some believe in fox possession."

I pulled back my head. "Is that what it sounds like—demonic possession?"

"Not necessarily. *Kitsune* possession can take three forms." One by one, he raised his fingers, counting off the ways. "Possession of an individual, a family, or a medium."

"A medium what?" I frowned.

"A channeler or psychic, someone who invites the *kitsune* to inhabit her body and use her voice to predict the future." His sniff passing for a laugh, he leaned closer as if taking me into his confidence. "Of course, the medium expects the *kitsune* to vacate her body afterwards, which is a leap of faith. Once in possession, the fox may stay." His voice became husky. "The *kitsune* is formidable."

Again, his tone caught my attention, and I did a double take.

In the lanterns' ruddy light, his silver hair took on a reddish hue, and his sky-blue eyes reflected red like the eyes of a roadside animal caught in a car's headlights. His ears pointy, his chin seemed long and thin, and his smile was a leer. In the gloom, he looked like a fox.

I covered my mouth with my hands, silencing a gasp, then stared down the path before us and glanced behind. *Nobody.* Eerie before, the solitude was alarming now. My imagination running rampant, I struggled to regain my composure.

Then we walked beneath an overhead streetlight, and the illusion vanished along with the shadows.

Relieved he once again looked human, I took a deep breath and resumed our conversation. "You'd mentioned three forms of *Kitsune* possession. What are the other two?"

"The *kitsune* can possess entire families." His mouth twisting, his grin was cynical. "Although some would say the families possess him since the household's members make the fox spirit do their bidding, either for their success or their enemies' demise. A fox spirit often lives with its family for generations—as long as the members care for it."

"I can understand the medium's issue with the *kitsune* not leaving, but *if* you believe in such things, this hereditary possession sounds like an ideal arrangement." Squinting, I hunched my shoulders. "What's the drawback?"

"Historically, people feared those families and wouldn't socialize with them or marry into them. Even today, their descendants have trouble finding spouses."

"Are you serious?" I glanced up from the uneven path. "Why?"

"Fox magic. The *nogitsune* were thought to steal from neighbors, cause illness, or possess people against their will." His unwavering gaze captured my attention.

For several moments, I was spellbound. Then breaking the connection, I peered at the paper lanterns illuminating the tunnel. The lamps' uncanny red glow generated a shadowy, surreal landscape that kindled my imagination. "How can you tell when people are possessed?"

"They all share an addiction…"

"For what?" I swallowed the sudden lump in my throat.

"Azuki beans, they crave azuki beans. They eat and eat but never get their fill."

Recalling how he had labeled the beans his favorite dessert, I drew a ragged breath. "You mean, people still believe in *kitsunes*?"

"Some do."

"Okay…" Uneasy with the conversation's turn, I redirected it. "Then what's the third form of *kitsune* possession?"

"Individuals. *Nogitsune* force them to behave any way they please—froth at the mouth, dance naked under the moon, shout obscenities, or speak fluently in a foreign language they've never learned." Taking a step closer, he leaned into my space.

Again, his gaze gripped me.

****

Without warning, my feet lifted off the ground. Rising, floating, I was buoyant, weightless. Physical boundaries held neither meaning nor reference. One leg walked in this world, while the other waded in liquid air. Stunned but euphoric as I levitated, I bent forward until prone, "swimming" through the air, my arms pulling me as if through water.

Is this an out-of-body experience? Fox magic? Is this shrine some mystical crossroads between gravity and time?

I took a deep breath to ground myself and began the descent from my emotional high. With my feet once more firmly planted on *terra firma*, I sighed, relieved. For however many hours it lasted—or how brief the instant—I had no choice but to acknowledge a shift as my consciousness swung from reality to a plane without linear time or physical constraints.

****

I glanced at my watch. *Only seconds passed.* Shaken though strangely unafraid, I gave a nervous laugh as I assessed the sensation.

Did it happen? Was it the power of suggestion? After all this superstitious talk, did I imagine it? I blinked, unsure. *And if it occurred, was it because of this mountain, this shrine…or this man?* I recalled his mesmerizing gaze just before I felt myself lift into the air. *Did he hypnotize me?* As the idea took hold, I uncurled my spine, scrutinizing him while my questions multiplied.

"So, if the *nogitsune* is the evil *kitsune*"—my words sounded disembodied in the dark, like a ventriloquist's voice—"what about the good *kitsune*? What do they do?"

"Where *nogitsune* are tricksters that swing between mischievous and malevolent, *kitsune* can be loyal friends"—he shrugged—"even lovers or devoted spouses." His arresting blue eyes searched my face. "When respect travels in both directions, *kitsune* can be powerful allies. Japanese literature is filled with spirit foxes who protect…and even intermarry…" Still eyeing me, he left his sentence hanging.

Intermarry? I tore my gaze from his, sorting my thoughts as I stepped carefully along the uneven path. "Are you saying *kitsune* shapeshifters are so convincing, they pass for human"—I paused—"even intimately?" My cheeks burning, I side glanced his way.

"So says a thousand years of *kitsune* literature." His eyes shimmered in the lantern light. "I call it kiterature." After a beat, his lips curved in a subtle smile.

He's joking. The tension broken, I laughed out loud, the sound echoing through the empty *torii* tunnel. *This whole conversation's been a put-on.* Chuckling at his expert timing and delivery, I laughed at my fears. "You had me fooled. Your stories are so entertaining—so credible—I believed you."

"Are they?"

"Entertaining? Credible?" I nodded. "Definitely."

"No." His face devoid of any humor, he stared through lusterless eyes. "Are they stories…?"

I blinked. *How much of tonight is real? Did I have an out-of-body experience? Did his fables—or this spooky atmosphere—trigger my imagination? Or did he work some magic?*

The hairs prickling at the back of my neck, I tensed as I glimpsed the vacant path behind us. Realizing my vulnerability, I craned my neck, straining to see ahead into the tunnel, beyond the curve. *How much farther to the main shrine?* I wiped a trickle of perspiration from my temple as I studied him. *What am I doing on a mountain at night with a stranger?*

Then voices broke the stillness as several people rounded the curve.

Weak with relief, I drew a deep breath as my knees

wobbled. Behind that group came another, followed by a steady stream of people. *Guess we were just ahead of the crowd.* "How much far—"

"This is the last series of *torii* gates before we reach the main temple." He resumed his stride. "If we pick up the pace, we'll reach the exit in a few minutes."

"I've enjoyed today." Still recovering from my last remnants of fear, I paused, unsure how to tactfully say goodbye. "But I don't think—"

"Why don't I call you a cab? Then tomorrow morning, I'll meet you at *Tenryu-ji* Temple in *Arashiyama.*"

How does he always divert the conversation? Pressing my lips together, I stifled a sigh. *It's like he reads my thoughts, then sidetracks me. It's unnerving.* "I don't think we—"

"You look exhausted—not that you don't look lovely, mind you."

His tone soothing and his smile benevolent, he seemed genuinely concerned.

Again, put off balance, I evaluated him as I weighed my options. *He's a knowledgeable guide. On my own, I wouldn't have seen or done half as much today, but he's...strange. Then again, if he'd help me cover as much territory tomorrow, the article will write itself.* Recalling the tight deadline, I glanced at my watch. "I have to—"

"Get back to your hotel." Tilting his head, he gave me a winning smile. "Another five- or ten-minute walk, and I'll have you safely in a cab on your way home."

*The way he skews the conversation is frustrating. He saps my strength, while he...*I gave him a once-over. "I'm exhausted, yet you look as fresh as you did this afternoon—not a hair out of place, not a wrinkle in your starched shirt."

"You're too kind." A faint smile played at his lips.

"No, while you look crisp, I'm wilted." *And I still need to transcribe my voice memos before turning in.*

"Guess I'm just strong as a fox." Though his face remained impassive, his eyes flickered.

"You mean, strong as an ox." *Or was* fox *tongue in cheek?* Tipping back my head to better view him, I gave a begrudging chuckle. *Maybe he's not as strange as I thought. Maybe he just has a quirky sense of humor— that or jet lag's making me too tired to think straight.*

The *Taiko* drums' rhythmic beat cut through my thoughts. Then the path widened into the main shrine's open plaza, where the festivities continued, and the lantern-lit courtyard teemed with people. I squeezed through the swarming throngs toward the exit and, within minutes, stepped into the cab, still debating. "Look, about tomorrow, I don't—"

"How 'bout we meet at *Tenryu-ji* Temple's main entrance?" He rushed his words as if racing me to the punchline. "If you want to beat the crowds and see everything *Arashiyama* has to offer, I suggest an early start."

Though his boyish face reminded me of an eager puppy, his cryptic behavior made me uneasy. "Let me think about it."

"Keep in mind, I can introduce you to Kyoto's soul." After closing the door, he came to attention and bowed stiffly. "The temple opens at eight-thirty. I'll meet you outside the main entrance." Then he took a step back and banged the taxi's roof twice.

But will I meet you?

Chapter 5—Tokyo

Tuesday Afternoon

As we walked past the paved piazza and through the main entry of the Tokyo Metropolitan Government Building, the ground wobbled. "What's that?"

"Maybe it's the subway"—Rafe shrugged—"or maybe it's a slight tremor."

"Tremor? You mean an *earthquake* when we're going to the forty-fifth floor?" Suddenly my breathing became fast and shallow, closer to panting. I swallowed to keep from voicing more fears.

"Relax." A faint smile lifted his lips. "Tremors are common."

"You're *not* helping…"

"Most tremors are too small to feel."

"I felt that one!" I looked around the bustling lobby. Hundreds of people went about their business as if nothing happened. *Am I overreacting?* "How many earthquakes does Japan get?"

"Every day?" He glanced at my face. "Two or three—"

"Two or *three!*" My pitch rose along with my blood pressure.

"Most amount to nothing. Just breathe deeply."

"Are you serious?" I tried to slow my breathing, but his statistics triggered my imagination.

"Want to take an express elevator and zip to the top, or would you rather 'savor the ride' on a local elevator?" As he pointed to the bank of elevators, the smile lines around his eyes deepened.

"Express." I took a deep breath. "I want this over with—done."

"Maybe not the best attitude for sight-seeing." He dipped his head, hiding a smile, as he led me to the observatory elevator. "After you."

I said a quick prayer before stepping inside the car marked *Observatory*. The starting jolt was subtle, but a sinking sensation in the pit of my stomach made me gasp, and I covered my belly with my hands.

"It's just gravity," he whispered.

Rolling my eyes, I deadpanned. After a moment, the queasy, dropping sensation left me until a few seconds later, when I felt another slight jolt, followed by the elevator's braking. I pressed my fingers against the side of the cab for balance. "I left my insides on the first floor."

Though he kept a straight face, his eyes danced. "Almost there."

The moment the doors opened, I rushed out. Then I glanced out the wall of windows, saw nothing but sky, and the building's height hit home, and I gulped air as if I were drowning.

"It's a cloudless day." He pointed. "Look! You can see Mount Fuji."

Sure enough. With Mount Fuji looming in the background, novelty overcame fear, and I drew closer to the window. "Look at that."

But as I approached the glass wall, the cityscape emerged far below, and I froze.

"Look at this map showing which buildings are which." Rafe turned me by my shoulders, redirecting my attention to a backlit photo of the scene below. Callout boxes identified the buildings of interest.

"Thanks." I breathed easier, focusing on the map instead of the window's bird's-eye view.

Gradually, he pointed out the connections between the photographs and the views as we slowly circled the observatory. "Here's the Tokyo Skytree and Tokyo Tower. Look. Here's the *Meiji* Shrine and the *Gyoen* National Garden."

I recognized the names of the last two and ventured peeks at the cityscape below, curious where I would visit tomorrow. Grateful for his unhurried approach, I smiled. Then my legs buckled. "What's that?"

"Just a tremor. The higher you go, the stronger they feel."

Again, I got a queasy, sinking feeling in my stomach as the entire building seemed to rock. I grabbed onto the metal railing and took a wide stance, using my "sea legs" as I would on a rolling ship.

Rafe braced himself with his left hand but stood facing me with his right arm outstretched, as if poised to catch me if I stumbled.

The building creaked and moaned, setting off surprised yelps and nervous hoots from the crowd. The lights on the ceiling began to swing, and the noise level increased with everyone talking at once. Then like a giant pendulum, the building stopped rocking and slowly started swaying in the opposite direction. This time, the crowd became silent while they listened to the structure's groans and creaks.

"Don't worry," Rafe whispered. "Japan's

skyscrapers are built on stilts, so the buildings flex but don't crack. The shifting is the tower's response to the earthquake's low frequency waves."

"The shockwaves?"

"Exactly." His smile was reassuring. "My guess is the epicenter is relatively far away, so we feel a rolling sensation. If the quake had been closer, we'd have felt a sharp jolt followed by stronger secondary waves."

I digested his logic. "What you're saying is, it could have been worse."

Then another jolt rocked the building, spawning shrieks and nervous laughter.

"Maybe I spoke too soon." His eyes widened as the shaking continued.

Though afraid of his answer, I had to ask. "What do you mean?"

"Instead of an aftershock, maybe what we felt before was a foreshock."

"So, *this* is the earthquake"—I swallowed—"*now?*"

"The main shock." He nodded as the tower began to sway.

The creaking and rumbling intensified as the seconds ticked by. Dust sifted from the ceiling, and the overhead lights swung independent of the high rise's slower tilt.

Hunching over, I ducked my head. "It feels like a giant's twisting the tower."

"Don't worry. *Tochō* was built to survive seismic activity." Still holding onto the railing with his left hand, he inched closer, protectively embracing me with his right arm. Head bent, he shielded me with his back.

Peeking over his shoulder, I glanced out the window. In what had been a cloudless sky, smoke rose in an eerie column. Worse, the twin tower beside us swayed in the opposite direction, doubling my sense of motion.

Several days earlier, as my plane waited for takeoff, another aircraft taxied by, and I had the impression that *my* jet—not the taxiing plane—was moving.

Then again that morning, while sitting on a stopped bullet train as another train whizzed past, I felt *my train* move. When I checked online, an article called the sensation an optical illusion, where visual clues of motion trick the brain.

The weaving tower beside us gave me the same unsettling feeling. Compounded with the actual swaying of their tower, the second tower's movement intensified my vertigo. Still gripping the metal railing with my left hand, I reached my right arm around Rafe's waist and held on for dear life.

After a minute, the swaying subsided, and finally the building came to a rest.

Weak-kneed and nauseous, I clung to Rafe, steadying myself as I gulped air. Then I became aware of our embrace.

"Sorry." With a self-conscious laugh, I let go his waist and straightened my spine. "I don't normally grab hold of men."

Loosening his protective grip, he put his hands on my shoulders and gazed into my eyes. "Are you all right?"

For that moment, he was the man I remembered loving. I stared back, dazed and flustered. Then the memory of the past years' pain shook me like another aftershock. *I'm in the middle of one dilemma. I can't deal with two.* I shrugged off his hands as I stepped back. "I'm fine. Thanks."

Still, his gaze locked onto mine.

Finally, I found my tongue. "How can the tower keep standing?"

"The bamboo that bends is stronger than the oak that resists."

"Sounds like a Japanese saying." I ventured a cautious smile.

"That's because it is." His cheek dimpled.

Then the ceiling fixtures began to swing.

My legs buckled, and I simultaneously grabbed the railing and Rafe.

Again, he shielded me with his body, holding onto the railing with one hand and my shoulders with the other as he huddled over me protectively.

The building rumbled and began swaying left and then swinging right, back and forth, back and forth.

With the movement, my nausea returned, along with a sensation of falling. *My equilibrium's off.* I tightened my grip on Rafe to steady myself.

Gradually, the swinging diminished, and I became aware of his subtle lime scent and the tickle of his breath on my neck. Uncomfortable with his nearness, I loosened my grasp on his waist, and when the swaying stopped, let go.

A fire alarm shrieked.

Fire! Hyperventilating, I eyed the elevators. *No, if they lose power, we'd be trapped.*

A backlit exit sign showed the stairs.

"We've got to get out!" My hands clenched into fists, and I started running toward the stairwell.

"No." He caught my arm. "Keep away from the stairs. In an earthquake, they can swing separately from the building and collapse."

"But the building's on fire!" I jerked away. "We've got to go. Now!"

"The fire alarm doesn't necessarily mean fire. Earthquakes often set off alarm systems and sprinkler heads. Japan's high rises are built to sustain earthquakes, and the aftershocks will stop soon. For now, our best bet is to stay put. Trust me. Try to breathe deeply." He grabbed my balled fist. "Watch me. Breath in through your nose for a count of three and then out through your mouth for another count of three. In and out. In and out. In and out."

I relaxed my fist and grasped his hand.

"But to be safe, let's step away from the windows."

I peeked through the window-wall at the city's skyscrapers, imagining a deluge of broken glass crashing to the streets below as the buildings collapsed. Breathing hard, I glanced at the overhead lights, alert to any telltale swinging.

"You haven't told me about your trip to Kyoto. Did you get to *Fushimi Inari*?"

"Oh, yes." I smiled as memories bubbled to the surface. "Have you seen the *torii*?"

Before I finished sharing the adventures, the elevator doors opened, and people got off as others boarded.

I glanced at Rafe. "Is it safe to go downstairs?"

"I think so. We haven't felt any aftershocks for a while." His smile was encouraging. "Are you ready?"

Lifting my gaze to meet his, I nodded. "Thank you."

"For what?"

"Talking me through my fears. You're good." Self-conscious, I chuckled. "I didn't even realize it 'til just now, but you kept my mind off the earthquake, the aftershocks, and even the forty-five stories between us and the ground."

"Glad to be of service." His face warmed into a good-natured smile.

Scrutinizing his expression, I reevaluated him. "When did you learn compassion?"

"Too late." His smile drooped, and his shoulders curled over his chest. As an elevator door opened, he gestured toward it, palm up, and stepped aside. "After you."

I silently gauged him through side glances on the ride down. *He* has *changed.*

****

Kyoto

Monday Morning

Rushing toward the temple, I glanced at *Arashiyama* Train Station's oversized clock. *Nine-thirty.*

Chase stood at the entrance to *Tenryu-ji*, waiting as promised.

Crap. Embarrassed, I shrank back, but not before his gaze caught mine.

After checking his watch, he sauntered toward me wearing an ironic smile. His greeting was cool yet cordial. "Good morning. I wasn't sure you'd come."

"I almost didn't."

"What changed your mind?"

"I thought you'd have left." *After an hour.* Nervous, I spoke quickly, my words clipped.

"I guess I didn't impress you yesterday with my tour-guide skills." His brows bunched above an otherwise stony face.

His wounded tone tugged at my conscience. Squirming beneath his stare, I swallowed hard, sorry that I'd disappointed him and sorrier to be called out. *He deserves better than he got.*

"I'd hoped you'd enjoyed our outing, but apparently you didn't." His bottom lip pushed forward in a pout. "I've been waiting over an hour."

"Sorry." Fidgeting, I studied my shoes.

"You weren't trying to avoid me, were you?" His tone lightened from sarcastic to playful.

I peeked.

"Child, you cut me to the quick…" Parodying the wizard from the *Wizard of Oz*, he wore a semi-indulgent smile. "What happened?"

"I overslept—never even heard the alarm go off." Though relieved at his reprieve, I pushed back. "But to be honest, you did frighten me last night with all your tales about shapeshifting and fox possession."

"Tales you asked me to tell, as I recall." Shoulders back, he stared me down.

"I did, didn't I?" Put off, I pressed my lips together. "But I only wanted your stories to take my mind off the boar, not keep me awake all night with nightmares."

"You got what you asked for."

"No, you delivered much more than I bargained for." *How does he always turn my arguments against me?* "I had so many weird dreams about *kitsune* that I got up and couldn't get back to sleep until six this morning." A begrudging smile made my lips twitch. "Though, one fringe benefit came of it. I not only transcribed my memos but wrote half of 'Kickin' Around Kyoto.' "

"See?" Chin high, he grinned. "I serve a purpose even while you sleep—or oversleep." Then his smile sagging, he drew his brows together. "I only want to help you, Ava, but if the topic bothers you, I promise no more talk about *kitsune*"—his lips curled in a half-smile—"that is, unless *you* bring it up."

"About that." I made a humming noise in my throat as I debated whether to share my idea. "I had a brainstorm for an article—the bar scene in Tokyo, but from the slant of a wolf searching for a stone-cold fox."

"*Cherchez la femme?*" He tipped back his head and laughed.

"That wasn't a joke. I'm serious."

"What prompted that idea?" He cocked his head.

"I was struggling to find a fresh angle for the article, so I searched *foxes* online, and the phrase *stone-cold fox* popped up."

"Okay…then what was the connection with Tokyo and the bar scene?"

"Wolf seemed the logical counterpart of fox." I shrugged. "And a college friend, who works as a hostess in Tokyo, has told me some humdinger experiences."

"You may find more subject matter than you want…" His smile evaporated.

"But what a unique angle, and…" I ignored his mood. "I could use your help. I apologize for making you wait, but could we still squeeze in everything *Arashiyama* has to offer?"

Shrugging, he lifted his hand loosely, palm up.

"I don't have a choice." I bunched my lips. "I have to leave tomorrow morning."

"It'd mean a nonstop, twelve-hour day." His forehead wrinkling, he surveyed me, seeming to evaluate my resolve. Then he glanced at his watch as he ran a hand through his thick, silvery hair. "If you're up for it—"

"Yes, absolutely." Though I'd had only three hours' sleep, it was enough. *Adrenaline will do the rest.*

"All right. We can start with *Tenryu-ji* Temple."

"Great! And while we're touring"—I grinned—"could you tell me how to spot a *kitsune*?"

He jerked back his head and stared.

"After you told me how they masquerade as people, I'm curious—*not* that I believe *kitsune* exist." I splayed my fingers like a guard halting a prisoner. "Don't get me wrong. This is purely an angle for an article, but *from that perspective*, how can you tell a disguised fox spirit from an ordinary person?"

"To begin with, fox spirits don't look ordinary." Again, he ran a hand through his thick shock of hair. "Since they can shapeshift into whatever disguise they want, they usually choose attractive faces and physiques."

"So, you're saying beware of handsome men?" A smile played at my lips.

"And beautiful women." Before handing our tickets to the temple guard, Chase pointed to the sign's instructions, translating. "Take off your shoes and leave them here."

Following directions, I crossed the tatami mats in bare feet and peeked inside shoji doors as I described the site in a voice memo.

"The expansive halls are starkly furnished except for wall-to-wall tatami mats and immense panoramic paintings on its walls. The Dharma Hall's mostly wood-paneled ceiling contains one massive image. Hovering above an ornate altar, black, gray, and white clouds ominously gather into a colossal cloud-dragon."

Awed by the painting's raw force, I caught my breath as I tucked away my phone. "Powerful art—but back to my question. How could you tell a disguised fox spirit from a person?"

"You can't." His sniff passed as a wry laugh. "That is, unless a *kitsune* in human form gets drunk or careless and accidentally reveals his true identity."

"What would give it away?"

Wearing a stern look as he inhaled, he seemed reluctant to answer.

"Don't you know, or is this classified information?" I grinned, maintaining eye contact as I teased. "Does it require a wink and secret handshake?"

He stifled a sigh as if debating.

"Come on." I flashed my brightest smile. "How can I write about a topic if I don't understand it?"

His eyelids fluttered as if conflicting thoughts crossed his mind like a kaleidoscope of butterflies. Then, meeting my gaze, he began slowly. "If it'll help your article, of course, I'll tell you." He leaned in, intimately close. "Remember, I'm always here for you."

Unsure how to interpret his words, I shrank back.

"Always watch for his shadow. If he's caught off guard or taken by surprise, the shadow reflects his true nature."

Reacting to his ominous tone, I cringed until mental images of Punxsutawney Phil made me chuckle. "So, what do I do? Wait for February second to see it?"

He cracked a wan smile. "Only what's solid casts a shadow. Illusion doesn't."

"Okay, so how do I maneuver him—"

"Or her."

"Or her"—I nodded politely—"in front of a light source?"

"Intense light casts the clearest shadows, so in daylight, it'd be the sun." He shrugged his shoulder. "Inside, it could be an exposed lightbulb, a spotlight on a stage, or even an overhead projector."

"Good stuff to know when writing fiction. Any final tip?"

"Besides shadows, watch for reflections." His gaze sharpened. "You'll see the actual image, not an optical illusion."

"Optical illusion." I frowned as my imagination took off. "What about photographs? Would it show up digitally?"

"I don't know, would it?" He gave me a sly smile. "Look, we're here for your Kyoto article. Let's finish 'Kickin' Around Kyoto' before we tackle 'Toolin' Around Tokyo.' "

"Good point." His advice made sense until his words sank in. "You said *we*. Are you planning a trip to Tokyo?"

"I have clients in the prefecture…This may be an opportune time to meet with them."

It "may," huh? Let him think what he wants, but he's not "tackling" Tokyo or anywhere else with me. Then taking my cue from his nonchalant expression, I dropped the subject and pointed at the inviting pond just beyond the open shoji doors. "That view's gorgeous."

As I padded barefoot across the hall's tatami mats toward the wooden deck, I recorded the article's notes into my phone.

"Swallows flit in and out of the veranda's ornately carved eaves, adding a dynamic dimension to the architecture's austere beauty. Just off the surrounding deck's rain-stained planks, a thicket of trees rims a small lake, their leaves varying shades of jade, emerald, olive, and lime green."

"That's the Sogen Pond Garden." Following my gaze, he described the arboretum. "Plum and cherry trees line its banks, but pines, maples, and hundreds of plants fill the garden beyond."

"Can we get a closer look?" I glanced from the pea-gravel path to our bare feet. "After we retrieve our shoes."

Several minutes later, as we strolled alongside the pond, he swept his arm across the vista. "This garden was designed almost seven hundred years ago. With only one exception, it looks the same now as it did then."

He paused, his eyes glazing over. "Originally, foxglove bloomed at the water's edge, but now it's bearded irises." As he stared, trancelike, he gave a yearning sigh.

"You sound homesick"—I tilted my head, watching him—"almost like you'd *seen* the earliest garden…been there…and miss it now."

"What?" He blinked as if emerging from his reverie, then scowled. "No, I've just seen woodblock prints showing how the garden's endured through the centuries."

Really? Recalling the previous night's disturbing sensations, I narrowed my eyes. *With him, anything seems possible—even a life that spans centuries.*

As we ambled along the park's paths, nature seemed to welcome us. Golden carp swam to the water's edge, opening and moving their mouths as if silently greeting us. Dragonflies fluttered above the pond's banks like old friends waving, and the birds chirped cheery hellos through the trees' canopy.

Never has the natural world treated me so hospitably. When I'm with Chase, it's as if animals don't fear me—or I'm invisible. He's my admission ticket into their world. Nature accepts me. Why?

As I collected my thoughts, I verbally sketched the scene in my phone app.

"The path loops around the picturesque pond, offering views of the well-kept gardens beyond. The air's scented with a woodsy fragrance, while azalea, wisteria, and camellias add subtle floral overtones. Along with their perfume, I breathe in the moment as I stroll through the bamboo grove's towering stalks."

Putting away the phone, I lightly ran my fingertips over the nearest bamboo trunk, caressing its cool, satiny finish. "I know bamboo is a kind of grass, but these trunks are so tall, they look like ancient trees."

"Illusion." His mouth curled into a twisted smile. "What you see isn't what it seems."

"You're saying it's more?" I squinted, trying to see beneath his polished façade.

"Nature—the natural world—is filled with illusion." He pointed at the sun overhead. "The sun doesn't climb in the sky. It doesn't rise or set. Those terms simply reflect our perceptions of a spinning universe."

"Are you talking about optical illusions?"

"Optical, olfactory, auditory—even tactile illusions." He turned toward me. "But add *deception* to illusion, and any psychological projection is possible—even what's considered supernatural. Think of hypnosis."

My mind shot back to the previous evening. *Was*

hypnosis behind that odd sensation of rising and floating? Did he mesmerize me somehow?

"Hypnotic suggestions alter sensory perceptions—sight, smell, hearing, touch—*and* sense of time..." His gaze penetrating, he scrutinized me. "Even what we view as 'reality' is open to interpretation. Everything boils down to personal perception."

"So, you're saying a thing isn't necessarily a thing. It's more a *think*." Though I grasped his concept, I sensed I was missing his point. "But why tell me this?"

His smile was enigmatic. "There are more things in heaven and earth, Horatio, than are dreamt of in your philosophy."

Stifling a groan, I shook my head. "Are you trying to tell me something or not?"

"I don't know, am I?" His eyes glittering in the mottled sunlight, he turned and resumed his stride.

He's beyond infuriating. I counted to three, debating whether to walk away, when I remembered my deadline. *I've got no choice. I have to depend on him just a few more hours, then I'll never see him again.*

Still ticked but emotionally exhausted, I followed a step behind him through the whispering bamboo grove. *Why does talking with him always drain me?*

"What about lunch before we cross the river and hike up Monkey Mountain?" At the park's exit, he turned toward me.

Noon already? I looked at the time and blinked. "This morning's zipped by." Then his words sank in. "What's Monkey Mountain?"

"You'll see..."

"Don't start this again..." His smile verged on a smirk, and his secrecy was getting on my nerves. "What is it?"

"If I tell you, it'll spoil the surpr—"

"What IS it?" *Enough already.*

"Okay, okay." His tone placated. "It's a park at the top of *Iwata* Mountain with a breathtaking panorama of Kyoto, where you can handfeed wild snow monkeys."

"Really?" Charmed by the image, I smiled. "That does sound like fun."

He lifted his brow as if to say *I told you so.* "I'm only trying to help you."

"Sorry if I overreacted." Regretting my outburst, yet frustrated with his annoying habits, I sighed. "But please...*please* stop begging the question or answering me with platitudes or being so darned cryptic about Eve-ry. Lit-tle. Thing." I squeezed my eyes shut and silently counted to three. Then I rubbed my temples to stave off a sudden headache. "Look, I appreciate your showing me around Kyoto, but I don't think we should..." I stifled another sigh, stopping before I said too much.

"Point taken." His mouth grim, he dipped his chin on his chest. "Apologies if I appeared condescending. That wasn't my intent." Respect glimmering in his eyes, he came to attention with a subtle bow. "Let's raise the white flag and have lunch in a traditional Japanese restaurant just off the temple grounds."

Chapter 6—Tokyo

Tuesday Dusk

On the first floor, Rafe turned toward me. "You'd wanted to experience *Kabukicho's* night life for your article. Would you like to visit the Golden *Gai*?"

"Sure!" I grinned at my premature enthusiasm. "What is it?"

"It's the 'Golden District,' where you poke your head inside doorways or peek up stairways and choose where to stop for a drink or a bite to eat. We can pub crawl to your heart's content."

"Sounds like fun." Then my smile faded as I remembered Chase's words.

"What?" He stopped.

"Chase didn't have the highest opinion of *Kabukicho*." I scowled. "And from what you've told me, neither do you. What don't I know?"

"*Kabukicho* is Tokyo's red-light district, but it has many areas. The Golden *Gai* is the"—he inhaled—"*least* dangerous."

"Dangerous?" *And Mia works nights...*"Why?"

"The Golden *Gai* is home to the less risqué entertainment—themed restaurants and bars, karaoke clubs, and cabaret shows."

"If the area isn't risky, why are you so against Mia working there?"

"She works in a rougher section of *Kabukicho*, and her job—hostessing—is on the fringe of adult entertainment—strip theaters, peep shows, 'soaplands,' 'lovers' banks, porn shops, sex telephone clubs, *pachinko* parlors, host or hostess clubs, 'bottomless' coffee shops with mirrored floors, and of course, love hotels. You can find anything in *Kabukicho*—for a price."

Guessing at half the terms, I got the gist.

"Mia makes good money, but she's treading on thin ice." He grimaced. "Hostesses have short careers, and if she's not careful, she'll become an alcoholic, addict"—he drew a deep breath—"or worse."

"What do you mean 'or worse'?"

"The *Yakuza* controls Japan's adult entertainment industry, and Atsuki is *Yakuza*." Rafe's eyes took on a pained gaze. "She could get hurt."

"Mia's a big girl. She can take care of herself." His words were chilling, but I trusted Mia's grasp of the situation. "Besides, I thought you said the Golden *Gai* was fun. You make the area sound like a den of iniquity."

"It's both." He gave a mirthless laugh as his expression soured. "What you find depends on what you look for." He recovered his smile as quickly as pulling on a jacket. "But if it's background information you want for your article, this is the place to find it. Ready?"

****

Kyoto

Monday Afternoon

The longer we delay the inevitable, the harder it'll be to say sayonara. I hesitated as we finished lunch, debating whether it was wise or fair to travel together when Chase and I clearly did not see eye to eye. "Perhaps it'd be best—"

"*Arigatōgozaimashita.*" The waitress presented the bill on a red lacquered tray with a smile and a graceful bow.

He reached for the check.

Beating him to it, I slapped my credit card on the tray.

"Thank you, but that really wasn't necessary."

"Nonsense." I waved away his objections with a flick of my wrist. "You've paid for everything else. It's only fair I pay for one meal, at least—make a token gesture."

"You misunderstand." He shook his head. "Our time together is rejuvenating. Each time I introduce you to something different, you make it an adventure, even if vicarious." The corners of his mouth sagging, he slumped in his seat.

His expression tugged at my conscience. *What do I say?*

"Let's climb Monkey Mountain together." He lifted his shoulders with an air of expectation. "It's steep, but I can walk you through it. After that, if you still want to part ways, it's your call."

Steep? My heart skipped a beat. *Maybe one last hike together...but then how do I know he'd leave?*

"I always keep my promises." His spine stiffened. "I have no option."

Is he reading my mind? Before I thought it through, his words registered. "No option?"

"Call it honor among thieves if you like"—his lip curled—"but it's a moral code I follow. If you can tolerate me a few more hours, I'll guide you up *Iwata* Mountain. Then if you like, we part company. You have my word."

His eyes hardened to blue ice. His tone and body language sent a chill through me, but the thought of scaling a mountain alone terrified me. I discretely patted my lips with my napkin, wiping away the fine beads of perspiration.

"You still have your natural curiosity"—his laugh was sarcastic—"yet you literally ooze fear."

If I weren't so afraid of heights…or if it weren't for this article's deadline…I'd tell him what I really think. My chest heaved in a stifled sigh. *I'm between a rock and a hard place…*

"Is that what you think of me? The lesser of two evils?" The color drained from his face. "Rather than climb alone, you're willing to endure my company."

I blinked. "Can you read—"

"Your thoughts?" He gave a quick, disgusted snort. "Your face is so expressive, mindreading isn't necessary."

He all but admits he can.

"*Arigatō.*" The waitress returned my credit card with a bow.

"*Gochisousama-deshita.*" Chase's head bobbed in a slight nod. After the woman left, he turned toward me, repeating the words.

"What does that mean?"

"It's a way to show appreciation for my meal, toward both the person serving and the person buying." Once again, his smile was polite and distant.

He's frustrating one moment and fascinating the next. I stifled a sigh, vacillating between distrust and dependence. *I could skip the mountain, but unless I explore and report Kyoto's highlights, my article won't sizzle. Better face it—with tonight's deadline—I need his help.* I took a deep breath. "Ready to climb Monkey Mountain?"

****

After scaling seven sheer flights of stairs, I followed Chase up a steep, zigzagging path. The more perpendicular the climb became, the more often I had to stop. And during a particularly vertical rise, I hunched over, bracing my hands against my knees. Exhausted, I gasped. "I've got to catch my breath."

"The next switchback has a bench. Just a few more feet."

I shook my head. "I can't go another step."

He scanned the rocky, unpaved path. "Come on." He held out his hand. "I'll help."

I hesitated only a moment before grabbing his hand as if it were a lifeline.

Like an electric jolt, his touch shook me to the bone. The instant our fingertips connected, a current surged up my arm and down my spine. His vitality seemed to course through my veins and into my bursting lungs and burning thighs.

"What just happened?" Stunned but revived, I stared at his drawn, washed-out face. In the dappled sunlight, his eyes seemed a faded blue and his smile lines deeper.

"I offered you a hand." His chin dipping on his chest, he gave me a wan smile.

"Maybe this climb is steeper than we realized." My hand still in his, I took a deep breath, filling my lungs.

"Apparently." His voice was a raspy whisper, as if he were exhausted.

Is it my imagination, or did I somehow tap into his strength? I let go his hand. "Thanks."

Several minutes later, I plopped on the bench and lay my head against the back rest.

"We're halfway up." Chase drew a ragged breath.

"What happened back there?"

He scrutinized my face. "Are you familiar with the term 'the laying on of hands'?"

"Sure." I nodded. "It's an energy transfer, like in a healing service."

"Energy can be transmitted through touch—or even proximity."

"Like a contact high?"

Nodding, he chewed the corner of his lip. "Have you ever been around someone that drains you emotionally or physically?"

"Yes, *you*." Still reeling from the most recent event, I thought back to that morning and previous evening. "For whatever reason, you sap my strength—except for a few moments ago, when it seemed your energy flowed into me."

"I wondered if you'd sensed it…consciously." He paused, tilting his head from side to side as if weighing choices. "Are you aware you're intuitive? In fact, you may be an empath."

"No…" I wrinkled my nose.

"You pick up emotional energy from those around you. You're sensitive to people's thoughts or moods. Energy vampires can drain you dry physically, mentally, emotionally—even spiritually." He paused. "Does any of this sound familiar?"

"All of it." *Energy vampire—that was Rafe. Everything had to be about him. With his rants and raves and daily dramas, he was the center of his universe. While I gave him my undivided attention, he depleted me. Then the one time I depended on him, he deserted me without so much as a phone call. He dumped on me— then dumped me.*

I sniffed, seeing the relationship for what it had been. *But what about Chase just now?* "Even if you're right, your characterization wouldn't explain the energy surge."

"As an empath, you have a heightened ability to give—and evidently *receive* energy. Negative energy drains you, while positive revives you. A moment ago, you absorbed my strength like a greedy sponge." His face drawn and ashen, his arms dangled at his sides.

Is it my imagination, or have his smile lines deepened into crow's feet? "Are you all right?"

"I'll be fine." What started as a wan smile morphed into a grimace. "Normally, I recuperate by feeding off others' energy, but this time, you've bled me dry."

"What are you talking about?" I straightened my spine.

"The West has tales of people changing into wolves."

"Werewolves."

"As you're aware, Japan has tales of foxes passing for human." His gaze intent, he tucked his hands under his armpits, his thumbs facing up.

"So?" Though his fixed blue eyes unnerved me, I returned his stare.

"So…" His face took on a triangular appearance— wide cheekbones and pointy chin. "A *kitsune* climbed my family tree."

"What?" My neck hairs stood on end. A primeval

voice screamed *Run!* But a macabre fascination glued me to the bench.

"Family legends say my great-great-great-grandmother was *kitsune* and passed for human."

"You're telling me you're"—I did the math—"roughly three percent *fox*?" I arched my brow.

"So I'm told." He rolled a shoulder.

"I'm a mutt—part Irish, part Polish, part everything else—but every bit human. You don't expect me to believe you're part fox, do you?"

"I knew you were sensitive the moment you petted that kitten yesterday." His pale lips turned up in a smile. "Since we met, I've fed off your energy—"

"Is this a joke?" I narrowed my eyes.

"No." He waved aside the idea. "I've already told you how I vicariously experience your impressions. The best way to describe this process is osmosis. Simply being near you, I absorb your energy—your *joie de vivre*."

Energy can be transmitted through touch—or even proximity. I mentally replayed his words.

"But a few minutes ago, you depleted me." Their sparkle gone, his eyes were a dull, matte blue. "And that's never happened before in my seven hundred and seventy-two years."

"Seven hundred…" Processing his words, I blinked, then burst out laughing. "You're such a pro at put-ons. I almost believed you. *Again*." Still chuckling, I tilted my head, studying him. "But we're back to where this conversation began. What was that energy surge I felt several minutes ago?"

"I told you." He spread his hands, palms up. "You're an empath, who's apparently turned the tables. You've learned how to reclaim your energy." A corner of his mouth lifted in a tired smile. "In fact, everything I've told you is the truth—just peppered with several half-truths. You decide which is which."

More tall tales...how can I believe anything he says?

****

Tokyo

Tuesday Sundown

Godzilla—the one landmark I recognized—peeked above the forest of vertical signs. As the shadows lengthened in the city's canyons, Tokyo's neon lights exploded like fireworks at Lunar New Year.

Kabukicho is a Japanese Vegas.

The cab skipped the flashy clubs and lounges, stopping instead at a narrow alley. Lining both sides were Red *chochin* lanterns and small signs in *kanji.*

Only an occasional English word or phrase gave me a feel for the neighborhood—*Bar, Open, No Charge, No Tax,* and *No Tattoo.* Rafe's concerns about Mia's *Yakuza* friend washed over me.

I poked my head in the first bar for a looksee, but the blaring, offkey karaoke pushed me back.

"Golden *Gai* has roughly two hundred bars to choose from, so don't feel you have to settle. Pick and choose." Rafe shrugged. "See what catches your fancy."

Comparing the bars as we checked out the area, I whispered a voice memo into my phone.

"Billboards, air conditioners, potted plants, and empty beer crates clutter the already narrow walkway as tourists brush shoulders with men toting briefcases, students wearing backpacks, women carrying shopping bags, and couples decked out for a night on the town."

Every so often, a hawker tried to lure us inside a dark doorway.

Rafe shook his head and kept walking. "Rule of thumb." He turned toward me with a crooked smile. "If they pitch you, don't go in. It's a trap. Once inside, you rack up hidden charges, then they lock the doors until you pay."

"Yikes." Relieved to have a knowledgeable escort, I gave a shaky laugh. "Glad you're with me." As I developed a feel for the neighborhood, I took notes for the article, verbally sketching the area's character into my phone. "Golden *Gai* is a time-warped tumble of closely-packed, closet-sized, and independently themed bars, all packed into six alleys."

The next bar sported chandeliers and flickering candles, and the bartender greeted us with a friendly smile.

Intrigued, I smiled back. "Let's try this place."

After ordering local beer, we found a tiny, candlelit table on the roof terrace. With a gentle breeze blowing, the evening was balmy, and the skyglow complemented the candle's glimmer.

Because of the closely spaced tables, wisps of conversations floated past, but without understanding Japanese, I heard only white noise. Speaking English ensured additional privacy, providing unexpected intimacy in a packed bar, and lulled into a sense of affable seclusion, I let down my guard. "Why did you move to Tokyo?"

"I mentioned how I'd found relief through the monthly healing services."

I nodded.

"After Ashley's death, I immersed myself in the church's outreach ministry, and when a foreign missionary assignment opened, I quit my job to accept it."

"But why?"

His eyes glazed over, as if he looked inward. After a moment, he refocused, and his gaze met mine. "I accepted partly because I want others to know the same peace those services gave me." Sighing, he bunched his lips. "But mostly I took the position because I blame myself for Ashley's death. I figured missionary work might compensate for it." He raised a shoulder in a semi shrug. "Thought *maybe* I could work off my penance."

I leaned back in my chair. "Odd the turns life takes." Then I recalled our earlier conversation. "But Mia said you worked in a language school. What's the connection between missionary work and teaching English?"

"ESL is the means for taking the good news to the people. It lets me connect with prospective believers who'd never set foot in a church. I meet them where they are—not where I am."

"But how?" I squinted, trying to imagine evangelization in a school environment.

"The classroom is non-threatening. ESL provides opportunities to share the good book. I teach English, and for this service, students are a willing, if not 'captive' audience at hearing God's word." He dimpled.

"It sounds symbiotic—first teach, then preach." I smiled at the rhyme. "So is your goal to tutor people or convert them?"

"My goal"—the corners of his lips rose in an enigmatic smile—"is to do God's will."

My eyelids shot up.

"What?" He chuckled.

Pressing my fingers to my temple, I rubbed my forehead. "You don't sound like the Rafe I recall."

"I'm not." His smile dissolved. "After what's happened, how could I be?"

"Good point." *How couldn't those experiences change him?* "Then let me rephrase the question. Is your *job* as a missionary to tutor people or convert them?"

"Who says tutoring isn't missionary work?" His lips curling in a half-smile, he challenged me. "A missionary is a person sent by the church"—he raised his index finger—"*but* called by God."

"But to do *what?*" Frustrated by his enigmatic response, I spread my hands wide.

"Win new believers, establish them in the faith, and then integrate them in a local church. But *how* a missionary accomplishes those three things is *what* he or she does."

Unable to follow, I shook my head.

"Some missionaries believe conversion is all that matters. For them, evangelizing is a numbers game. They speak to as many people as they can, get as many converts as possible, then leave. Get in—convert—get out." He sipped his beer pensively, as if gathering his thoughts. "Others believe that anything and everything done for prospective converts is mission work."

"For instance…"

"Dig wells, set up medical centers, establish schools, modernize agricultural methods, or a thousand other things, *but* they don't proselytize."

"So—"

"Don't get me wrong!" He waved his arms as if

banishing any unintentional slurs. "I don't belittle their good works in the least, but they have to be careful their work for God doesn't become their God."

"Okay." I glimpsed the evening's subtle skyglow before searching his face for the answer. "So, the *purpose* of mission work *is…?*"

"One: Preach the gospel." He held up an index finger. He added another finger. "Two: Make disciples of any converts, and three"—he held up a third finger, emphasizing his point—"establish effective churches." He sat back with a sheepish grin. "At least, that's my explanation. Whatever *means* a missionary uses to accomplish those three goals is *what* he or she does."

There's the old Rafe—the grad student who held forth Friday nights at Tootsie's. How he'd loved to take center stage…I'd tuned out the drama then, but now he's channeling it into evangelization. Smiling at his conversion, I sat back and sipped my beer.

"Returning to your original question. What's the connection between missionary work and teaching English?" He peered into my eyes. "For me, ESL is the catalyst for meeting and making converts."

For the first time that day—the first time in two years—I looked into his eyes. Flickering with the intensity of hazel neon signs, his eyes riveted me to my seat, and for an instant, warm memories mingled with endorphins.

Then I blinked, breaking the spell. "Your passion for your ministry is obvious. Sounds like you've found your calling."

"The path leading me here was circuitous, to say the least." He rubbed his hand across his face.

I stared into the table's flickering candle as I

considered his words. "Maybe the end justifies the means."

"You're saying my ministry is Machiavellian?" His brow puckered.

"No." I turned toward him, squirming that my words came out wrong. "I mean…the path leading you here was a rough road, but it was the *means* that led you to this profession—this *end*—so the end justifies the means. Good comes of bad."

"Maybe you're right." A slow smile relaxed his face.

"But just because you're enthusiastic about your religion doesn't mean others will leave their religion for yours." Chase and his god *Inari* came to mind. "Traditionally, isn't Japan Shinto?"

He nodded. "Depending on the survey, up to eighty percent of the Japanese practice Shinto, but in Japan, few people identify themselves as belonging to a single religion."

"Why is that?"

"Most combine Shintoism with elements of Buddhism, creating a syncretic faith. Folk Shinto has no formal rituals. It's the 'way of the gods.' Instead of one God, it has many *kami*—spirits that manifest in rocks, trees, rivers—even animals."

"Animals?" Chase's stories of fox messengers and auspicious cats came to mind.

"The Japanese revere nature and natural phenomena. The underlying Shinto mindset accepts all things and beings as *potentially* sacred. As a missionary, I find this openness fertile ground for planting spiritual seeds." He stopped speaking and pressed his lips into a grimace. "But enough of me on my soapbox."

I sipped my drink, peering through the dappled light as I recognized the old Rafe speaking from a new platform.

He leaned forward. "What have *you* been doing?"

"After graduation, I took an entry-level job as an editorial assistant."

"Sounds like your career got off to a running start."

"If you call administrative duties like collating printouts for meetings a 'running start.' " I snickered. "At least, I got my foot in the door."

His warm laugh embraced me.

"But after a year, I began writing display copy and editing *The Mailbag*, the online magazine's contributors' pages. Two months ago, I started writing social copy, and last week, I landed this job as the food and travel correspondent—my first international assignment."

He held up his beer in a toast. "Hear, hear."

I smiled as we clinked bottles.

"You've done well."

Weighing reality against the outward appearances, I wrinkled my nose.

"No, seriously, you're doing what you set out to do, and for that, I applaud you." He drained his beer. "Want another, or do you want to bar hop."

"I definitely want to see more of *Kabukicho's* nightlife for the bar-scene slant of my 'Toolin' Around Tokyo' article"—I grinned—"from the perspective of a wolf searching for a stone-cold fox."

Chuckling, he did a double take. "Well, Stone-cold Fox, I'll hold Golden *Gai's* wolves at bay, while you keep an eye out for a storyline."

My gaze caught his, and for a moment, my pulse fluttered as old feelings resurfaced. *Oh, no, you don't.*

Betrayed by my body, I looked away, annoyed. *Don't ever forget what he did.* Then recalling his circumstances, I turned back, studying the face I'd once loved—and recently despised. With smile lines and a touch of gray at his temples, he looked different. *He is different.*

Pushing back my chair, I forced a bright smile. "Yes, let's see what else the Golden *Gai* has to offer."

We walked into the warm night lit with neon and LED signs. Somehow, the lights seemed charismatic, adding to the evening's charm. Slightly buzzed from the beer on an empty stomach, I glanced sideways at Rafe, thinking how natural it seemed walking at his side, as if time—and Ashley—had never separated us.

Flamenco music streamed onto the street, and I peeked inside the building to see brick archways and dark wooden tables.

"Would you like a taste of Spain? Maybe duck in for a sangria?"

I shook my head. "No, I want to experience Tokyo tonight, not Barcelona."

We bypassed dozens of tiny bars, each playing distinctive music and sporting a different theme. Then retro music from one pub caught my attention and I peeked in. Middle-aged men sat at a bar, building plastic toys, and I shook my head. "Nope."

Seventies punk music blared from another. I kept walking. Another bar boomed out death-metal music with heavily distorted and low-tuned guitars. I picked up the pace, hurrying past.

Then the driving beat of eighties' rock 'n' roll grabbed me, drawing me down a narrow stairway wallpapered in a leopard print. Inside the bar, multicolored bottles of sake and beer lined the walls, and cushioned chairs in faux leopard upholstery beckoned.

I grinned. "Want to try this place?"

"Sure." He glanced at the brew selection. "Looks like they've got local stout."

We ordered dark beer at the bar and found a corner table.

"From here, you can see everyone." Rafe slowly turned, scanning the small bar, while he held his hands alongside his eyes as if slicing the room into thin, visual wedges. "Each scene is a vignette, telling a different story. From this perspective, you can watch what develops between each of the wolves and stone-cold foxes."

"I'll drink to that." Chuckling, I clinked my bottle against his as I glanced at the patrons. Eavesdropping was out of the question. Without understanding Japanese, I missed the linguistic subtleties, but body language was the vernacular. Speaking loud and clear, the customers' postures and subtle movements indicated the intensity of the chase as it distinguished the pursuer from the pursued.

Then I caught Rafe mirroring me. He leaned his chin against his hand or stretched his shoulders whenever I did and inclined his head when I spoke. When my leopard-print coaster slipped to the floor, he nearly tipped over his chair, scrambling to retrieve it.

I tapped my finger to my face, musing. *Maybe I don't have to look farther than the tip of my nose...*

He leaned across the table. "Want to order appetizers?"

Chapter 7—Kyoto

Monday Afternoon

When we reached the summit of Mount *Iwata*, the vista opened before us. Trees and rocks no longer obscured the view, and I could see through the clear mountain air for miles.

Chase pointed out the temple we'd visited that morning and Mount *Inari* in the distance.

Then a monkey strolled near us, casually sat down, and began eating an apple slice as she nursed a baby at her breast.

"Look at that." Not believing my eyes, I glanced around. "No cages, no fences—are these monkeys wild?"

"Only people are caged here." As his eyes flickered with their former sparkle, he pointed to a small, framed building. A heavy-gauge, chain-link grill covered its open windows. "Inside, you buy snacks for the monkeys and handfeed them through the grate."

"Why can't you feed them out here?"

"If the park allowed that, the monkeys would associate people with food. They'd not only become dependent on humans, but they'd mob the visitors." He motioned toward the mother monkey with his chin. "This way, they associate food only with that building, so they remain wild and leave us alone."

"Clever…and humane." I scanned the area.

Monkeys scrambled up the building's wire-enclosed windows, sat on the roof, climbed trees, groomed themselves, or chased each other.

"I've never seen anything like it—dozens, maybe a hundred or more monkeys just roaming freely."

"Want to feed them?" The color returning to his face, he started toward the building at a fast clip.

"Definitely!" Energy replenished, I felt buoyant, nearly skipping as I followed him inside.

We purchased small bags of sliced fruit and peanuts in the shell, then stood near the fenced windows.

Instantly, tiny arms reached between the chain-links for handouts. With hands smaller than a newborn baby's, the monkeys gently slipped the nuts and apple slices from our fingers.

Fascinated by their light, delicate touch, I compared the simians' tiny fingers to ours. "They feel amazingly human."

"The gap between humans and animals is less than you might think"—his gaze caught mine as we left the building—"often negligible."

"Is this another of your jokes?" I tossed my chin, not trusting him to be serious.

"No." He shook his head. "All living creatures are made from the earth's elements, so most of the DNA is shared, just in varying proportions. It's the behavior that differs."

"What do you mean?"

"Think of water, ice, and vapor. Ice is frozen in one place. Water's liquid and moves about, as does vapor, but vapor isn't solid." He leaned toward me. "They all have the same atomic structure. The only difference is their behavior at varying temperatures."

"Now you're comparing animals to water?" I rolled my eyes.

"No, I'm simply saying the difference between humans and animals isn't necessarily genetic. *Behavior* can determine the differences."

"How far do you take this comparison?"

"You mentioned how the monkey's fingers felt human."

"The similarity is ironic." I shrugged. "That's all."

"We have more in common with animals than not. For instance, chimpanzees share nearly ninety-nine percent of human DNA. That's *close* on the genome scale." Head back, he raised his brow, challenging me. "Amino acid data shows human and chimpanzee beta globin to be identical, while human and red fox beta globin share over ninety-one percent agreement."

"Your point?" Frustrated with his statistics, I frowned.

"As long as the DNA is similar—and the right situation presents itself—animal behavior apes human behavior." He grinned. "Pun intended."

"You've lost me." I scratched my head.

"Think of all the stories you've heard of ape-like humanoids—Bigfoot, Sasquatch, Yeti—or the West's werewolf stories about bi-pedal, shapeshifting creatures that are half man and half wolf."

"So…"

"Japan and China have the same half-human, half-beast, shapeshifting stories—but of werefoxes or *kitsune*." Tilting his head at an impudent angle, he met my gaze. "Now, if the DNA between humans and apes *or* between humans and foxes is as close as science proves, why couldn't these beings shapeshift?"

"Because shapeshifters exist only in stories." I jerked my chin. "Anyone who believes those tales is either a child or a fool."

"Really?" Crossing his arms, he smirked. "The oldest text about werewolves is 'The Epic of Gilgamesh,' written over four millennia ago. Whether you believe in werewolves, you've got to agree the belief is persistent." He arched his brow. "Makes you wonder about its authenticity, doesn't it?"

"Nope. It's nothing but hogwash." I scowled. "Why all this talk about werewolves and ape men?"

"You started it with your comment about the monkey's fingers." His tone teased. "How did you phrase it? 'They feel amazingly human.' "

"Next time, I'll think twice about speaking my thoughts." I curled my lip.

"No, don't ever let me curb your natural curiosity. That's what's so refreshing about you—your genuine interest." His gaze homed in on mine. "You force me to view everything from an unfamiliar perspective."

"It's the other way around. You're..." His blue eyes deepened into a hypnotic indigo. The longer I stared, the more spellbound I became.

"You were saying?"

"What?" I blinked, disentangling my thoughts. "I was saying...you're the one who makes me view the world another way."

"Even if you call my ideas hogwash?" His eyes twinkled like faceted sapphires.

"I don't always agree with you, but I always learn something...and..." Again, I paused, tongue tied, caught in his gaze.

"And what?"

"My life is richer." The words began rolling off my tongue as if they had a mind of their own. "In fact, in some ways, I'm sorry to leave tomorrow."

A gasp escaped. *I never meant to say that. Until I heard my words, I never thought that. What is going on with me?* I tried to look away but found it impossible.

"I share your sentiments." He leaned into my space. "Shall we discuss this over dinner?"

"Oh." The word came out a groan. "I can't. Thanks for asking—but my article's due tonight."

He peered into my eyes as if evaluating my words. Then a smile swept across his face so warm that it could have melted Mount Fuji's snow cap. "But it's early, and this is your last night in Kyoto."

"I've really got to get back…" His glistening eyes sucked me into his moving stream of consciousness. The mind-numbing rate of imagery left me no time to absorb it. Mesmerized, I peered into his face as innumerable film clips of places and events bombarded me.

I took a step back and found myself in an eddy, removed from his turbulent flow of thoughts. I breathed deeply, recovering. "I have to finish that article."

"Have you ever tried Kobe filet mignon?"

"Can't say I have." Swallowing a smile, I held up my hands, stopping him. "Look, I know what you're doing."

"What?" Palms up, he spread his arms. "I'm simply asking a question."

"A question that no doubt leads to a tutorial about Japanese culture or Kobe beef with a recommendation that I highlight it in the travel article—"

"I want your article to be a feature story." His gaze

met mine. "Let me help you."

Have I misjudged him? Though not physically attracted, I was grateful for his mentoring, but a question nagged. "Why?"

"Why what?"

"Why would you want to help me?"

"Why not?"

"What's in it for you?"

"I've already told you—the pleasure of enjoying life again." His eyes soft and dewy, his gaze verged on tender. "A better question would be, 'What do *you* gain from our time together?' I want our relationship to benefit you as much as me."

Relationship? "You mean friendship."

"I'll take friendship…" His eyes took on an icy glint.

He played me for a fool. Worse, I fell for it. Thrown off-balance, I retreated behind crossed arms. "Acquaintanceship better describes our encounter."

"Acquaintanceship, friendship, relationship…a rose by any other name would smell as sweet." His hand slid down my shoulder, lingering at my elbow. "Now about the Kobe steak dinner—"

"I should get back to Kyoto." *Did I imagine it, or did he just fondle me?* Straightening my spine, I shrugged off his hand. "Thank you for a lovely day, but…" I sighed. "Good evening." Chin high, I turned and walked away without a backward glance.

I didn't misread the situation, did I? Second-guessing myself, I stared down the steep labyrinth of intertwining paths, and my knees buckled. *Which trail leads back to town and the train station?* I took a deep breath, bracing myself, but broke out in a cold sweat.

"Are you sure you don't want a trail-mate?"

"No, thanks." Shaking my head, I let him pass. Then as second thoughts crept in, I threw aside any dignity. "Wait!"

"Change your mind?"

Head down to hide my scowl, I nodded.

"Always glad to help a damsel in distress."

Humiliated yet indebted, I resented his glib answer and hugged the edge of the narrow path, as far away as possible. "We're back to 'why?' "

"Why? I enjoy your company…"

His earnest tone forced me to peek.

"Usually." His face broke into a mischievous grin.

Is he mocking me? Half tempted to turn back, I paused mid-step. *Sincere one minute and sarcastic the next, he waffles so much, I can't tell when he's serious or teasing.*

"I'm serious."

Is he reading my mind again? I spun toward him.

"I mean it." No hint of irony, his eyes were wide and solemn. "I enjoy spending time with you…"

"Usually." I smirked, neither believing nor trusting him.

"Look"—he glanced at his watch—"we have to take the same train downtown. Let's be civil until then."

"At least 'til we reach the *Arashiyama* station." Though I resented my reliance as I followed him down the jumble of switchback paths and sheer stairways, I had to agree with his logic. *Glad I didn't walk alone. I'd have taken four times as long to pick my way through this maze.*

When we arrived at the train station an hour later, I bit my lip, sorry to end our travels on a sour note.

"Thanks again for your help in Kyoto."

"It's been my pleasure." His tone was polite but distant. "Best of luck."

I raised my hand in a parting wave as I turned toward the ticket counter. But when I found my assigned seat, I mentally groaned.

Chase sat in the seat beside mine.

"We can't go our own ways." My sniff passed for a laugh. "Life keeps throwing us together."

"You often meet your fate on the road you take to avoid it." His shoulders rounding, he clasped his hands.

"Another old Japanese proverb?"

"Nope"—he shook his head—"French."

"Everything happens for a reason, or so they say."

"Do you believe that maxim?"

Tilting my head, I considered it. "Guess I do since I don't believe in luck or coincidences."

"Fate leads the willing and drags along the reluctant."

"Japanese proverb?"

"Nope"—his cheekbones rose in a restrained smile—"Seneca."

"All I know is we keep running into each other."

"Fate brings people together no matter how far apart they may be."

"That sounds Japanese."

"Nope, Chinese." His laugh was good-natured—an old friend sharing a private joke.

The warmth of his laughter surrounded me like an *obi*, that broad sash that encircles kimonos. I chuckled at our inside joke. *I'm going to miss his camaraderie in Tokyo.* Then reminded of the timeframe, I sighed.

"What?"

"I just thought of all I have to do tonight—finish the article, pack, take a nap before catching the morning train—then start all over in Tokyo."

"You'll do it." He gave me an encouraging nod. "I have confidence in you."

"Wish I did." Jet lag catching up, I felt depleted.

"Where are you staying in Tokyo—*Ginza, Shinjuku, Harajuku*?"

"*Shinjuku.* I'm staying with a college friend in *Kabukicho.*"

"*Kabukicho*?" Holding back his head, he looked down his nose. "Really..."

"Why? What's wrong with *Kabukicho*?"

"Nothing, I'm just"—he shrugged—"surprised."

"Surprised by what?" Bristling beneath his cynical gaze, I stiffened. "What's wrong with *Kabukicho*?"

He drew a deep breath as if debating how to proceed. "It's Japan's largest red-light district—mostly bars, hostess clubs, *pachinko* parlors, and 'love' hotels."

"Oh." I blinked as his words sank in. "Now it makes sense. My friend's working this summer as a hostess."

"Is she?" His brows shot up. "Does she know hostess clubs are at the edge of the *mizu shobai*—the water trade."

"What's the water trade?"

"It's a euphemism for Japan's sex industry—from the shogun era, when bathhouses were built as much for sexual pleasure as bathing."

"Mia isn't involved in any of that." Loyalty made me rush to her defense. "She taught English as a Second Language when she first moved to Tokyo, but hostessing paid double or more, she said—plus it gave her time to research."

"Research what?" He cocked his brow as if confused.

"She's finishing her doctoral dissertation in Modern Japanese Studies." I lifted my chin, proud of my classmate. "Mia's an ABD PhD—a doctor of philosophy, all but dissertation."

"Really?" This time, his pitch rose on the first syllable instead of the second, and jerking back his head, he seemed impressed rather than condescending.

"Yes." I rotated my tense shoulders to loosen them. *Why does he always tick me off?*

"Do you plan to cover *Kabukicho's* nightlife in your travel article?"

"Only what I'd mentioned earlier, writing about Tokyo's bar scene—"

"Oh, yes"—ducking his head, he smiled—"from the perspective of a wolf searching for a stone-cold fox."

"Otherwise, I haven't had time to think about it." I shrugged. "This assignment was last-minute. I barely had time to research Kyoto's sights before I left, and I have to finish writing 'Kickin' Around Kyoto' tonight before I even think of 'Toolin' Around Tokyo.' "

"Would you like me to recommend a few places of interest in Tokyo?"

"Any ideas would save time researching." Grateful, I clicked my phone app and held my cell close to his lips. "I'll transcribe your suggestions later."

"As long as you'll be in *Shinjuku*, definitely take in the *Gyoen* National Garden, and stop by *Takeshita-Dori* in *Harajuku*." Then he held up his index finger as if remembering another place. "Don't miss *Yoyogi* Park, especially the *Meiji Jingu* Shrine's inner garden. It's supposed to be a 'power spot.' "

"Like the highest peak of *Inariyama*?"

"Yes, like *Ichinomine...*" His eyes dimming as his lips enunciated the word, he dipped his chin.

"Sorry." I gritted my teeth, kicking myself for reminding him of his breakup. Then I forced a grateful smile. "But thank you for your travel tips."

"Remember, begin in the National Garden." His eyes danced like candle flames in a draught.

"Why?"

"Its entrance is closest to *Kabukicho*." He shrugged. "The gates open at nine. Then if you exit the gardens at *Sendagaya* Gate, it's a short walk to *Takeshita-Dori*, which leads you right to *Yoyogi* Park's entrance. After you tour the *Meiji Jingu* Shrine, walk the length of the park, and the path leads you back to *Kabukicho*."

"So, it's a loop?" I nodded, seeing the efficient use of time.

"Exactly."

I smiled as I put away my phone. "You've come to my aid once again." Then sorry I'd turned down his invitation, I grimaced. "If I didn't have this deadline, I really would like to have dinner, but I've got to finish this article tonight."

"I understand." He waived off my apology. "As you said, everything happens for a reason."

After the train pulled into the station and we walked to the exit, I extended my right hand. "Thank you again. I'm so glad we met." My gaze connected with his as we shook, but when his hand lingered, I pulled away.

"As am I." He gave me a polite bow and left without a backward glance.

I watched Chase until he disappeared into the crowds. *Was he being friendly or forward?*

Chapter 8—Tokyo

Tuesday Evening

Appetizers turned into dinner, then after-dinner drinks. With eighties' music playing in the background, the bar's patrons often joined in the refrains, singing a phrase or two in English. Their enthusiasm contagious, I sang along.

While singing one chorus, Rafe caught my gaze as if serenading me. "Let's give it a shot."

As he drew me into the moment, I studied him. *Is he hinting he wants to start over?*

After-dinner drinks turned into dessert and coffee, then multiple coffee refills.

Before I realized it, the stools were stacked on the bar, and the bartender was sweeping the floors.

"Everyone's left." Rafe nodded toward the empty tables. "Guess we're closing the place."

I glanced about the empty pub and laughed. "You're right."

The bartender opened the shutters, and light streamed through the windows.

"What time is it?" Shading my phone from the sunlight, I glanced at the display. "Five o'clock!"

"Where'd the night go?" Rafe grinned.

I smiled back, sharing a comfortable camaraderie. Our evening's conversation had answered the haunting questions, and as my bitterness dissipated, the resentment had subsided.

The morning was balmy, and the sky was an azalea blue. Rather than take a cab, we walked to Mia's apartment, strolling side-by-side through the Golden *Gai's* narrow streets, then dodging the crowds along *Shinjuku's* boulevards despite the early hour. Saying little, yet much, we reminisced as we rubbed shoulders and bumped elbows.

Feels like old times. I swallowed a nostalgic smile.

When he dropped me off at the front door, Rafe whispered a husky, "Good night." Dimpling, he glanced at the bright sky. "Or should I say good morning?" Then he leaned toward me in a parting kiss.

Unprepared, I stiffened and pulled back.

He recalibrated and kissed the side of my cheek. "Maybe we could see each other again while you're in—"

A tiny but penetrating sound pierced the traffic's din and air conditioners' drone.

"What's that?" Perking my ears, I strained to hear.

The high-pitched cry seemed to come from behind a raised bed of azaleas.

"There it is again..." Walking past Rafe, I followed the faint sound to a silver-gray kitten with crossed blue eyes, black-tipped ears, and a kinked tail. *Another Siamese? Wait a minute...*I caught my breath. *It can't be...can it?*

The kitten's hind right paw hung limp. When I gently touched its foot, it whimpered and pulled back. "You can't possibly be the same kitty I saw in Kyoto...can you?" I picked it up, cuddling it. "But two of you with the same markings and the same sore paw…?"

"Did you find a stray kitten?"

"Yeah. This kitten's the spitting image of one I saw in Kyoto." Gently molding it to my chest, I turned toward Rafe. "I think it's the same cat…"

"Can't be." Shaking his head, he gave a soft laugh. "Kyoto's three hundred miles away."

"But its markings are the same." I fingered through the silky fur, and the feline began purring.

"It looks like a hundred other Siamese cats." He swallowed a frustrated groan as if not wanting to argue. "What makes you think it's the same one?"

"Its hind right paw's hurt." As the kitten began kneading my breast with its front paws, I gently stroked its glossy coat. "Besides, it acts like it knows me."

"A coincidence." Rafe all but rolled his eyes. "No kitten could travel three hundred miles in two days—especially with a sore paw."

"It's possible. I've read of cats hitching rides in car engines." I shrugged off the unlikelihood. "Whatever the reason, it showed up here, and this time, I'm not letting it get away."

He scratched his head. "What are you going to do with it?"

"Get it to a vet as soon as a clinic opens, but for now…" I suddenly realized the responsibilities involved. "I have to get a litter box, food—"

"What'll Mia say? Are pets even allowed in her building?"

"Yikes, I didn't think of that." I sucked in my breath and stepped back from the street as a black limo pulled alongside.

The chauffeur jumped out and opened the

passengers' compartment door.

"What've you got there?" Three-inch heels and long legs first, Mia climbed out. "A kitten?"

A moment later, a Japanese man wearing a dark suit, charcoal shirt, and coal-black tie emerged from the limo. After removing his sunglasses, he made a beeline for the cat, then turned toward me. "*Shamu neko?*"

"Sorry, what?" Shrugging, I shook my head.

He glanced at Mia. "Cat from *Tai*?"

"Yes, from Thailand"—she nodded—"a Siamese kitten."

"*Nani*?" He squinted.

"Baby *neko*…kitten."

"Ah, kit-ten." Nodding, he surveyed the cat at my chest, then reached out to pet it. His shirt sleeve rode up, exposing a gold Rolex and tattoos beginning at his wrist. "I like cat."

The kitten stopped purring. Hissing, it swiped at his hand and squirmed, struggling to jump away.

"I do, too." Tightening my grip, I returned the fellow cat lover's smile.

"This is my friend, Atsuki." Palm up, Mia gestured toward him and then Rafe. "You've met before."

Lips pressed tightly, Rafe gave him a curt nod.

"And this is Ava, another friend from school."

"You look like picture with Mia-*san*."

"Picture?" Turning toward Mia, I squinted. "What picture?"

"You know—the one you, Rafe, and I took outside the student union just before graduation." She rummaged in her bag for her wallet and opened to an old photo, with me standing in the middle.

Just before my birthday. The memories returning, I

scowled. *Just before Rafe—*

"Glad to meet."

"What?" At Atsuki's words, I whipped my head toward him. "Nice to meet you, too." Then remembering my mission, I turned to Mia and lifted the kitten's limp hind leg. "It's paw is hurt, and I want a vet to look at it." Mentally crossing my fingers, I hoped my friend wouldn't object. "Would you mind if I keep the cat a day or two—at least, until it's healed?"

"The condo allows pets"—Mia winced—"but my lease doesn't…"

"I take care." Atsuki held up his hand as if to stop further discussion. Then he spoke in Japanese to his chauffeur, standing at attention near the limo.

"*Hai.*" The man gave a stiff bow, hopped into the driver seat, and pulled into traffic.

"My driver back soon. Bring cat food." Atsuki gave a slight bow.

"Thank you." Impressed with the animal lover, I smiled. "That's so thoughtful."

"Nothing." Atsuki waved his hand as if thanks were unnecessary. Again, his jacket and shirtsleeve rode up, exposing his tattoos.

Rafe glowered at Mia.

Wriggling, the cat strained to escape.

"Can we take this conversation inside?" I tightened my grip as I started for the entrance.

"Sure, I'll get the door." Keycard in hand, Mia glanced at Rafe. "Why don't we all come inside for coffee while we wait for Atsuki's driver?"

"Thanks." I breathed a grateful sigh. "This kitten won't settle down, and I don't want to lose it again."

"Again?" Mia's forehead wrinkled as she led us to

the elevator.

"I'd swear this is the same cat I saw two days ago in Kyoto." Hunching my shoulders, I grinned.

"Kyoto! It's what—four hundred kilometers away?" As the elevator doors closed, Mia glanced at Atsuki.

He shook his head. "Four hundred, eighty."

"I know the idea's farfetched." I gave a self-conscious laugh. "Riding here on the bullet train took two and a half hours, but I *still* say this is the same cat I saw in Kyoto."

"*Hai*." Atsuki nodded slowly as if confirming a suspicion. "Cat sometime more."

"What do you mean?" I caught his gaze.

"Cat sometime messenger—*Inari kitsune*."

"*Inari*? *Kitsune*?" Mia shook her head as she led us to her apartment. "What are you talking about?"

"Fox spirit."

"Rafe, you've studied other religions." Mia turned toward him. "Do you know anything about fox spirits?"

"Not much." He shrugged. "Just that *Inari* is the Shinto god *or* goddess of rice, and a *kitsune* can be an actual fox *or* a supernatural messenger."

"Now that you mention it, I vaguely recall reading about *kitsunes* in Modern Japanese Studies, but I'm unfamiliar with Shintoism's various *kami*." Mia scratched her head. "Refresh my memory."

"Originally, *Inari* was the concept of a successful rice harvest. Over time, devotees fleshed out that belief, and *Inari* became the androgynous god of wealth."

"And the *kitsune*?"

"The relationship has always been cooperative. Initially, foxes kept rice fields free from rodents, ensuring good crop yields. Eventually, people humanized the foxes into guardians and agents."

Though Atsuki wore a bland expression, the veins stood out on his neck. "That what *gaikoku hito* think?"

"Foreigner." Translating, Mia winked at me as she closed the door behind us.

"Japan's history of foxes is complex." Rafe's nostrils flared. "I've only mentioned the basic fox mythology—"

"No!" Atsuki's dark eyes blazed. "Fox spirit more—"

"Does everyone want coffee?" Interrupting with a smile, Mia turned toward him. "Or would you prefer sake?"

"You know what I like…" Atsuki's gaze leveled with hers.

Mia gave an evil laugh as she reached into the cupboard for a bottle of sake and a ceramic cup the size of a shot glass.

Rafe pressed his lips together, scowling as he stifled a sigh.

The kitten hissed, flicked its tail, and swiped at Atsuki.

"Hey, simmer down." Getting a firmer grip on the tiny cat, I sat on one of the breakfast barstools. "What's gotten into you?"

"Feisty little thing, isn't it?" Mia stated more than asked before turning her attention to Rafe and me. "What can I get you two? Sake? Beer? Coffee? Tea?"

"Coffee sounds good." I covered a yawn. "Sorry. It's way past my bedtime."

"And speaking of time, it's late. I should leave."

"Already?" Mia's brow puckered. "You just got here."

"Some of us have day jobs." Rafe shot Atsuki a sharp look.

Atsuki's smile faded as his dark eyes narrowed.

"Come on. Join us in a cup of coffee." Turning on the electric tea kettle, Mia brought out cups and instant coffee. "The party's only getting started."

"I have a nine o'clock class." Rafe shook his head.

"Stay." The word escaped my lips before I realized it. Surprisingly, I didn't want the evening to end. "At least, stay until Atsuki's driver comes back with the cat food." I appealed with a smile.

"Maybe a few minutes." Rafe met my gaze, his face softening into a gentle smile. "Then I really do have to go."

"*Kanpai*." Atsuki raised his glass, tipped back his head, and downed the shot.

As Mia refilled his cup, she turned toward me. "What did you two do tonight?"

"You mean, last night." I glanced at the clock and chuckled. "Rafe helped me research my article in Golden *Gai*." After describing the bars' decors and music, I suppressed another yawn. "I never expected to stay out all ni—"

The teakettle's whistle interrupted.

"Coffee will revive you." Mia stirred the instant coffee in the cups. Then she opened a package and arranged its contents on a plate. "Ava, have you ever tried sweet *senbei* crackers?"

"Nope."

"The word *cracker* is misleading. They're made with *zarame*, raw sugar, and they're closer to cookies than crackers." She passed the sugar-coated wafers. "Try one."

I cautiously nibbled a thin, crisp disk. The first taste was the sugary coating, but as I chewed, I noticed a soy flavor. "Delicious, both sweet and savory. I'd call it a crookie."

Mia chuckled as she passed the plate to Atsuki. "You know, studies show links between diets and temperaments."

He helped himself to a cracker.

"Foods are categorized as sweet, sour, salty, bitter, or spicy." Mia counted off each food group on her fingers. Then she passed the plate to Rafe. "People characterized as sweethearts like sweets. Sourpusses prefer acidic foods. Bitter people choose tart flavors."

"So basically, people are sweet or savory." Ava nodded.

"Or you could divide them as sweet and *un*savory." Rafe glanced at Atsuki before he bit into a cracker.

At its crunch, Atsuki's dark eyes flashed. "You—"

The intercom rang. "*Riku*," said a voice over the speaker.

"My driver." Atsuki motioned to Mia with his fingers. "Buzz."

Moments later, a knock sounded at the door, and Mia opened it.

With a deep bow, the chauffeur presented six bulging shopping bags.

"*Motte kite*," said Atsuki. "*Sorekara kuruma no naka de matsu. Haru o tsutaeru kanojo no rīsu o henkō suru neko o kyoka suru.*"

The only word I caught was *neko*—cat.

"*Hai.*" The driver brought the bags to Atsuki, gave a stiff bow, turned, and closed the door behind him with another deep bow.

Loosening his tie, Atsuki smiled as he gestured to the bags. "For you, Mia-*san*. You keep cat. I fix."

"Thanks, Atsuki-*san*." A sultry smile flirted at Mia's lips as she peered through her mascaraed eyelashes.

"Thank you, Atsuki." I echoed her words. "I appreciate your help."

Wearing a magnanimous smile, he gave a slight nod in acknowledgment. Then with a wide sweep of his hand, he gestured to the gifts. "Please take."

After finding a cat carrier, I secured the kitten. Then Mia and I knelt on the floor, sorting through the bags of food and litter, bowls, plush cat bed, litter pan, scratching post, catnip, calming diffuser, toys—and a gift certificate at a local veterinarian.

"Wow. You outdid yourself. Kitty has more than enough supplies and toys for weeks." After scanning the voucher, I grinned at Atsuki. "And the clinic opens at eight. Thank you again."

"What you name kit-ten?"

I thought of Chase and smiled. "Ichiro."

Cocking his brow, he gave a sly, self-satisfied smile. Then he turned toward Mia. "Now I leave. You have guest."

Rafe stood from the barstool. "I'd better be—"

"No." Mia scrambled to her feet. "Keep Ava company while I see Atsuki downstairs." The same sensual smile ghosted her lips as she caught Atsuki's smug gaze.

"*Sayonara*." After crossing to the door, Atsuki gave me a fifteen-degree bow with his hands stiffly at his sides.

"Thank you again." I rose and shook his hand. "I'm speechless at your generosity."

Again, he waved his hand as if no thanks were necessary, and his shirtsleeve strained, exposing his multicolored tattoos.

Rafe exhaled, stifling a sigh. "*Sayonara*."

His eyes glittering like black ice, Atsuki stared hard at his antagonist. Then he turned away. "Mia-*san*, walk with me."

"Back in a minute," she called, closing the door behind them.

"What a nice guy." Turning to Rafe, I gestured to the goodies spread across the floor. "Can you imagine the cost?"

"Probably no more than a meal at one of his favorite restaurants." Rafe's lip curled. "This display is nothing but a grand gesture to win Mia's—and your—gratitude. Be careful. The *Yakuza* don't give unless they expect something in return."

"No." I shook my head. "Atsuki's simply an animal lover."

He sniffed. "Watch your step."

I glanced at the kitten. "Just hope the cat doesn't jeopardize Mia's lease—"

"It won't."

"What makes you so sure?"

"Atsuki gave his driver orders for Haru to change her lease."

"Who's Haru?"

He shrugged. "Probably one of his soldiers"—his eyes narrowed—"or maybe the apartment's leaser." He blinked. "Or maybe Atsuki owns this place, and Haru's his lawyer."

"I just hope…" Stifling a sigh, I lifted the kitten from the carrier and cuddled it. "You don't think Ichiro will cause any trouble, do you?"

****

Humming an eighties' tune while I showered, I replayed the night's events, chuckling as I recalled singing along in the Golden *Gai* bar. Then, while drying off, I thought of Rafe's serenade. "Let's give it a shot." *Was that an invitation?*

I pulled on an oversized t-shirt, then groaned as I set the alarm for seven-thirty. *It's six-thirty now—barely long enough for a catnap.*

The kitten watched me through enormous blue eyes, meowing as he rubbed against his crate's frame.

"Poor baby. Is that cage scary?"

As if he understood, he mewed.

I reached into the crate to pet him. "Would you rather sleep with me, Ichiro?"

Purring, he head-butted my hand, then rubbed back and forth against my arm.

"It's almost like you're answering me." I lifted him from the crate, cuddling him to my chest. Then I slipped between the sheets and turned off the light.

The kitten crawled on the pillow, purring in my ear as he kneaded my neck and shoulders with his silky paws.

"That actually feels good." I chuckled at the irony, then exhausted from the long day, fell into a deep sleep.

I found myself walking in a forest of pine, maple, plum, and cherry trees. When I came to a shaded, grassy slope, I sat beneath a flowering cherry tree. A gentle breeze fluttered against my cheek.

No, not a breeze, Chase.

He caressed my cheek as he swept my hair behind my ear and whispered sweet nothings. His breath tickling, he nuzzled my neck.

Goosebumps slid down my spine.

Then he massaged my shoulders and my back.

The tension released, I felt as languid as a cat basking in the sun. I stretched and lolled on my back.

Ever so gradually, his fingers slid over my nipples, circling and gently pinching my areolas to erection. Then he lifted off my shirt while he tongued and suckled at my breast.

As latent yearnings awakened, I arched my back, enjoying the waves of sensation. With a shudder, I moaned, pulling him toward me in a deep kiss.

His growing erection pressing against my groin, his hands cupped my bottom as he rolled me on top.

I eased myself onto him, undulating rhythmically until he filled me. Then riding him like a racehorse, I galloped to ecstasy in wave after wave of wanton bliss. The deeper he plunged into my soul, the greater the thrill.

Bbbrrringg, bbbrrringg, bbbrrringg.

The alarm jolted me awake. As I woke, the heat rose to my cheeks, and I scanned the surroundings to get my bearings. Mortified, I cringed beneath the sheets. *What have I done?* Then relieved to see only the kitten for a bed partner, I gave a nervous laugh. *It was a dream—just a dream.* Drawing a ragged breath, I regained my composure.

The kitten uncurled from between my legs. Purring as it kneaded my thigh, it watched me through heavy-lidded, blue eyes.

Embarrassed by the sensations it elicited, I scrambled to my feet. *Did the kitten trigger those dreams?*

****

I held the kitten while the veterinarian listened to its chest with a stethoscope, then palpitated its neck, stomach, and legs.

"Just a sprain. Otherwise, as healthy as can be." As the vet vaccinated the cat against distemper, he added, "Come back in two weeks for the feline leukemia vaccination."

"I'm leaving in a few days." *Maybe Mia will adopt him.* "But I'll tell my friend."

Mia was still asleep when I dropped off the kitten. Whispering, I scratched behind his ears before closing his crate's door. "You have food, water, and litter, Ichiro. Be a good boy, and I'll be back in a few hours."

Chapter 9—Tokyo

Wednesday Morning

I grabbed a cab to *Gyoen* National Garden and arrived just as the gates opened at nine.

"Fancy meeting you here."

Hearing English startled me. Then recognizing the voice, I spun around. *Chase?* "What are you doing here?"

"Playing a hunch you'd start your city loop here."

"What a surprise." I blinked, not believing my eyes.

But there he stood, handsome in his tailored silk suit, pale blue shirt, and iridescent blue tie. With his violet-blue eyes glinting and his silver hair gleaming in the morning light, he looked radiant.

Seeing him reawakened the physical sensations of the recent dreams. The pit of my stomach still quivering from its aftershocks, I squirmed and breathed deeply, reminding myself that nothing happened. *It was only a dream.* "What are you doing here—both here in Tokyo *and* the garden?"

"Like I said, I have clients…"

"And…?

"*And* this proved an opportune time to meet with them." His blue eyes stared into mine.

His gaze spellbinding, I forced myself to break the visual link. "That doesn't explain how you timed this encounter." Then I recalled the itinerary he'd suggested. *The gates open at nine.* "You! You planned this 'chance' meeting, didn't you? You recommended—"

"I may have inadvertently mentioned—"

"And I blindly went along." Huffing, I pursed my lips. *Why are his suggestions so compelling?* I remembered the sense of swimming through the air and his words afterwards. "Hypnotic suggestions alter sensory perceptions…" *Does he hypnotize me? Cast a spell on me?*

Palms up, he spread his hands wide. "You said you liked the idea because the tour's loop was the best use of time." He stared into my eyes.

As if peeking through a keyhole, Chase seemed to peer inside my psyche, then alter my memory.

The longer I stared back, the truer his words rang. I found myself nodding, even agreeing. "That's true…I remember saying, 'You've come to my aid once again.' "

"And that's what I intend to do—help you with your 'Toolin' Around Tokyo' article."

"That's so sweet…I…" My words drifted away as my memory returned. *Wait a minute…What is it about his power of suggestion?* I shook my head. "No!"

"Didn't I live up to my promise to help you with your 'Kickin' Around Kyoto' article?"

"Yes…but I didn't invite—"

"That's what I'll do again—help you write the best travel article that's ever been published." His eyes snapping, he smiled. "I'm here to help…like I did in Kyoto. Is that all right?"

His gaze homed in on mine, intensifying—like a light getting brighter or a sound growing louder.

As I shaded my eyes from the sun, his penetrating stare seemed to cloud my thoughts. I nodded as I began to see his point. "That'd be great..." *Wouldn't it?* I blinked. *Why didn't I see his perspective from the start?*

"Good." Wearing a smile, he handed me a ticket and a brochure. "Here's a diagram of the park." He traced his finger along one of the map's central paths. "Since the roses are in bloom, might I suggest the French Formal Gardens' rose beds?"

Though he asked a question, his tone was commanding.

"Sure..." I shrugged. "You knew your way around Kyoto, and I don't have an agenda, so lead on."

His face relaxed into a benign smile, like a tutor fondly gazing at his student.

"Did you know *Shinjuku Gyoen* was once the Imperial Household garden?"

"All this?" Fingers splayed, I spread my arm, gesturing to the surrounding greenspace and trees. "This park is huge."

"Almost a hundred and fifty acres. No one was allowed in it except the royal family"—he snickered—"and an occasional fox."

"Fox?" Again, I shaded my eyes from the glaring sun to peer into his face. "How would you know whether—"

"But the park's best known for its cherry blossoms in March and April. I wish you could see the trees in the spring. With all their buds and blooms, they brim with life—like you."

"Me?" His description made me pause, and I studied him through narrowed eyes. *Is this a quirky pick-up line?*

His smile drooped as if he sensed my reserve—or

read my thoughts. "Am I being too forward? Too direct?"

"Honestly?" I opened my mouth, meaning to speak my mind, but on second thought sighed.

"I see." He glanced away, his gaze landing on the frothy hydrangeas. "I've visited this park many times, but through your eyes, it's like viewing it for the first time." He gestured to the surrounding gardens. "I've seen it all—done it all—and for so many decades that..."

The light in his eyes blazed into a blue flame, then went out like a snuffed candle, leaving behind opaque, soulless slits. "Life's become monotonous, and truth be told, I'm..." He grimaced and started over. "Life's empty. Apparently, it has been for some time. I just didn't realize how hollow it had become until I saw Kyoto through your lens."

His words sound sincere, yet so farfetched, I can't take him seriously. I scrutinized his youthful, unlined face, comparing his features to his silver-gray hair. "Except for your hair, you don't look old at all." I attempted a smile. "Yet to hear you talk, you've been around for—"

"Centuries..." He straightened his spine. "At least, it feels that way."

"Why?" I peered through my lashes. "How old are you? *Really.*"

"I told you. Seven hundred and seventy-two next winter." His eyes grazed mine.

"Okay." I gave a dry laugh. "I forget how sensitive you are about your age."

"I'm an old man, weary of this world." His shoulders slumped briefly. Then brightening, he quirked a brow. "But you make life fresh again."

Ill at ease, I fidgeted. "Why do you do that?"

"Do what?"

"Compliment me all the time. You make me uncomfortable."

"Why do you call the truth flattery? Everything I've said is true"—he rocked back on his heels—"except for a handful of fibs. You decide which is which."

How can I trust him when he talks in riddles? He wants something from me, but what? I tilted my head, studying him in the morning light—then gasped.

As the July sun bore down, I took a step to the left to study him from another perspective. I took a step to the right and swallowed hard, recalling our earlier conversation. *Only what's solid casts a shadow.*

"What?" His brows pulling together, he scowled.

My pulse raced as I stared at my own long shadow on the sidewalk and compared it to his. The shape of his silhouette wasn't a man's, but what looked like an upright creature's with muscular thighs, bony shins, and a bushy tail.

"Your shadow…"

"What about it?" He glanced down and paled.

From a clear, blue sky, a cloud suddenly appeared, obscuring the sun, and the shadows dissolved.

"For a moment, your shadow looked like a…" Realizing my mouth was open, I pursed my lips.

"Like a what?" His icy blue eyes penetrated.

"A…" My voice a hoarse whisper, I swallowed and tried again. "A fox."

"Odd what shapes shadows take, isn't it?" With a laugh, he turned my attention to the map, tracing his finger along one of the routes. "We're here, and the French Formal Gardens are there." Glancing up, he pointed to the tree-lined path on our right. "This way."

Dual rows of big-leafed sycamores overarched the path, and the trees' cool shade beckoned.

But still troubled by the shadows, I looked from the map's two routes to the actual paths. The sheltered trail was twice as long, while the shortcut on the left was direct but sunny. *One path shady and one bright.* As I scrutinized his profile's upturned nose and pointed ears, our earlier conversation came to mind about light sources exposing fox spirits. *In daylight, it'd be the sun.*

The hairs lifted on my arms and the nape of my neck. My knees went weak. "You're not trying to avoid sunshine…are you?"

He chewed his lip.

He is *a kitsune.* I froze…afraid yet intrigued.

"Is it obvious?"

Comic relief? His inane answer broke the tension, and I gave a nervous giggle. "Yeah."

"Decades ago, antibiotics made me sun sensitive." He frowned. "Sorry, I didn't mean to burden you with my phototoxicity issues." He stepped to the left. "If you like, let's take the sunny path. A few minutes of sunlight shouldn't—"

"Oh, no. Please don't." *He looks so young, I keep forgetting he's old…or so he says…*Flustered, I gripped his shoulder, restraining him, but the gesture reminded me of the dream. Recoiling, I dropped my hand. "I didn't…" I took a deep breath and started again. "I mean, no need for you to be uncomfortable." *Just to prove some dumb point.* "Let's take the path you suggested."

"It's all right. A few minutes' sunlight won't kill me." His jaw stiff, he eyed me. "What do you think I am? A vampire?"

"Of course not." His tone made me flinch. *I sound like an idiot.* "No, this path is fine. Besides, who doesn't prefer the shade in July?"

As we approached the boulevard, the sycamores' mottled and peeling bark caught my imagination. "Don't the tree trunks remind you of Army fatigues? You could stand against them and be completely camouflaged."

He snapped his head toward me. "Why do you say that?"

"Their blotchy colors are the perfect disguise." I squinted, unsure he understood the term *fatigues.* "You've seen Army uniforms, haven't you?"

"Of course, but why did you say *I'd* be completely camouflaged?"

"I meant you in general...anyone." Again, I stared as I walked, suspicious. *Why would he think I'd mean him specifically?* Then his pointed ears caught my attention, and I began questioning his long, thin chin and toothy grin.

The tree branches overhead diffused the bright sunlight. Instead of steady shade, the canopy created a strobe effect with flashes of glare and gloom.

In the fluttering shadows, his face alternated between that of a man and a fox.

I gasped, then covered my mouth with my hand.

"What?" A sunbeam pierced the trees' canopy, illuminating his face, and Chase's attractive features reemerged from the flickering shadows.

"Sorry, guess I'm a little high strung this morning."

Heels clicking together, he tipped his shoulders in a formal bow. "Apologies if my unexpected appearance upset you."

"You were a surprise."

His smile was indulgent—a teacher humoring a favorite student.

My qualms blew away with the summer breeze, and I walked beside him in affable silence. The only sound was the breeze whooshing through the sycamores, covering the urban din of *Shinjuku.*

"Who's Rafe?"

"What?" I turned toward him so fast, my neck snapped. "How do you know about Rafe?"

"You mentioned him." He faltered as his shoe scuffed against the path. Then resuming his gait, he shrugged.

"No, I didn't." Squinting, I slowly shook my head.

"You must have. How else would I know his name?"

"That's what I'd like to know—"

"Don't you remember? You mentioned him in Kyoto." He stared into my eyes.

"I did?" I searched my memory and again shook my head. "No, I didn't."

"Yes, you did. Think back to the night before you left, when you told me about your friend, who works as a hostess."

I reran our conversation. "No, I never mentioned his name." But the more he stared, the more I wavered. *Did I?*

"Sure you did—when you told me your idea for an article on Tokyo's bar scene—from the perspective of a wolf searching for a stone-cold fox…remember?"

"Not really…though…" His mesmerizing blue eyes made concentration difficult. Frowning, I scratched my ear as a dim recollection began to emerge. "Now that you mention it, I vaguely—"

"It was just before I told you about *Gyoen* National Garden…*Now* do you remember?"

His gaze intense, he stared me down.

"Sort of…" I recalled the conversation about Mia and his suggestion to visit the gardens. Then I blew out my frustration in a deep sigh. *Why do I doubt Chase?* "I must've forgotten mentioning him." I shrugged, caving in the battle of wills. "We went to school together. Rafe's an old friend."

"*Just* an old friend?"

As a woman pushed a stroller past us, the fine gravel beneath the baby buggy's wheels crunched and crackled.

Like a hypnotist's fingers snapping, the sound woke me from some torpor. I blinked at the red, pink, white, yellow, and orange-pink blossoms and buds that surrounded us. "We're at the rose garden already?" I glanced from the map to the sycamore path behind us. "Guess I was so caught up in our discussion, I didn't pay attention to the trail."

"Nothing like friendly conversation to pass the time." He pointed at the orderly rows of blooms. "These are the floribunda roses."

I nodded vaguely, retreating into the role of sightseer while he guided me among the roses, each variety more fragrant than the last. I breathed in their heady scents, filling my lungs, and as my head cleared, my memory revived. *No. I never mentioned Rafe, yet Chase nearly convinced me I did.* "Why—"

"It's a five-minute walk to *Sendagaya* Gate. Though the gardens have much more to see, the spring flowers are fading, and the chrysanthemums haven't begun blooming."

"Why did you—"

"Then it's a short stroll to *Takeshita-Dori*."

Let it go. I blew out my frustration. "Taka what?"

"*Takeshita-Dori*. Lined with boutiques and cafes, the street's a mecca for the younger set." His eyes flashed. "Who knows? You might spot a cosplayer or two."

Again, I contrasted his unlined face with his hair. "For someone so insistent he's ancient, you seem to know a lot about adolescents."

He grinned, looking only slightly older than a teenager himself except for the silvery hair.

I returned his irresistible smile as we passed through the gate, then was assaulted by the city's street noise. "Didn't realize how quiet the gardens were."

"What?" His hand to his ear, he turned toward me.

I raised my voice to speak above the traffic's din. "With the trees blocking the sound, I forgot we were in Tokyo."

Outside the walled garden, high-rise buildings loomed high overhead, providing narrow strips of shade from the July sun. I sidestepped pedestrians dodging the harsh noon glare.

"*Hatonomori-Hachiman* is a Shinto shrine along the way. If you like, we can escape the sun and noise for a few minutes, and you can climb Mount Fuji."

"I can *what?*" I spun toward him thinking I'd misheard.

"The shrine has a *fujizuka*—a small replica of Mount Fuji." A mischievous gleam flickered in his eyes. "It's only sixteen feet high, but some believe climbing the mound benefits the pilgrim as much as scaling the mountain."

"Why use the word *pilgrim?*"

"Many believe Mount Fuji's sacred. Some consider it the entry to another world."

Entry to another world...that's Chase. He's my ticket to understanding the Japanese culture.

"Just as climbing Mount Sinai to watch the sunrise is a pilgrimage for Christians, scaling Mount Fuji is a religious experience for Shinto believers, but not everyone gets that opportunity. An urban *fujizuka* is far more accessible, and *Hatonomori-Hachiman* is Tokyo's oldest."

Within minutes, Chase ushered me into a narrow park wedged between high rises, where trees and grass provided relief from the concrete canyons. A red gate announced the shrine. "Once you pass through the *torii*, you enter the sacred space."

I grasped the cement railings, molded and painted to resemble rough-hewn wood as I climbed the *fujizuka's* stone steps. At the mound's peak, I viewed the greenspace below. "Last night, I saw Mount Fuji in the distance, and now I've climbed a mini version."

"Wouldn't climbing the original be better?" His eyes glittered in the filtered sunlight.

"Of course, but how—"

"Mount Fuji's only hours away—a daytrip from Tokyo..." He tilted his head, as if gauging his words' effect.

"I'm on a tight schedule." I shook my head. "I leave—"

"Request an extension." Stepping closer, he peered into my face. "Convince your publisher that staying another day would be cost effective."

"I *could* write a third article..." I began formulating my argument, then waved away the thought. "No, my publisher would never approve it."

"Try." Though his face was expressionless, his gaze bore into me, as if he stared into my future.

Despite the day's heat, a shudder slid down my spine. "I wouldn't know what to say."

"Tell them you can take a train from *Shinjuku* and be back in time for dinner."

"Visit Mount Fuji?" Faltering beneath his stare, I chewed my lip. The idea appealed to my wanderlust. Then as practicality set in, I wrinkled my nose. "No, they'd never agree. Changing flights would cost a fortune."

"Tell them missing this opportunity would cost more. If they want you to make the most of your time here, they need to extend your stay." He leaned into my space. "Your publisher isn't even paying for your hotel. You're staying with your friend, right?"

"True..." Uncomfortable with him so close, I stepped back.

"That savings alone should offset any penalty fees."

Maybe...no. I shook my head. "The Travel Department would never extend my per diem."

"Another day's expenses would be a small price for a third article." He spoke in a soothing voice, his gaze never wavering. "Even if they don't agree to the idea, stay. Travel as my guest. Go on. Text them *now*."

Spellbound, I focused on his eyes, seeing nothing else as I fumbled for my phone. Then logistics came to mind. "I can't text them from Tokyo."

"Sure, you can." His gaze drilled into me. "Dial zero-one-zero, then one and the number."

"That's it? But what if...? How...?" His stare seemed to puncture every argument before I formed the words. Dreamlike, I brought up my phone's text function. "What should I say?"

"With two more days, I can write a third article. Please change my flight date."

Breathing uneasily, I punched the keys, then hesitated, my finger poised over the *send* button. "No, I shouldn't—"

"Hit *send*."

"My publisher will never agree." I groaned, not wanting to jeopardize my job, yet—

"Do it." His eye contact strong, he spoke with quiet authority.

Against my better judgment, I hit *send*. "With the time difference, I won't hear back until late tonight." The deed done, I rubbed my forehead. "Now I'll worry all day, wondering whether I did the right thing."

"Trust me." He gave my shoulder a reassuring shake. "You did."

After walking several minutes, Chase turned down a street lined with fashion boutiques and trendy shops targeted at teens. As if by magic, the already crowded sidewalks swelled with Tokyo's teens.

"Let me guess—*Takeshita-Dori*?" I raised my voice over the crowd's drone.

He gestured with his chin, indicating a group of youngsters.

Dressed in love beads and mismatching tie-dyed top and skirt, one girl looked like a flowerchild lost in time. Another resembled a pirate with a shark-jaw jacket, green-striped top, and fuchsia fishnet stockings.

A third girl in pink hair and a cat-ears headband wore a gingham minidress with a strawberry motif and carried a white muff that resembled a cat's paw.

"No introverts here." Swallowing a smile, I followed Chase and, several blocks later, left the shoulder-to-shoulder crowds of *Takeshita-Dori* for a wide pedestrian thoroughfare.

An immense *torii* rose before us. Beyond, a tunnel of enormous trees lined the broad path, where people sauntered, rather than squeezed between throngs of people.

"This is *Yoyogi* Park. About halfway through, we'll see the *Meiji Jingu* Shrine. Then the park's far border ends near *Kabukicho*."

"We're making the loop." Nodding, I recalled the itinerary.

Several silent minutes later, Chase turned onto a side path and pointed to a steeply arched bridge. Including the arc and the water's reflection, the two halves formed a perfect circle. "Have you ever crossed a moon bridge?"

I caught my breath. "It's like something from a fairytale—no, science fiction—a portal to another world."

"I've never looked at it that way." As he led me up the steps, he paused and about-faced. "You did it again."

"Did what?" I blinked.

"Made me see this bridge from your perspective." His eyes blazed like hibachi flames.

My solar plexus tingled. My belly quivered. Blood rushed through my veins like a burning torrent. *What's happening?* Swallowing hard, I looked to him for clues.

His silver hair gleamed in the afternoon light. The toned muscles of his forearms, biceps, and chest strained against his silk jacket. Standing on the step above, he leaned toward me.

Snared in his gaze, I felt naked…vulnerable. I lifted

my lips to his, my body working independently of my mind. *What's going on?* Vivid scenes from last night's dream flashed before my eyes. My cheeks burning, I inclined toward him, powerless to resist.

He leaned closer, pausing millimeters from my lips.

His breath tickled, heightening the suspense. Unsure what to expect—either from him or myself—I was giddy with anticipation.

The glint left his eyes, and the heavy atmosphere seemed to lift.

"You have a leaf in your hair."

What? The baffling daze broken, I blinked.

He reached his hand toward me. "Do you mind?"

Do I? Uncertain, I faintly shook my head.

His fingers stroked my hair in a shameless caress.

The tiny hairs on the nape of my neck bristled, and a pleasant shudder raced down my spine.

"A souvenir of today's excursion." Wearing only a suggestion of a smile, he handed me the leaf and stepped back. A faint scent of ginger lingering, he continued up the arched bridge and paused at the top.

As my mind cleared, I laughed at my overactive imagination. *What did I think—that he was going to kiss me?*

"My favorite part of the shrine is the inner garden's 'power spot.' "

"Like Kyoto's *Ichinomine*."

"Exactly." A smile ghosting his face, he turned toward me as if pleased I'd made the connection.

I squirmed beneath his approval. *What is it about him that's so...compelling? I'm not attracted, am I?* I tore my gaze from his, glancing at the surrounding trees to gather my thoughts.

"Refreshing view, isn't it?"

His words startled me, and a nervous laugh escaped. "Picturesque." Feeling susceptible, I turned and resumed the walk.

"*Kiyomasa's* Well is considered a spiritual 'energy spot.' " He spoke in reverent, hushed tones. "Especially on a lucky day like today…"

His husky whisper piqued my interest. "Why is this a *lucky day*?"

"According to the Buddhist calendar, the date's auspicious."

"But this is a Shinto shrine." I frowned, trying to recall the religions' distinctions. "Isn't following the Buddhist calendar contradictory?"

"No, it's syncretism, a blending of religions, the middle way. One enhances the other." Shrugging, he glanced at the surroundings. "And here we are."

A bamboo fence cordoned off a rocky grotto. Several feet below the path, clear water burbled from a stone-lined cylinder, and a queue of people stood patiently in line.

"What are they doing?"

"Waiting their turn to make a wish." Getting in line, he stepped into the grotto and waved me over. "Decide for yourself whether this 'power spot' works…"

"But I don't practice either Buddhism or Shinto." Shoulders stiffening, I hung back.

"It's simply making a wish at a wishing well." He rolled a shoulder, but his gaze remained steady—watchful. "That's all it is—neither religious, nor sacrilegious."

"Somehow, this seems different." My conscience uneasy, I made a humming noise in my throat.

"You've made a wish when you've blown out birthday candles or thrown coins in a fountain, haven't you?" Chin high, he challenged me through narrowed eyes.

"Sure." I shrugged.

"This is no different."

"Then why are they *praying* before the well?"

As each person approached the well, they knelt as they touched the clear water.

"They're not praying." His face relaxed into a mild grin. "They're connecting with the water's energy. Then as they make a wish, they take a selfie."

"You're kidding me…" I did a double take.

"Nope, a picture's part of the experience—an absolute must." His high cheekbones lifted in a smile.

"Why?" Fascinated, I stepped closer.

Immediately, a man joined the queue behind me, and behind him, another couple.

Whether intentional or not, I'm in line. I glanced at the grotto's tiny dimensions. *And I'm trapped.* Traffic flow was in one direction, and the only exit was on the opposite side, creating a moral dilemma.

"A photo captures the moment of that connection." His violet-blue eyes sparkled. Warm and inviting, his smile was disarming.

Making a wish isn't praying to other gods. But when my turn came, I crouched instead of knelt as I dipped my hand in the well's chilly water.

"Now make a wish."

Prompted, I closed my eyes, held my breath, and crossed my fingers. *I wish my publisher would extend my stay.*

"Quick! Take a selfie."

Silly superstitions. I laughed at myself and my qualms, then snapped a selfie, climbed out of the well, and joined Chase on the path above.

As I reached him, my phone buzzed.

"Who could that be?" I glanced at the text and caught my breath.

"Anything wrong?"

"I hope not. It's my publisher." Anxious that my request had backfired, I grimaced. But after reading the message, I laughed out loud.

"Good news?"

"*Definitely.*" I turned my phone toward him.

Publisher—*Your ticket was a flexible fare, so the Travel Department's agreed to extend your stay two days. Make sure your third article's as good as the first—*

"*Now* do you believe in this 'power spot'?" Lifting up on his heels, he wore a self-satisfied grin.

"That text was a coincidence"—I tossed my chin—"nothing more than a well-timed twist of fate."

"*Well*-timed—I get it." His smile widened. "The takeaway from this experience—always ask for what you want."

"If you hadn't insisted, I never would've asked, and if I hadn't asked…" Amazed at the power of a simple request, I barked a laugh.

"Seek and you will always find a way." His eyes glittered. "Mount Fuji doesn't seem quite so distant now, does it?"

"No…it doesn't." Suddenly, the impossible was within reach. *And I have Chase to thank for it.* Then I thought of the logistics and, chewing my lip, speed-dialed my hostess. "I'd better let Mia know—and ask if

I can stay another day."

She answered on the first ring.

"The strangest thing just—"

"Ava? Something terrible has happened."

"What?" The panic in Mia's voice frightened me. "Are you all right?"

"I'm fine, but Ichiro's gone."

"He's not in his crate?"

"No. I've turned my apartment upside down, and he's gone."

"Oh, no." *I closed his crate door, didn't I?* Shutting my eyes, I groaned. *He can't have gotten out...can he?* "Don't worry. I'll help you find him. I'll grab a cab and see you in a few minutes."

"Anything wrong?" His forehead wrinkled.

"The cat got out."

"Don't worry." He dismissed my fears with a wave of his hand. "Cats have a way of appearing in the unlikeliest places—closets, drawers, even kitchen cupboards. You'll find Ichiro."

"I hope so." Only half listening, I agonized whether the cat's escape was my fault. Then his words sank in. "How do you know his name? I never told you."

"Sure you did." He shrugged. "You must have."

"No, I said *the cat* got out." I shook my head.

"Then I must've overheard you speaking on the phone. You said, 'Ichiro's not in his crate.' "

"No, I didn't. I distinctly remember—"

"Let's not argue semantics." He arched his brow. "Don't you have more pressing matters?"

"Good point." Grimacing, I looked left and right. "What's the quickest way out?"

Ten minutes later, I flagged a cab, jumped in the

back seat, and handed the driver Mia's business card with her address. Then my hand on the door, I turned to Chase. "Thank you for today's tour, but I've got to run."

"I'm heading to *Shinjuku* myself." He smiled as he hopped in and shut the door. "Mind if we share the cab?"

"Of course not." I slid over. Then sitting on the edge of the seat, I smacked my head with my hand. "I forgot to tell Mia why I called. I'm just worried I didn't close Ichiro's crate."

"Relax. Like I said. Cats have a way of appearing in the unlikeliest places." He spoke in a low, soothing voice. "Just sit back and unwind."

His tone calming and words reassuring, I sank back.

"That's better." His tone was sing-song, almost as if chanting. "You'll find Ichiro. All's well. Just close your eyes and let go."

Suddenly exhausted, I rested my head against the seat. With a yawn, I shut my eyes.

"Breathe deeply. Focus on expanding your chest and filling your lungs."

As his voice lulled me, the tension slipped away, first from my head, neck, and shoulders and then throughout my body in a cascading effect. I felt as languid as if I'd sipped wine on an empty stomach.

"Good, the stress is leaving your body." He spoke barely above a whisper. "We never did get to that steakhouse in Kyoto. Now with your two-day extension, you have time for dinner in Tokyo."

My eyelids flew open. *What?*

"Doesn't filet mignon sound good for dinner—especially since we didn't have lunch?" His face was so close, I felt his breath.

"I…" I tried to break the mesmerizing gaze but

could not look away.

"After a busy day, wouldn't a relaxing meal help you unwind?" He spoke in comforting tones that dispersed any nagging concerns.

A steak dinner does *sound delicious.*

The cab stopped, and the driver spoke in Japanese.

I glanced out the window and recognized Mia's building. *Seems like we just left the park.* Groggy, as if I'd woken from a deep sleep, I reached into my purse for the fare.

"I've got it." Chase gently laid his hand on mine as he paid the driver.

"No, it isn't necessary…" My hand limp, I tried to object, but I felt so lethargic, I could barely rouse myself.

Palm extended, he helped me from the backseat. Then he walked me to the apartment door. "Shall I pick you up tonight at seven?"

I didn't agree to dinner, did I? I shook my head, trying to remember. *What's wrong with me? I'm so tired.* I drew a shaky breath. *Too much walking, I guess—*

"Seven?"

His sharp tone shook me from my misgivings, and his raised brow demanded an answer. "Seven…sure…"

"Until then." He gently squeezed my fingertips goodbye, then raised his hand in a parting wave as he strode off and disappeared into the crowd.

Chapter 10—Tokyo

Wednesday Afternoon

I rode the elevator to Mia's apartment in a foggy haze. As I pressed the keycard to the scanner, the door swung wide.

"There you are! Why didn't you answer my texts?" Still in pajamas, her hair disheveled, Mia was wild eyed. "I can't find the kitten. How did he get out?"

Though posed as a question, her accusation woke me from my stupor. All sense of peace and wellbeing dispelled, I glanced at the clock. "We spoke less than thirty minutes ago…"

"I'm sorry." Mia put her hand to her temple and sighed. "I'm just so worried about Ichiro." She gulped. "I've looked everywhere."

"Relax, we'll find him." I glanced about the efficiency apartment. *A search can't take more than a few minutes. Just hope I didn't accidentally let him out.* "I'll start in the kitchenette."

"And I'll check my bedroom…for the fourth time." Mia's shoulders sagged.

I opened each of the drawers and examined the contents, searching in and between the linens, kitchen utensils, pots and pans. I rifled through the cupboards, checking behind the boxes of cereal and canned goods, then looked under the sink and behind the refrigerator.

Where is he?

"Any luck?" Mia poked her head around the corner.

"No. You?"

Grimacing, she shook her head. "I'll try the bathroom…again."

"I'll check the alcove." I glanced inside my suitcase and opened each drawer, thinking Ichiro might have crept inside. *No luck.* I crawled under the bed and flashed a light behind the headboard. *Nothing.*

Just as I was about to give up, I noticed a tissue box on the desk, and Chase's story flashed through my mind: *Always sleep in a tiny space. Ichiro wouldn't be in there…would he?* I lifted the box, weighing it with my hand. *Feels heavy.*

A tiny mew escaped. Then the kitten's silky head popped up, and he began mewing loudly.

"You found him?" Mia ran in.

"Yup. The little stinker used the tissue box as a hideaway bed." I lifted the kitten, cuddling him.

"Thank heaven!" Mia gave a deep sigh. "I didn't know what to tell Atsuki."

"Who cares what he thinks?" Her overreaction was getting on my nerves.

"I do."

"Why?

"*Because* Atsuki takes an interest in this little guy." Mia gently took the cat. "And what Atsuki likes, I like."

"Since when?"

"I don't know…recently. Actually, since last night…" Her brow wrinkling, Mia mumbled while she walked into the kitchenette.

"What?"

"Something happened, but I can't quite

remember…" She set the kitten on the counter, and what started as a dismissive chuckle developed into adenoidal braying. "I must've had too much Saki last night."

"Why? What happened?"

"Atsuki said something about cats…and foxes…I can't recall."

*Cats and foxes again…*My ears perked.

Mia took a bowl from the fridge and set it in the microwave. "I'm reheating azuki beans. Want some?"

What did Chase say about azuki beans? "Sure."

Wailing in a high-pitched howl, the kitten paced back and forth on the countertop.

"What's wrong with Ichiro? Is he hurt? Maybe he's hungry." I brought his food bowl, but he continued pacing and meowing. "He isn't eating—but look. His limp's gone." I scratched behind his ears. "Guess all he needed was a nap on his tissue mattress."

At my touch, the kitten began purring and head-butting my hand.

"You little narcissist. What you really wanted was attention." I glanced at Mia. "Which reminds me. The vet wants Ichiro back in two weeks for a vaccination, so if you're planning to adopt—"

"Of course, I'll adopt him *and* take him to the vet." She opened the microwave door, stirred the azuki beans, tasted them, and set the timer for another minute as she licked the spoon. "I love azuki beans…can't get enough."

What was it about those beans?

Again, the kitten paced back and forth on the countertop, yowling at the top of his lungs.

"What's wrong with him?"

"Maybe he wants azuki beans." Mia opened the

microwave, felt the beans' temperature, then spooned some into the cat's bowl.

He wolfed down the beans, flicked his tail, and stared at Mia with his big, China-blue eyes.

Chuckling, she spooned more into his bowl. Then she split the remaining beans between two plates and carried them to the breakfast niche. "The chopsticks and napkins are in the second drawer on the left."

"Got 'em." I joined her at the small, brushed nickel table. "Before I forget. My publisher extended my stay. Would you mind if I stay here another two nights?"

"You're welcome here as long as you want. I like having a roommate."

"Thanks." Relieved, I returned her smile as I crossed that hurdle off my mental list.

Mia glanced about the chic apartment, her smile contracting into a tight-lipped pout. "With you here, I don't feel quite so—"

The phone rang.

Her face lighting up in an expectant smile, Mia scrambled to reach the phone on the first ring. "*Moshi-moshi.*" Then her smile withered, and she handed over the phone. "It's for you—Rafe."

Caught with my mouth full, I gulped the beans. "Hi."

"Hey, you, ever try *tonkatsu?*"

"No." His buoyant greeting made me grin. "What is it?"

"It's a tempura pork dish that melts in your mouth. I know a little ramen shop not far from Mia's place that makes the best *tonkatsu* in *Kabukicho*." His cleared his throat and mumbled. "That is, if you'd like to try it…for dinner tonight…"

He left his invitation hanging as if unsure I'd accept. His insecurity was disarming. The old Rafe had been self-confident to a fault. *He* has *changed.*

"I'd love to go, but..." I stifled a sigh, sorry I'd accepted Chase's invitation. *I did...didn't I?* Squinting, I tried to recall whether I'd agreed or been coerced. Either way, I was obligated. "I'm really sorry, but I have other plans."

"Oh..."

Less a word than a guttural grunt, he sounded like he'd had the wind knocked out of him.

"Maybe another time."

"But you're leaving tomor—"

"No!" Excited by the possibilities, I sat up straight. "My publisher's extended my stay. I'll be here another two days."

"That *is* good news." His smile came through his voice. "Maybe you'd like to go for dinner tomorrow?"

"Sure." My pulse raced at the thought of seeing him, and a warmth coursed through my veins.

"My classes end at four. How 'bout I pick you up tomorrow at five?"

"Perfect. See you then." *Why's my stomach doing somersaults?* I handed Mia the phone.

"What are you beaming about?" Mia smirked as she returned the phone to its cradle. "Old feelings returning?"

"No, not at all." I tossed my chin. "I'm just glad for the chance to say goodbye."

"Me thinks the lady doth protest too much." Mia gave me a knowing smile as she wolfed her beans.

"You must've been hungry."

"I just love azuki beans...can't get enough." She

eyed my full plate.

"Want mine? I'm not that hungry. Besides, I'm going to dinner soon."

"Yes! That is, if you're *sure*..." Grabbing my plate, Mia began gobbling the beans. Then chopsticks suspended midair, she paused. "What's wrong?"

"The way you're inhaling your food, you'll have to let out your clothes." I chuckled.

"I swear, these azuki beans are addictive." The kitten pawed at Mia's leg, and she rolled her eyes. "I'll save you some, Ichiro. Relax."

I scoured my memory. *What did Chase say?* Then checking the time, I gasped. *Dinner! He'll be here soon, and I still have to type my notes.* "Do you mind if I use the desk?"

"Make yourself at home." Mia glanced about the untidy apartment. "Besides, I need to put everything back after rummaging through it."

"Let me help. I brought Ichiro here, so I'm responsible." *And I might've left his cage open...*

"No, I made the mess." Mia turned my shoulders toward the desk. "Go. Write your article."

After transcribing my notes, I still couldn't recall Chase's caveat about the food cravings, so I searched online. Most articles promoted the beans' health benefits—helped resist sugar cravings and lowered cholesterol—but one site linked them to fox possession.

Chase's words returned like a recurrent nightmare. *The idea's ridiculous, but why is Mia suddenly so fond of azuki beans?*

****

The intercom rang at six-fifty-five.

That must be Chase. I buzzed him in and, moments

later, answered the knock at the door.

A delivery boy held out a long rectangular box. "*Eiba Nishi?*"

I stared blankly.

"*Hai. Arigatō.*" Intervening, Mia accepted the package, closed the door, and handed over the box. "For you. *Eiba Nishi* is Japanese for Ava West."

"Me?" *Who'd send me a gift?*

"Who's it from?" Mia's eyes twinkled. "Your friend, Chase?"

"That'd be my guess." I opened the white box to find one perfect, long-stemmed red rose on a bed of feathery green fronds. Lifting the rose, I breathed in its sweet fragrance, then read the card aloud. "If I had a rose for every thought of you, I'd have a garden. Until tomorrow. Rafe." Hand to my chest, I caught my breath. *Rafe?*

"Wow. Someone's smitten." Mia chuckled. "What happened between you two?"

"Nothing." I shook my head as I silently reread the card.

"Maybe *your* old feelings haven't returned, but his have." Mia grabbed a bud vase from the cabinet, half-filled it with water, and placed it on the breakfast bar. "Here you go."

"Perfect. Thanks." I arranged the rose with the greenery and then stood back to admire it.

In a flying leap, the kitten bounded onto the bar and sent the glass vase crashing to the tile floor.

"Ichiro, no. Bad cat!" I picked up the kitten, scolding it as I apologized. "I'll get you a new vase. Let me put him in his crate, then I'll clean up this mess."

"Don't worry over spilled water. Besides, he didn't break the vase." Mia sopped up the water with paper towels and refilled the vase. "See? Good as new."

"Thanks." Double checking that the kitten had food, water, and litter, I locked him in his crate, making sure the bolt was in place. "Don't know what got into him."

"Who knows?" Mia laughed. "Cats are crazy…but adorable."

The intercom buzzed.

I glanced at the time—seven sharp. "That has to be Chase." I spoke into the intercom. "Be right down."

Three minutes later, I stepped off the elevator and into the lobby. "Hi."

"You look radiant." As he gazed at my face, his almond-shaped eyes narrowed. "Any particular reason for your…rosy glow…?"

His sarcastic tone made me do a double take. "Why do you ask?"

"You always look fresh…as a rose…" He paused, staring hard. "But tonight, you have an air of mystery about you…a certain *je ne sais quoi*…yet you come off smelling…like a rose…"

Rose. I fidgeted beneath his scrutiny. "What're you getting at?"

"Maybe it's the devilish glint in your eyes— disguised guilt?" His lips curled in a callous smile. "Anything happen since I last saw you?"

"Nothing that concerns you." Irritated with his insinuations, I pressed the elevator button. "If this is your idea of table talk, I'm sorry to cancel our dinner plans, but I've lost my appetite."

The elevator door opened.

"No, please don't go. I'm the one who's sorry. Can you forgive an old man's insecurity?"

His dejected appeal made me pause. One foot in the

elevator, and one foot out, I side glanced at his sagging head and rounded shoulders. *He does look old.* I stifled a sigh. "No more cross-examinations?"

"Only scintillating dinner conversation." He wore a stoic, wounded smile.

"Promise?"

"My word of honor." Hands stiffly at his side, he bowed at a respectful, forty-five-degree angle.

But will he follow through? My turn to appraise him, I debated whether to go. *I don't recall agreeing to din—*

"I always keep my promises." Gradually straightening his spine, he came to attention. "I have no option."

Is he reading my mind? Then his words registered. "That's the second time you've said you have no option. Why?"

"Honor. Without your word, what have you?" Chin high, he stood ramrod straight.

Though skeptical, I nodded. "Okay, lead on."

We grabbed a cab and ten minutes later walked into an intimate, dimly lit restaurant.

"This is Tokyo's finest Kobe steakhouse. It serves *haute cuisine,* seats only six, and is rated three Michelin stars." He spoke over the soft jazz playing in the background. "Reservations are booked a month in advance—and the reservations line is open only two hours a day."

"Booking a table sounds next to impossible." Skeptical, I arched my brow. "If the restaurant's that exclusive, how does it stay in business?"

"Its only problem is turning people away. Each seat receives nearly a thousand requests a month." A smile started at the corner of his mouth and spread across his face. "And you don't book a table. You reserve a seat at the counter."

"Are you serious?" I pulled back my head to study him. *A seat at a counter...? Sounds like a dime-store luncheonette.* "If this place is so trendy, how did you get reservations on such short notice?"

"The chef's an old friend..." Barely hiding a self-satisfied smile, he adjusted his diamond-studded cufflinks.

I contrasted the décor of the restaurant with a roadside diner. Instead of a chipped Formica counter, polished granite topped the chic bar. In place of white stoneware and chintzy flatware, each setting included a metal charger, folded linen napkin, champagne flute, oversized red wine glass, chopsticks, steak knife, and a variety of forks. Instead of bar stools, six sumptuous armchairs lined the counter.

My eyes took a moment to adjust to the adjacent kitchen's low light before copper pots gleamed from behind the counter. Then a grill, stove, and brick oven came into focus. I spun toward him, unconvinced despite his hype. "No matter how upscale the trappings, this place still reminds me of a diner."

"The concept is restaurant as theater." In the dim light, his eyes glowed a midnight blue. "As the chef grills the dinner, the preparation is the show, and the steak is superb."

Speaking in Japanese, a man wearing a tall chef's hat, white apron, and double-breasted jacket placed his hands on Chase's shoulders, greeting him like an old friend. Then with a wink, he rolled out the armchair at the counter's end and seated me. Gesturing for Chase to sit at my left, he spoke in excellent English. "So, you don't have to share your beautiful lady with anyone else."

"This charming *itamae* is *Ginji*." Chase grinned as he turned toward me. "And this 'beautiful lady' is my friend, Ava."

"*Eiba,* welcome to my humble kitchen." The chef acknowledged me with a thirty-degree bow. "Please sit back and make yourself comfortable."

As I sank into the armchair's plush cushions, I relaxed into its comfortable fit. Unlike the oversized chairs in the States, I did not have to sit on the edge for my feet to touch the floor.

"Prosecco to start the evening?" The chef popped the iced bottle's cork and, without waiting for an answer, poured its bubbling contents into our champagne flutes. "What would you like for dinner?"

"*Omakase.*" Chase half-turned toward me but eyed the chef, seeming to speak for his benefit. "I recommend you leave your choice to Chef *Ginji.* He knows today's specialties better than anyone."

I arched my brow at the idea of anyone ordering for me—even the chef. The idea smacked of male control. *But this entire trip, including this meal, is a fact-finding mission.* I shrugged and raised my hands, palms up. "When in Rome...or Tokyo..."

"Excellent choice. You won't be disappointed." With a smile, the chef lifted a glossy, purple vegetable from a basket. "Your first dish is Chinese eggplant, teppanyaki style, in a light garlic sauce, followed by miso-glazed Japanese sweet potatoes." He flourished a purple yam and began flamboyantly slicing and dicing the vegetables.

During the performance, I sipped Prosecco as I

made small talk with Chase.

Before my glass emptied, *Ginji* snapped his fingers, and a young man instantly refilled it. By the time the first dish arrived, sizzling and steaming, I was pleasantly buzzed.

I bit into the tender slivers of eggplant, garnished with paper-thin rings of red pepper, and detected the licorice flavor of star anise with just a hint of garlic. "Delicious."

Ginji again motioned our server to refill my glass.

The moment Chase and I finished the first course, the chef replaced it with the second course. Diced and grilled into crispy chunks, the sweet potatoes were caramelized in a soy and brown-sugar sauce, then sprinkled with sesame seeds.

The food delectable, the service was impeccable, and with my wine glass always full, I found the company charming.

True to his promise, Chase's behavior was sterling. Dressed in a perfectly fitted, blue silk pinstripe suit, he exuded an air of reserve and controlled power.

A gleam below his starched cuff caught my gaze. Surprised to see no dial face on his gold skeleton watch, I watched the mechanism's coils tick off the seconds. *Time*...I glanced from Chase's smooth hands to his boyish face. *Except for his silver hair, he looks so young in this light—as if he's prematurely gray.* I drained the last of the sparkling wine and was mildly disappointed as our server whisked away my flute.

Then with a nod and a knowing smile, he half-filled my oversized wineglass with Merlot, its color a rich, burgundy red.

The chef continued the show, meticulously slicing

the thick chunks of marbled Japanese beef.

Whispering, Chase leaned toward me. "Watch *Ginji's* grilling technique over his charcoal-fired brick oven. After searing the steaks, he'll place them in a cooler part of the oven to roast until they're done to perfection: Crispy on the outside but moist and tender on the inside." His gaze met mine. "What do you think so far?"

"The food's exceptional." I filled my lungs with the tantalizing aromas of wood smoke and roasting beef. "I can smell the steak from here." With an anticipatory groan, I sat back, propping my elbow on the arm of my chair. "I can't wait to bite into it."

"Soon enough." His blue eyes blazing like the gas stove's flames, he leaned close and spoke in a hoarse whisper. "*Ginji's* mastered the art of building a crescendo of anticipation until the culinary experience climaxes with the entrée."

His words had a risqué ring. *Was that a double-entendre?*

As if in answer, he ran his finger along my arm.

Yanking my elbow from the chair's arm, I sat up straight, and focused on the chef. But in my peripheral vision, I glimpsed Chase subtly motion the server to top off my glass.

As the man approached with the wine, I covered my glass with my hand. "No, thank you." I glanced at the chef. "Could I have water instead?"

Ginji snapped his fingers and spoke in Japanese. Moments later, the server placed a water goblet before me, opened a chilled bottle of sparkling water, poured, bowed, and left.

Check mate. I smiled sweetly at Chase.

He half grinned, half leered before downing his wine and motioning for more. Then he lifted his glass in a toast. "Check mate."

His words made me gasp. *Can he read my mind?*

"*Bon appétit.*" The chef placed a picture-perfect tenderloin before me—crisp, browned, and still crackling from the oven.

Nodding my appreciation, I turned my attention to the sizzling steak.

"Enjoy." With a slight bow, the chef about-faced and busied himself in the kitchenette.

"The *Kobe-gyu* is a feast for the eyes and the palate."

I bobbed my head but could not face Chase. Instead, I concentrated on cutting into the meat with the steak knife, but it was so tender, a butter knife would have sufficed. I took a bite, and the meat melted in my mouth. Chewing was hardly necessary.

"Notice the fine texture, unparalleled marbling, and rich flavor…as well as that deep azuki bean color."

Recalling his earlier words about the beans, I spun my head toward him. "Azuki?" Mia's recent craving came to mind.

"Yes, the steak's rich, red color." He pointed at the meat's rosy hue with his knife. "You should include Kobe beef in your travel article."

"Definitely."

"How's your tenderloin?" His gaze tracked mine and lingered.

"Beyond delicious."

His expression warm, he seemed to hang on my words.

Relenting, I returned his smile. "I don't believe I've ever tasted any cut this tender or juicy."

"Good." He leaned sideways, tilting his head toward my ear and speaking quietly, as if in an aside. "I was afraid you weren't enjoying it."

"This meal is a foodie's dream come true." *Maybe I've misjudged him...again.* "Thank you for introducing me to yet another aspect of Japanese culture. Once again, I'm indebted."

"Entirely my pleasure. Since the timing was wrong in Kyoto, I'm glad we're able to share this meal here." His eyes flashed, and his nostrils flared, giving his face an inviting, open expression.

Except for his silver hair, Chase looked like a young man in the restaurant's dim lighting. Amused at my overactive imagination, I gazed at his unlined face. *He can't read my mind any more than I can read his. Where do I get such absurd thoughts?*

We no sooner finished the steaks, than the chef served iced dishes of citrus sorbet.

"Tokyo has many *Inari* shrines, but the *Kaichu Inari* Shrine is nearby." His watch flashed as he straightened his tie and smoothed his lapel. "Would you like to visit it after dinner?"

"Wouldn't it be closed?"

"No, the shrine's open twenty-four, seven, every day of the year." He glanced at the time. "Besides, eight-thirty's early."

I don't have a deadline tonight, and I'm caught up with my notes from today. I shrugged. "Sure, why not? It'll be Tokyo's answer to Kyoto's *Fushimi Inari* Shrine."

As we left the restaurant, we walked past a convex antique mirror.

Still buzzed, I giggled at our distorted,

disproportional reflections. His ears looked pointed, like an elf's. *No, like a fox's.* Startled, I gulped.

"What?"

"I…I thought I saw…" Fingers shaking, I pointed at the mirror.

"What?" He glimpsed the mirror.

His reflection was normal.

"Nothing." Relieved, I giggled and shook my head. "Just that convex mirror playing tricks on my eyes." *Or too much wine…*

A short ride later, the cab stopped in front of a narrow alley squeezed between high rises. Then I noticed the *Inari* fox statues lining its length with the nearest statue holding a baby fox beneath its paw. "I don't recall the *Fushimi Inari* Shrine having statues with fox cubs. The ones I saw held jewels in their mouths."

"A kit symbolizes fertility, while a gem represents wealth." He led me to another fox holding a rolled-up paper. "This scroll indicates a message from *Inari*—"

"With the *kitsune* as the message bearer." I nodded, beginning to understand.

"You *are* learning." His slow smile raised his high cheekbones, and his face assumed the indulgent expression of a doting tutor.

I smiled back as vague memories of a blue star on my second-grade homework came to mind.

"About tomorrow…"

"Yes?"

"I thought we could finish touring Tokyo by early afternoon, make it an early night, so you can finish the 'Toolin' Around Tokyo' article. Then in the morning, we'll catch the first train to Mount Fuji."

His tone stated more than asked, as if he had worked

out the best itinerary and his question was rhetorical—merely a formality.

Reminds me of the chef ordering for me. Bristling at his show of male control, I wrinkled my nose.

Then stepping closer, Chase homed in on my face, his eyes darting left and right as he took in my features.

The effect of his full attention was captivating. I lost my train of thought, and any critical thinking evaporated. "I'm sorry. What did you ask?"

"Does that schedule work for you?" His gaze penetrated as if he intuited my thoughts.

"Sure." I spoke too quickly, giving my assent before I'd had time to think it through. *Why did I agree so fast?* I mentally ran over my schedule and deadlines. Then I dipped my chin, swallowing a grin. *Ironically, the timetable's perfect—even leaving time for dinner with Rafe.* At the thought, a warm tingling raced through my body.

"Did you hear me?"

Emerging from my reverie, I peered through my lashes. "I'm sorry. What was that?"

"I *said*"—his eyes narrowed—"tomorrow, we'll tour Tokyo's two tallest towers—"

"I've been to one of them."

"Really?" He arched his brow. "Which one?"

"*Tochō.*"

"The government building." Looking down his nose, he gave a disdainful sniff. "*Tochō was* Tokyo's highest tower…thirty years ago. I'm talking about the Tokyo Tower and Skytree." Then his eyes darkening to a stormy blue-gray, he examined my face. "Who took you to *Tochō*? Rafe?"

"Who promised no more cross-examinations?"

Stepping back, I jerked my chin.

"You're right. No more questions."

His sigh sounded like a deflating balloon.

Why does he always spoil an otherwise lovely evening? "I think it's time to hail a cab."

"As you wish." He bobbed his head in a stiff bow.

We left the shrine, walking past one dark storefront after another without seeing a taxi.

Watching our reflections in the glass windows, I felt I was streaming live video. Then gradually, the reflected image seemed off kilter—a subtle misrepresentation of what my eyes perceived—like a TV's sound out of sync with its picture, where the actor speaks before his lips move.

At first, the distinction between reality and its reflection was negligible, but with each passing window, the difference became more pronounced until I realized the discrepancy. *Something's behind Chase...beneath his jacket.*

An image of the snow monkeys came to mind, their tails swinging at their legs as they walked upright. *He has a tail!* Like in a waking nightmare, I tried to scream, but only a strangled yelp escaped.

"Are you all right?" He spun toward me.

Instantly, the illusion vanished, and I gulped as my adrenaline spiked. "I thought..." I shook my head. "I must've had too much wine..."

"Why do you say that?" His breathing labored, he stiffened.

I know what I saw...but that's impossible. I gave a nervous laugh at my overactive imagination. "All these tales about *Inari* and *kitsunes* are making me jump at every shadow and reflection..." Confused, I turned toward him. "That's all it is, isn't it?"

"Of course." He glanced at the store window, then regarded me through stern, narrow eyes. "What else could it be?"

"I don't know…"

"The dark plays tricks on the mind. What the eye can't detect, the brain fills in, sometimes leading to fantastic delusions."

"That wasn't the case." My palms perspiring in the hot July evening, I shook my head, questioning what I'd seen. "I could've sworn you had a—"

"Plus, manga and anime put their own spin on *kitsune*. If you're a fan of either, who knows what fantasies you might imagine?" He hailed a cab and opened the door. "Hop in. It's time to get you home to Ichiro."

"You're probably right…" As I stepped inside the cab, his words registered. "How *did* you know the kitten's name?"

Chapter 11—Tokyo

Wednesday Evening

I froze as I entered the apartment.

Magazines were strewn across the floor. Clothes were heaped on the beds. The cabinet doors stood wide open, and all the drawers were overturned, their contents jumbled together on the floor.

Someone's ransacked Mia's place.

Sobbing came from the bathroom.

Mia? I tried the door, but she was slumped in front of it. Anxious, I slammed my body against the door until it opened enough to squeeze through. "Are you all right?"

She huddled in a fetal position, staring at nothing as her tears dissolved her mascara and slid down her cheeks in dark streaks.

"What happened?"

She turned red eyes toward me. Between sobs, she tried to catch her breath, but her words were lost as new rounds of weeping gripped her.

I grabbed a tissue from the ripped-open box on the floor, crouched beside her, and put my arm around her shoulders. "What happened?"

Her back pressing against the door, Mia crossed her arms over her knees and choked out the words. "The kitten's...gone." The last word a loud wail, she hid her head in her arms.

"That's it?" *Are you kidding me?* I let out a disbelieving groan. "Ichiro's probably hiding again, although I'm *sure* I locked him in his crate." Relieved Mia was safe, I changed mental gears. "Did you check all the tissue boxes?"

Head still bent, she nodded.

"He's here somewhere. I'd bet money on it." Then I glanced at the time. "How come you're not at work?"

"I couldn't go like this." Sniffling, she whimpered. "Besides, I don't want Atsuki to find out."

"Who cares if he finds out?" Scowling at her reaction, I scrambled to my feet and offered her a hand. "Come on. We'll find Ichiro, and then I'll help you straighten the place. Did you move his crate?"

Sniffling, she stood and gestured toward a pile of clothes. "It's around the corner."

Neither the dry cat food, nor the litter had been touched. *What's going on? The lock's still latched, but…*I pulled the crate's door, and the bottom half gave. "That little stinker. He pushed the door from the inside and squeezed through." Demonstrating for Mia, I tugged the door's bottom corner, showing his escape route. "Let's put everything away, so we're sure he isn't hiding in this mess."

We systematically repacked each drawer. After double-checking the corners of the cabinets before closing each cupboard door, we restacked the scattered magazines and rehung Mia's clothes in the closet.

Then just as I was about to latch the closet door, I checked Mia's shoe collection. Inspecting them, pair by pair, I turned the shoes upside down, working through the stilettos, pumps, loafers, and sneakers. Finally, I upended the fleecy slippers.

Out slid Ichiro, protesting loudly.

Chuckling as I cuddled him, I scolded the escape artist. "You have a plush kitty bed. Why do you sleep in shoes and tissue boxes?"

"You found him?" Mia ran in. "Where was he?"

"Curled up in your slipper's toe." I handed him over. "From now on, we'll have to barricade his door or lock it with a bungy cord."

But later, as I reworked my notes for the Tokyo article, an annoying thought hammered at my brain like a mallet to a gong. *Why have I never seen Ichiro and Chase together—either in Kyoto or here in Tokyo?*

The minute I left Chase at Fushimi Inari, *the kitten appeared, and moments before I reconnected with Chase, the kitten ran away...limping. Then Chase hobbled, saying he'd wrenched his ankle while I was gone. Ichiro's escaped twice now, and both times, I've been with Chase.* I scowled at the possibility. *Do they alternate guard duty?*

****

Thursday

The next morning, Chase and I ate breakfast at a small neighborhood restaurant. Dozens of vividly painted paper parasols dangled upside-down from the ceiling, the only Japanese element in an otherwise nondescript diner.

Smorgasbord style, I helped myself to a buffet of salmon, rice, fermented soybeans, miso soup, tofu with bonito flakes and scallions, pickled vegetables, dried seaweed, and *dashimaki tamago*—a paper-thin layer of scrambled eggs, rolled and sliced.

As we sat at a Western diner booth, eating with chopsticks and short, thick-handled spoons, I smiled at the juxtaposition of cultures.

"What are you grinning about?"

"Bamboo chopsticks and fifties' pleather booths…East meets West." Then pausing, I recalled my questions from the night before.

"What?" His backbone stiffened, and he sat up straight.

Shaping my thoughts into diplomatic queries proved difficult. Instead, I blurted them out. "Why don't I ever see you and the kitten together?"

"You've never invited me inside your friend's apartment." He rested his chopsticks on his plate.

"Even at *Fushimi Inari*, I was either with you or the kitten—but never both." I peered into his eyes. "Can you explain that?"

"Who can control cats?" Spreading his hands, he smiled. "They come and go as they please."

"True, but this is more than coincidental. It's as if you and the kitten swap places—almost like you take turns watching me. I can't help feeling you're linked somehow." No matter how far-fetched the idea, I refused to back down. "How else could you guess the cat's name or know about Rafe?"

"You should write fiction, not travel articles." Smoothing his tie, he chuckled. "You have the most fertile imagination."

The heat rose from my neck to my cheeks. Head bowed, I mumbled into my plate. "Laugh if you want, but the only connection is the kitten." I glanced up. "How else could—"

"Simple." His gaze determined and his voice calm,

he spoke slowly, enunciating each syllable. "You mentioned their names, both Ichiro's and Rafe's."

"No, I didn't." But under his mesmerizing gaze, I wavered. *Did I?*

"Sure you did—you told me about Rafe when you shared your idea regarding the bar-scene article...remember?"

"No..." His piercing blue eyes made concentration difficult. I bunched my lips as a dim recollection emerged. "Though, now that you mention it, I vaguely—"

"Then you *do* remember?" His gaze intense, he stared me down.

"Sort of..." Taking a deep breath, I blew out my frustration in a deep sigh. "I must've forgotten."

"As you forgot mentioning Ichiro." He leaned across the table, glaring like a Deva demigod guarding a temple door. His eyes were so wide, they protruded.

Maybe I did... Shrinking from his glare, I sat back, blaming myself. *Why do I question Chase's memory?* "That must be it..."

"It's been a hectic week. Details are bound to slip your mind." His scowl relaxed into his tutor smile, and he gestured to the traditional Japanese buffet. "How's breakfast?"

The atmosphere lightened.

I blinked as if waking from a nap. "Delicious." The matter resolved, I returned his smile.

"Good." He took a small brochure from his vest pocket. "Next on the agenda is the Skytree. At six hundred and thirty-four meters, it's Tokyo's tallest tower."

"Meters..." A queasy feeling started at the pit of my

stomach. "That converts to how many feet?"

"A little over two thousand or just under seven football fields."

Squirming at the height, I gave a sickly laugh. "That's up there."

"We'll visit the observatories, but then..." He smoothed his tie as he read from the brochure. "We'll get a bird's-eye view of the tower's steel beam and girder construction from the outside."

"*Bird's-eye*?" Suddenly nauseous, I imagined being suspended in thin air. "You mean dangle from a harness system?" The undigested breakfast began weighing heavily on my stomach.

"Not exactly." He rolled his coffee cup between his hands. "We'll explore the tower from an open-air deck."

I gave a nervous laugh. My palms clammy at the thought of hanging above Tokyo, I wiped them on my thighs. "Can't we just view everything from the observation decks? Look at it through safety glass?"

"I thought you wanted to impress your editor with a unique story angle." Tossing his chin, he challenged me.

"The idea sounded good at the time." I winced.

"To review Tokyo's top attractions, you have to experience them."

Squeamish about visiting the city's tallest building, I groaned.

"And to do *that*, you need to step out of your comfort zone." His face warmed into an encouraging smile. "Cheer up. We won't go all the way to the top. The *Tembo* Galleria is just four hundred and fifty meters, or about four football fields."

Curling my toes, I cringed. "Instead of the nearly seven..."

"Don't worry." He leaned across the table with a reassuring smile. "I'll be right beside you, walking you through each step."

His help at Mount *Inari* came to mind. *But that was climbing on* terra firma, *not swinging from the rafters over Tokyo*. I took a deep, centering breath. "If I fall, I swear I'll haunt you."

An hour later, I stepped inside the priority elevator, glanced through its glass walls and ceiling, and said a quick prayer. The starting jolt was subtle, but then the sinking sensation in the pit of my stomach made me grasp my belly with both hands.

"It's—"

"Gravity. I know." I forced a wan smile. As we climbed above the city, the LED display indicated the car's progress. After a moment, the queasy, dropping sensation left me until a few seconds later, when I felt another slight jolt, followed by the elevator's braking. The LED display read 350 meters.

A recording announced, "*Tembo* Deck."

My knees rickety, I walked stiffly, putting one foot in front of the other as I stumbled from the elevator.

"These windows circle the tower with a three-hundred-and-sixty-degree panoramic view."

Too scared to lift my eyes to the surrounding scenery, I gazed at my feet.

"Look." He gestured toward the floor-to-ceiling windows. "You've got to see what you write about."

I peeked at the walls' broad spans of glass, winced, and looked away.

"Are you all right?"

"Not really." My breathing shallow, I placed my hands on my upset stomach.

He gestured toward a floorplan of the *Tembo* Deck's three-story layout. "We're on its highest level. A restaurant and café are on the next floor." He turned toward me. "Would you like to sit down or get something to calm your nerves?"

I shook my head, too queasy to speak. "No, let's just get this over with…"

"The deck's lowest level features glass floor panels, where you can see all the way to the ground. Would you rather start there?"

"Definitely not." My laugh a groan, I cringed. "I'll just peek out the window and leave. The sooner I'm on solid ground, the better." I crossed to the window wall and gripped the metal railing, white-knuckled. After a few minutes, I loosened my grip. Gradually, my pulse slowed, my nausea subsided, and I forced myself to gaze out.

"See Mount Fuji on the left?" From behind, Chase reached around me, lightly grazing my shoulder while he pointed. "That's where we're going tomorrow."

I caught the subtle scent of ginger as his body heat enveloped me, arousing both exhilaration and panic. His breath on the back of my neck raised goosebumps, and his touch sent a pleasant shudder down my spine. Reliving the dream, I recalled the searing heat of his caresses, and an involuntary gasp escaped. My heartbeat quickening, I spun toward him, stopping just millimeters from his lips.

Standing sternum to sternum, he locked his gaze onto mine. "Take my hand." Despite his commanding tone, the corners of his eyes crinkled.

Reacting to both his air of authority and persuasive smile, I grabbed his hand as I would a hanging strap on the bullet train and held tight.

Instantly, a warmth surged up my arm, flooding my body with a sense of invulnerability. *What's happening? What is it about his touch?* I glanced at my hand in his.

He gently squeezed it as if urging me on.

Suddenly freed from my fear of heights, I grinned. A fearless yet insatiable curiosity overtook me, and I was impatient to explore. "Come on!"

Holding hands, I led him from one view to the next until we made the rounds. My acrophobia forgotten, I beamed as an impish thought came to mind. "Let's stand on the glass floor." Every cell of my body alive, I threw back my head and laughed. "I want to walk where others fear to tread."

I grabbed his arm and took the elevator two levels lower. As the other visitors sidestepped the clear panels' edges, I boldly strode onto the glass floor and peered between my feet at the ground far below.

Chase flashed a smile. "Are you ready for the next observation floor?"

"Absolutely." The longer I held his arm, the more confident I became.

"If you like the *Tembo* Deck, you'll love the Galleria." His eyes sparkled in the sunlit room.

"Why?"

"With your unbridled enthusiasm, the question is…" My hand on his arm, he squeezed his elbow to his side, drawing me closer. "Why wouldn't you?"

Intoxicated with the novelty of my newfound courage, I laughed.

Then as he led me into the glass-walled elevator, he gave my arm an affectionate squeeze.

Stiffening at his caress, I glanced at my arm

interlocked with his. *What am I doing?* As inconspicuously as possible, I slipped from his grasp and stood apart.

As if mildly surprised, he arched his brow.

I turned away, watching the floors whiz past through the elevator's glass walls and ceiling, until the LED display read 445, and the elevator stopped.

A recording announced, "*Tembo* Galleria."

The doors opened, and I froze.

Passengers in the back said, "*Sumimasen*. Excuse, please."

I swallowed, too petrified to move.

"This way." Leaning over in a whisper, he took my arm.

Again, my fears vanished at his touch. Stunned at the abrupt change, I glanced at my arm firmly tucked in his. "What—"

"Let's not block the door." He led me to a sloping, spiral ramp. "Welcome to the world's highest skywalk."

Highest skywalk...a moment before, his words would have terrified me, but now, they challenge me. What's happening? I glanced at the steel and glass walkway wrapping around the tower's center. Again fearless, I stared out the windows at Tokyo's smaller skyscrapers far below. *They look like dominoes.*

Beyond, Mount Fuji loomed on the horizon. *I can see for miles.* I turned toward him. "How far is Mount Fuji from Tokyo?"

"About a two-hour train ride." He smiled a toothy grin, his white cuspids glistening in the morning sun.

What pointed canines... A primordial fear flashed through me, and I shuddered. *But such a foxy smile...* The hairs tingled on the nape of my neck as his sheer animal magnetism pulsed through me.

"Instead of climbing a *fujizuka,* tomorrow we'll scale Mount Fuji."

The blood whooshed through my veins, and I felt a head rush at the idea. "What an amazing adventure." Intrigued, I turned back to the mountain and eyed its surrounding greenery. Like a topographical map, the distant scene contrasted the land's natural features against the urban areas' gray concrete. "The mountain looks like it's floating in a sea of green."

"Interesting that you compare the area to a sea. *Aokigahara* is often called the Sea of Trees"—he shrugged—"or Suicide Forest."

"Why?" Though I suspected the reason, I had to ask.

He sucked air between his gritted teeth, making a hissing sound.

"*Aokigahara* has become a popular suicide destination."

An image of Rafe's wife came to mind, and I shuddered as goosebumps broke out on my arms.

"So many suicides occur there that authorities posted signs asking desperate visitors to seek help, yet they find dozens of bodies annually."

"Is this a new trend?"

"The numbers have soared in the last decade, but *Aokigahara* has a long history." Shaking his head, he frowned. "Whether fable or fact, traditionally, it's where people abandoned their elderly relatives. According to local legends, the forest teems with the ghosts of those left to die."

"Senicide?" The hair rising on the nape of my neck, I shivered.

"The Japanese call it *oyasute*." He nodded.

"How long ago was that?"

"Supposedly, the practice ended in the 1800s, but as recently as last year, a woman was arrested for abandoning her father at a gas station."

Ghosts, abandoned parents left to die, suicide victims…"Can we change the subject?"

"Of course. Let's walk to *Sorakara* Point, the Galleria's highest point, and then…" Holding back his head, he studied me. "Are you ready for the Terrace Tour?"

****

The moment I walked onto the open-air deck, the wind assaulted my ears. The required hard hat did little to dampen the deafening roar. Buffeted by the gusts, I gazed at the tower's steel framework from the inside out. *This is like standing beneath a steel bridge, looking up at its underpinnings.* "How high are we?"

"What?" He cupped his ear and leaned closer.

"How high is this deck?" I stood on tiptoe and shouted in his ear.

"A hundred and fifty-five meters"—his eyes twinkled—"roughly one and a half football fields."

"Note the narrow catwalk." Speaking through a microphone, the tour guide directed our attention above.

How easy it'd be to slip…or jump. Again, Rafe's wife came to mind, and I viewed the maintenance walkway from another perspective. *What an opportune place to commit suicide.*

"This terrace surrounds the tower's *Shinbashira* or core pillar." The guide pointed out the immense column, then glanced at the group. "Are you familiar with the design of the five-storied pagoda?"

I shook my head.

"Japan is earthquake prone, yet five-storied pagodas have withstood earthquakes since ancient times. Why do these wooden structures survive? Because they contain a central pillar—just like this tower—to neutralize any swaying during earthquakes."

The tour guide pointed over the railing. "Now look below at the Sumida River."

I glanced at the ribbon winding through the city and, despite the handrails, suddenly felt dizzy. Weaving on my feet, I grabbed Chase's arm to steady myself and gave a nervous laugh. "Not for the faint of heart."

"Are you all right?" Again, he pressed his elbow to his side, drawing me closer.

"I'm okay..." But even to my ears, my voice sounded shaky.

"When the tour ends, let's grab a bite to eat."

****

A half hour later, we walked into the tower's restaurant. Tables set with metallic chargers and sparkling wine glasses lined the circular window wall. Sunshine permeated the dining room from all sides, lending the room a cheery glow.

As the hostess showed us to our seats, I glimpsed the next table. "Mia?"

Her mouth full, Mia looked up from her plate of tofu and azuki beans. She chewed quickly and swallowed. "What are you doing here?"

"We just finished the terrace tour." I turned toward Chase. "I'd like you to meet Mia and—"

"Ichiro." Sneering, Atsuki spat out the name. "How auspicious..."

"You two know each other?" Confused by Atsuki's cool reception, I looked from one man to the other.

"We're old friends." Chase bared a toothy smile.

From their stony glares, I suspected they were anything but.

"It's a pleasure meeting you." Chase turned his attention to Mia. "Ava's told me so much about you. I feel I know you."

I have? I blinked, unable to recall any such details.

"I see you haven't lost your penchant for azuki beans." Chase turned from Mia to Atsuki. "Enjoy your meal." With a parting wave, he crossed to our table and pulled out my chair.

"How did you know of Mia's fondness for azuki beans?" Searching my memory, I frowned as I took my seat. "I never told you."

"Sure you did…" He slid in my chair, then sat across from me. "Remember?"

"No." I shook my head. "I never mentioned it."

"Ava, how disappointing. You forget so many of our conversations…" He tsk-tsked while he stared into my eyes. "You told me when we discussed the Kobe beef's rich red color. Now, do you recall?"

"I recall *thinking about* Mia's craving when you compared their colors, but nope." Certain my memory served me correctly, I met his challenging gaze. "I never *mentioned* it."

"Sure you did." His gaze was unyielding. "Think back."

I tried to remember my exact words, but his penetrating stare made concentration impossible, and I lost focus. Surrendering to a sudden headache, I closed my eyes and massaged the bridge of my nose. "Maybe I did, after all." Then I exhaled, blowing out my frustration. "Besides, what difference does it make?"

"Exactly." Smiling, he handed me a menu and sat back.

A tap on my shoulder startled me.

"See you at the apartment." Mia stared absently, her gaze following Atsuki's retreating figure.

"When will you be back?" I tried to make eye contact.

"Late." With a careless wave, she called over her shoulder as she dashed after him.

How odd. I stared after her, listening to her stiletto heels echo on the tiles as the waiter approached.

After the man took our orders, Chase leaned across the table, engaging me with his smile. "After lunch, what's next?"

Though flattered as I basked in his undivided attention, I squirmed beneath his leveled gaze. "You'd suggested seeing the Tokyo Tower. Are you still up for it?"

"Are you up for climbing it?"

"What!" Any remote sense of wellbeing dissolved. "*Climbing* it?" Images of King Kong scrambling up the Empire State Building shot through my mind.

"Not *scaling* it, if that's what you think." He threw back his head, grinning. "It's only six-hundred steps to the main deck. We climbed more than that on Monkey Mountain."

"True." Remembering past successes, I took a deep breath. "And stairs have walled stairwells, so how high we climb won't matter because I won't see."

"Ah, but these stairs are *outside* the tower"—he lifted his brow—"and, instead of walls, they have chain-link mesh."

"Outside?" I gave a sickly laugh as I recalled the

open-air deck. "I've barely recovered from the last tour's gusty winds."

"Not gusty, think of it as *gutsy*." Pulling a brochure from his vest pocket, he wore a mischievous smile as he read. "You'll feel the *bracing* wind on your face as you climb…"

He's always pushing me to new heights—literally. Unsure whether to laugh or cry, I groaned. "What am I getting myself into?"

"You're not getting yourself 'into' anything." He shook his head. "Instead, you're breaking free of your fears." Returning the brochure to his vest pocket, he homed in on my face. His eyes darted left and right as he regarded me. "With me to guide you, you'll scale heights you never dreamed possible."

"Heights…?" My chest tightened.

"Not elevation, I'm speaking allegorically." He reached for my hand.

His hypnotic voice lulling, I became tangled in his gaze and did not recoil.

"With me at your side, you'll achieve all the goals you've imagined."

"Goals?" The word roused me from his spell.

"I can help you accomplish anything your heart desires. What do you want?"

I tried to look inwardly, but I couldn't break his gaze, and he spoke before I had time to think.

"Ah…your travel articles." He nodded knowingly as if he'd peeked into my psyche. "You want literary success?" His smile intensified into a leer. "How does the Pulitzer Prize sound?"

Me? How could I win the Pulitzer Prize? With my inexperience, I laughed at the idea.

"Yes, *you!*"

I tried to look away but was unable to break his penetrating gaze. *Is he reading my mind?*

"I have ways to compensate for any…journalistic shortcomings." He stared hard. "Or is it travel? Do you want to see the world? I can take you places you've only glimpsed in travel posters." He pulled my hand to his chest. "I can make your dreams come true—*any dream.* Tell me what you want, and it's yours." His hold tightened on my fingers.

Wincing, I extracted my hand. Then free of his grip, reason returned, and I snickered. *I've heard come-ons before, but this one…*

"What?" He gave me a blank stare.

"You sound like a casting-couch agent. 'Stay with me, babe, and I'll make you a star.' " Chuckling, I sat back. "How naïve do you think I am?"

"I don't think you're naïve at all." A deep V showed between his brows. "I simply want you to be happy." His eye contact remained steady as he leaned toward me. "I want *to make* you happy."

I analyzed his calm exterior. *Corny as he sounds, I almost believe him.*

"Am I wrong to help a person pursue their dreams?" His eyes widened.

"No." I shrugged. "Of course not, but you come on so strong, your words sound…preposterous."

"So now you're calling me absurd." The corners of his mouth sagging, he leaned back in his chair.

"No, I didn't say *you* were preposterous—only your words." *Geesh.*

"They're the same. A man's only as good as his word." He pressed his lips into a thin line and stared at the table.

"Look, I was only—"

"Your dinner, miss." The waiter placed my entrée on the metal charger.

"Thank you." I peeked at Chase, but his gaze remained fixed on the tabletop.

The waiter served him, bowed, and left.

I stole glances, trying to attract Chase's attention. *Is it a cultural thing? Is criticism considered rude?* After several silent minutes of nibbling at my seafood platter, I sighed. "Look, I didn't mean to insult you. It's just that your words sounded so farfetched, I have a hard time taking them seriously."

"So, you don't take *me* seriously?"

"That's not what I said." I huffed out my frustration. "Just don't make such outlandish promises—"

"Like what?"

"Like me winning the Pulitzer Prize, for instance." Laughing at the idea, I shook my head.

"What's so outlandish about encouraging a friend to chase her dream…follow her heart?"

"Nothing's wrong with encouraging, but *promising*…" I drew a deep breath. "That's something else altogether."

"What would you call it?" His pinched face challenged me.

"Hyperbole…a hollow promise, at best." *Call a spade a spade.* "At worst, it's a lie that raises false hope."

"I call it bold vision to encourage your aspirations. Ava, I have faith in you. I want to help you in any way— in *every* way—I can." He set down his fork and reached across the table.

Relieved he was no longer annoyed, I clasped his

hand.

"Let me put it this way." His gaze tender, he enveloped my hand between his. "Follow your dream wherever it takes you, but since it's led you to me, allow me to help."

My defenses crumbling, I smiled. The warmth of his hands spread up my arm to my chest. Then flushing, I recalled the heat of the dream and tried to pull away.

"What?" His eyes sparkling like tanzanite, he held tight.

Trapped. I tugged harder, but my hand was firmly wedged between his.

"No, don't run from whatever it is you're feeling." He tightened his grasp. "Tell me." He pressed his thumb against the mound in my palm, massaging it. Then he began lightly tracing the crevices between my fingers with his middle finger.

My fingers spread open at his touch. My pulse quickened as I caught my breath. Memories of the dream flooding my mind, I sensed a sudden moisture between my legs.

What's happening? Pulling away, I pressed my knees together and tightly crossed my ankles.

"What thoughts are running through your mind?" His heavy-lidded gaze silently urged me to confess.

Do I tell him? No...where might that lead? I gave a nervous laugh.

"What?" He leaned toward me.

A faint scent of ginger wafted across the table, and I inhaled its peppery fragrance.

"You can tell me...anything..." A mischievous gleam animated his dark eyes as he cocked his head. "Is this something naughty?"

"No!" I gave an embarrassed giggle as I fidgeted.

"Then tell me."

"It's nothing really." Shrugging, I lifted my palms. "Nothing worth mentioning."

"Tell me, anyway." He reached for my hand and gently tugged.

I shivered at his touch, the pit of my stomach shuddering in pleasurable spasms. I gasped.

"What?" He fingered my hand. "What has you so flustered?"

Recalling the magic his fingers conjured in my dream, I squirmed. "Like I said, nothing." I tried to pull from his grip.

"Oh, no you don't." My hand firmly within his, he shook his head. "Not until you tell me what's on your mind."

This is ridiculous. "Fine." I drew a deep breath. "If you must know, you appeared in a dream."

"Did I?" Lightly massaging my palm, he grinned. "Tell me more. What was the dream about?"

"Nothing…random, disconnected thoughts." I forced a shrug. "I can't remember."

"Yet you're blushing." His eyes snapped.

"You were simply one 'actor' in my dream's cast of thousands. Nothing more. Nothing less." I swallowed. "Now let go my hand."

"Why don't I believe you?" His gaze dropped to my chest as he continued kneading my palm.

I arched my back, remembering how his fingers had caressed my breasts. Swallowing a moan, I pulled with all my strength and wrenched free. "What you believe is none of my concern." I straightened my shoulders. "If you want me to respect your words, you have to respect mine."

"Point taken."

Reverting to his impenetrable façade, he wore a bland smile. Gone were the bedroom eyes.

I sat back, relieved to be free from his grasp. Then I congratulated myself on my moral victory. *Round One: Ava.*

Wearing an amused expression, he cleaned his plate. "What're you grinning about?"

I gave a dry laugh. "I'm wary of what to expect next. You're a chameleon—one person one minute and another the next."

"Not really." He set down his fork and gave me his full attention, the blue of his eyes intensifying. "You'll find me a good friend—a *loyal* friend, who'd never leave you hanging or stand you up…who'd never leave you."

Rafe. My sense of wellbeing dissolved. Dropping my smile, I kicked myself. *Why did I ever tell Chase about him?*

"I understand what it is to lose someone, and I'd never cause that pain." He reached across the table for my hand. "Ava, I'd never let you down…never hurt you. I'd always be there for you." He gently squeezed my fingertips. "You can always rely on me."

I stared at my hand in his, amazed at the sensations his touch elicited. I felt cherished. *Whatever my battles, my challenges, he'd protect me.* I took a contented breath.

"I can be a good friend." He folded his hands around mine. "Trust me."

But can I?

Chapter 12—Tokyo

Thursday

An hour later, I gripped the round metal handrail as I clambered up the red-painted stairway. The wind whipped at my hair and whistled past my ears. The vista transforming as I climbed higher, I stole glimpses of Tokyo Bay through the red tower's steel construction.

The chain-link mesh surrounding the outdoor stairway lent a marginal sense of security, and I climbed the first sets of steps quickly. But once I rose above the surrounding buildings' rooftops, the queasiness returned, and though the howling wind from the bay offset the afternoon heat, it did little to alleviate my nausea. My sweaty palms slipped on the metal handrail.

"Are you all right?"

"Not really."

"You seemed to be doing so well, I never thought to offer you my hand." Chase reached out.

What will his touch do this time?

The moment our hands clasped, his energy fortified me. No longer nauseous or frightened, I beamed, intoxicated with my new-found courage. *Whatever the reason for his power…I like its effects.*

"Better?"

"Much!" I tightened my grasp and sped up the red stairway, barely stopping to catch my breath. As I climbed, the tower's crimson-red beams and girders seemed oddly familiar. *They remind me of something, but what?* I smiled at the memory. *Of course, the vermillion torii of* Inari Fushimi.

My adrenaline flowing, I glimpsed Chase from the corner of my eye. *How lucky to have crossed paths. Seems I've known him for years, but was that only four days ago we met?*

****

"Five hundred, ninety-eight...five hundred, ninety-nine...six hundred!" I laughed as I reached the last step. Breathless from scrambling up the stairway, I grinned as we stepped onto the glass-walled main deck.

Mirrored, V-shaped supports and a dazzling ceiling of geometric mirrors glittered in the afternoon sunlight, reflecting Tokyo's skyline in a shimmering kaleidoscope of images.

"You make everything fun." I turned toward him while we queued for our certificates of completion.

"And you make everything new." He squeezed my hand. "Even an old man."

"Old man..." I chuckled at the incongruity of his assessment. "Why do you insist you're old?"

"Because it's true." He shrugged.

"You never paused on the climb. You're not even breathing hard." I shook my head at the irony. "You're in amazing condition, yet you call yourself old. Why?"

His gaze earnest, he gave a wistful sigh. "Because I am..."

His tone tugged at my heart. "You don't look old—or act it."

"Ava, there's something I've meant to tell you...something you should—"

"Next, please." The uniformed attendant at the counter beckoned with a smile.

I left the queue to receive my souvenir certificate.

Then the attendant bowed politely and turned toward Chase. "Next, please."

As my phone buzzed, I stepped away to read the text.

Rafe—*I want to be your favorite hello and your hardest goodbye. See you at five—*

How sweet. My stomach fluttering, old memories resurfaced. Then I glanced at the time. *Four already? He's meeting me in an hour.*

"Anything wrong?" Certificate in hand, Chase rubbernecked to see my phone.

"No, why?" I returned my cell to its holster.

"You look flushed."

"I do?" I put a hand to my face, then shrugged. "I just realized the time."

"Why?" His eyes narrowed. "Do you have to be somewhere?"

His penetrating gaze unnerved me. "I…uh…" I swallowed hard. "I need to finish the 'Toolin' Around Tokyo' article tonight. We probably should make an early night of it since we're catching the first train to Mount Fuji."

"I hope"—he spoke slowly as if letting each word sink in—"you're not meet—"

"You planned the itinerary." Chin high, I met his cold, accusing eyes. "I'm just following your schedule." *That's true.* I crossed my fingers. *Isn't it?*

****

I caught a cab from the Tokyo Tower, arriving at Mia's apartment at four-forty-five. *Barely time to change. Would a scarf jazz up my basic black dress?* Pausing to breathe in the scent of Rafe's rose, I checked on Ichiro and went cold. His crate was empty.

Not again. I know I locked it. Chase's tales of shapeshifters and supernatural foxes disguised as cats came to mind. *Every time Ichiro gets out, I'm with Chase. Are they watching me in shifts?*

I held my breath as I checked behind his latest hiding place: The automatic waterer. "Ichiro?"

The kitten mewed and looked up with sad, puppy-dog eyes, the exact shade of blue as Chase's.

"You little escape artist." Releasing a relieved sigh, I lifted him onto my bed. *What was I thinking?* I shook my head, chuckling at my overactive imagination. But as I unbuttoned my blouse, the hairs prickled the back of my neck, and I whirled about.

The kitten's eyes were as wide as one-yen coins.

Is it watching me undress? I chuckled at my imagination. *This is ridiculous.* But as the cat's gaze followed my every move, the hairs lifted on my arms. Shaking off a chill, I carried my dress into the bathroom and shut the door.

Seconds later, the door creaked open.

"Mia?" Wearing just bra and panties, I reached for a towel.

The kitten padded in and jumped on the sink.

"Oh, Ichiro, you silly cat." I laughed as I scratched behind his ears.

Purring, the kitten never took its gaze from me as it eyed me from toes to nose.

Almost as if it's giving me the once-over. This is too weird. Again, I hid behind the towel. "Out!" Shooing the cat, I locked the door.

After dressing, I peeked out, saw the cat asleep on my pillow, and rolled my eyes. *How ridiculous to think this kitten is anything but adorable?*

The front door opened and slammed shut.

"Mia?" I spun about. "Is that you?"

"In the flesh." Grinning from ear to ear, she bounded across the apartment. "Good, you're home!" Mia hugged me. "I'm *so* glad to see you!" Then noticing the kitten, she picked it up and cuddled it to her chest. "Ichiro, you pretty kitty…" Pouting, she held it at arm's length and surveyed it. "But you're a tommy." Hugging it again, she cooed. "You handsome tom cat, you…"

"Someone's in a good mood." *Better than earlier, that's for sure.* I recalled her odd behavior at lunch. "What happened?"

"Nothing." Beaming, Mia shrugged.

"If your smile were any brighter, I'd have to wear sunglasses." I chuckled. "Did you win the lottery or something? What's going on?"

"Nothing." Twisting her jaw, Mia set the kitten on the bed. "I'm just happy…very, *very* happy!"

"That's an understatement."

Mia smacked her lips, then swallowed hard.

"Can I get you something to drink?"

"No, why?" Her eyes red and glassy, Mia gazed vacantly.

"I don't know…you sound dry." *Something's off.* "Are you okay?"

"Yeah." Mia sucked her teeth. "Sure."

When the intercom buzzed, I checked the time: Five o'clock sharp. "That's Rafe." I pressed the speaker. "Down in a minute."

Mia licked her lips.

"Are you sure I can't get you a glass of water or something before I leave?"

"No." Mia smiled through teeth clenched so hard, her jaw seemed locked. "I'll see you after work. Then you can tell me *all* about your date." A giggle began in her throat, quickly spiraling into a high-pitched laugh.

"What's so funny?"

Mia laughed so hard, tears ran down her cheeks, and she collapsed on the bed, sending the kitten scampering.

I raced toward her. "Are you all—"

"I'm fine. In fact, I'm leaving in a few minutes myself. Just came home to change." Sitting up, she pointed to the door. "Now, go! Have a fabulous time— and tell Rafe hi...*hi*." What began as a giggle became another round of shrill laughter.

After I closed the door, I paused before boarding the elevator.

Mia's penetrating cackle spilled into the hall.

Should Mia be alone? But she's leaving for work soon...and this is the last time I'll see Rafe... His single rose and hard-goodbye text came to mind, and I swallowed a groan. *If I only had more time...*

When the elevator doors opened, Rafe's radiant face greeted me.

That's the gentle glow I remember. The memories flooded back.

"Evening, Foxy Lady." Leaning toward me, he kissed my cheek.

Foxy Lady... The tingling from his breath on my neck sent pleasant shudders down my spine as I breathed in his tangy lime scent. "I'd forgotten that nickname."

He shook his head. "Term of endearment." He glanced at his watch. "Not to rush you, but if we're going to catch the train, we've got to hustle." Grinning, he opened the door.

"Where are we going?"

"First stop, *Shinjuku* Station." Reaching for my hand, he hurried me along.

"We're taking a train?" His hand felt natural in mine. *Like old times.*

"Not just any train, mind you, but the Romance Car." He flickered his brow *a la* Groucho Marx.

"To where?" His mischievous smile sent butterflies fluttering in my stomach.

"To *Katase Enoshima.* Let me put it this way. Do you like seafood and beaches?"

****

Settling into the coach seat, I stifled a sigh.

"Anything wrong?"

"Sorry, didn't realize I was 'thinking' out loud." I bunched my lips, unsure where to begin. "Mia's been acting strange the last day or so."

"How so?"

"She's developed a sudden fondness for azuki beans—more of an addiction, really." I counted off her odd actions on my fingers. "She flies into a panic if the cat escapes. She worries what Atsuki will say, *and* she's moody. One minute, she's morose, and the next euphoric. Then five minutes later, she's paranoid."

"Food cravings and mood swings..." Shaking his head, he grunted. "Is she high?"

I remembered Mia's delight at telling Rafe *hi.* "Maybe...I met her at lunch, and if she wasn't scarfing down azuki beans, she acted dazed—robotic." I turned toward him. "Then just before you picked me up, she verged on hysteria."

"So, she's either zoned out or ecstatic. I'm no expert, but I'd guess she's on something." His nostrils flaring, he inhaled. "And I'd bet Atsuki's behind it. I never trusted him. I've tried to talk sense into her, but..." Shrugging, he spread his hands.

"I don't understand it, either, but I agree." I sighed. "Somehow, Atsuki has his claws in her." *As well as a history with Chase...*

Chapter 13—Katase Enoshima

Thursday Evening

As the train pulled into *Katase Enoshima*, the station's green and gold-tipped roof rose above its red and white walls.

The winged façade caught my imagination. "Isn't that charming?"

"It's designed to look like *Ryūjin's* legendary, coral castle."

I squinted, trying to place the name. "Who was *Ryūjin*?"

"A *what*, not a *who*, he was a sea-dragon of local legends." Rafe winked. "Some say he was the basis for Godzilla."

"What a fantastic way to introduce travelers to the area's folklore." Still eyeing the colorful building, I flung my arms wide as I inhaled the fresh sea air. "I love the scent of salt air. It's exhilarating."

"Why's that?"

Throwing back my head, I breathed deeply, filling my lungs. "It smells of faraway lands, distant ports, and journeys with destiny…"

"Aren't you the romantic this evening?" The corners of his dewy, hazel eyes creased in a smile.

Suddenly nostalgic, I sighed. "Maybe it's being seven thousand miles from home…with someone I thought I'd never see again." Old memories rushed in like gale force winds.

"Ava, I've wanted to…" His gaze locking onto mine, he stopped mid-sentence. "If you only knew…" His lips moved as if he were about to say more.

"Go on…" Tantalized, I leaned toward him.

He shook his head. "Nothing." Pressing his lips together, he retreated behind a melancholy smile.

Why does he tease me, leading me on just to leave me hanging? Again? Chase's words came to mind. *"I'd never let you down…never hurt you."*

"How 'bout dinner first, then a stroll on the beach?" He reached for my hand.

Disappointed that Rafe paled in the comparison, I pretended not to notice his outstretched hand. Instead, I adjusted my purse strap.

Polite chit-chat and a short cab ride later, I followed Rafe up a stairway to a seaside restaurant perched above the treetops. The bistro's window wall offered a bird's-eye view of the island and the sea beyond.

After the waiter seated us at a table overlooking the bay, he spoke in Japanese while gesturing to the window's expansive vista.

Translating, Rafe pointed to the sea beyond. "From here, you can see the entire *Shonan* coastline. And that's *Sagami* Bay."

As the waiter took our drink order, I watched large black birds ride the air currents outside our window, swooping and circling.

"What kind of birds are those?"

"Black kites." His gaze followed them. "They catch prey in their claws while in flight."

*Catch prey in their claws…*Instead of entertaining,

the birds' acrobatics reminded me of Atsuki with his claws in Mia.

Disillusioned with Rafe's dangling carrot, on-again, off-again flirtation, I scowled. *He implies so much...then never follows through. I can't rely on him. He always leaves me teetering on the brink.* Chase's words echoed through my mind: *"You'll find me a good friend—a loyal friend, who'd never leave you hanging or stand you up..."*

"Would you like an appetizer to start?"

Dissatisfied, I shrugged. "If you do."

"What's wrong?"

Should I confront him on our last night together? I clasped my fingers tightly, debating. "You started to open up before, then stopped cold. I don't know if you're holding something back or backing out on me...again." Wincing at my outburst, I bowed my head. "Tonight's not the night for arguments." *But his behavior is so aggravating.* I forced myself to meet his eyes. "Sorry, but we need to clear the air."

"Okay, where do we start?" He put his hands on the table and leaned across. "For two years, I've realized I was an idiot. I threw away the best thing that ever happened to me." He reached for my hand. "You."

"*Anata wa appeitzers ga hoshīdesu ka?*" Bowing politely, the server handed Rafe a menu.

He snatched it with his extended hand.

Glad for time to consider Rafe's words, I welcomed the waiter's interruption.

"Would you like to try turban shells?" He glanced from the menu. "They're sea snails, a local delicacy." His gaze searched mine. "And they're delicious."

"Sure, I'll view it as another gastronomic adventure

and add it to my article." *And Rafe didn't order for me. He asked first.* In this comparison, Rafe's rating climbed.

He ordered in Japanese and, after the server left, turned back, dimpling. "Where were we?"

"You threw away the best thing that ever happened…" I swallowed a smile.

"Oh, yeah…" Inhaling, he bent his head. When he looked up, his eyes glistened. "After I married Ashley, I struggled to put you out of my mind, but the harder I tried, the more you filled my thoughts. When I moved to Japan, I thought I'd closed that chapter. Then two days ago, you appeared like a page from the past. I have so much to say, but so little time to—"

"*Anata no wain, sensei.*" A second waiter appeared with two glasses and the wine.

"*Arigatō.*" Stifling a sigh, Rafe nodded.

I clenched my jaw.

The man uncorked the chilled bottle of Asti as beads of condensation trickled down its sides. Then he poured the sparkling wine into slim flutes, bowed, and left.

Wearing a wry smile, Rafe lifted his glass. "To us."

I clinked glasses and took a tentative sip. The bubbles tickled my nose, and after a sticky July day, the icy wine was refreshing. I took a long draught. Tipping back my head, I closed my eyes as a contented sigh escaped. "Hits the spot."

"If only it were so easy to quench a deeper thirst…"

Intrigued by his wistful tone, I opened my eyes.

"I blew it." His posture hunching, he shrugged.

Like champagne gone flat, any feelings of wellbeing fizzled. "Yeah, you did." The memories rushed back. Recalling the pain he inflicted, I felt anything but charitable. "Sounds like you had a rough go of it, but *darn it, Rafe!* You got yourself into that mess. You're the one that married her and left me..." I gave a dry laugh. "I almost said 'standing at the altar,' but you never even proposed. You always left me hanging. Scratch that. *Leave* me hanging...like you did a few minutes ago."

He stared at the table.

The silence deafening, I spat out the challenge. "Got anything to say?"

"Not really." The corners of his mouth turning down, he shook his head.

"I didn't think so." Angry that he had ghosted me two years before and ticked he didn't have the moxie to speak now, I bristled. "I can't even get a rise out of you." I took a deep breath and blew it out, releasing steam.

"I hurt you. Deeply. I get it, and I'm sorry. I never meant to leave you hanging." His chest rose and fell as he smothered a sigh. "I handled it badly—"

"Badly?" I swatted the air. "That's an understatement."

"I can't change the past or wish away your wounds." He grimaced. "But I can mend the present."

"How?" Still fuming, I folded my hands to keep them from shaking.

"By being direct. By having the courage to be vulnerable—instead of cowering behind self-doubts, afraid of intimacy. By showing my true colors." He snorted. "*Yellow.*" Then he stared into my eyes. "By admitting I love you."

My head snapped back. I gazed skyward as I collected my thoughts. Then carefully controlling my voice, I faced him. "How do you expect me to react to that?"

"Say you love me, too."

"Unbelievable!" I groaned. "Do you really think three little words will make everything all right? Life doesn't work that way."

"Then what way does it work?"

"*Not* by ignoring two wasted years, and *not* with tired platitudes."

"Then how about this? I love the lilt in your voice. I love the way you tackle mountains and skyscrapers despite your acrophobia. I love the lemony scent of your hair when you turn around quickly, and I miss talking with my best friend." Palm extended, he reached across the table. "I have only a few hours to show you how much I regret the past."

His dimpled smile tugged at my heart, and his outstretched arm beckoned. Unable to resist, I reached for his hand.

"But I promise. If you'll give me the chance—"

"*Motto wain?*"

Flinching, I pulled back.

Our server remained expressionless as he refilled our glasses, apparently oblivious of any interruption.

"*Arigatō.*" Rafe nodded to the man before turning toward me with a wink.

I swallowed a smile, waiting until the server bowed and left. Then I lifted my glass in a toast. "To our waiters' impeccable timing."

"I'll drink to that." Rafe clinked his glass against mine and, pausing, stared into my eyes. "And us."

I met his gaze and recognized his tender look of love. The memories rushed in, washing away the years of hurt.

Our server returned with two steaming plates. After refilling our glasses, he bowed and soundlessly retreated.

Baffled by the shells, each the size of a fist, I stared. "How do we eat these things?"

"Slide the shellfish out, twisting as you go." Demonstrating with his fork, he teased the seafood from its shell. "Some believe sea snails are aphrodisiacs." His eyes twinkled.

The heat rising to my cheeks, I gave a nervous laugh as I followed his instructions.

"Just saying." He grinned. "Now drizzle lemon juice and soy sauce over it."

Gathering my courage, I popped a sliver in my mouth, and after a moment's deliberation, smiled. "Chewy—but delectable."

We shared tiny plates of sashimi, chatting while we viewed the bay.

Then after a final toast, Rafe turned toward me. "Instead of *looking* at the beach, how would you like to walk it?"

"Sand and surf after seafood?" I stole one last glance out the window, then turned toward him with a grin. "I always prefer entering the scene to being a spectator."

"Let's give it a shot." Palm extended, he sang the line from the eighties' tune as he stood.

The song jolted me back to the Golden *Gai. He* does *want to start over.*

I clasped his hand, and an ebb and flow of energy passed between us in an equal exchange of yin and yang. Suddenly, everything made sense—*we* made sense. Our melding completed a circuit—closed a loop. *By each supplying what the other lacks, I complete him, while he fulfills me.*

I contrasted the sensations with Chase's manipulative energy flows. *Exchanges with Rafe balance...harmonize. They don't exploit.* With the insight came a natural high, an "ahhh" moment, and I glimpsed him from the corner of my eye. *Am I falling in love...again?*

Holding his hand as we walked, our arms swinging freely between us, I heard the surf before I saw it.

The waves boomed against the boulder jetties. Seagulls cried overhead as the sun dipped toward the horizon. Further down the beach, breakers pounded the sandy shore.

Inhaling the brisk sea air as I viewed the scene, I rephrased my earlier words. *I'm in a faraway land and distant port.* Am I *on a journey with destiny?* I glanced sideways at Rafe, noting his profile's tawny glow in the late-afternoon sun.

A breeze swept off the sea.

Despite the July temperatures, I shivered and turned toward the blue vista.

Several surfers rode the waves, while swimmers splashed in the shallow water, and diehard sunbathers lolled on the beach's mineral-rich sand.

"This shore's great for strolls—so rejuvenating." Glancing from the sandy expanse and blue horizon, I turned toward him. "This island seems a million miles from Tokyo, yet it's only an hour away."

"It's a popular romantic getaway."

"Why?" I winked. "Because the train from Tokyo is called the 'Romance Car'?"

"That express coach took its name from a local legend." His face warmed in a smile. "According to the myth, the love goddess *Benzaiten*—*Benten*, for short—created this island. Considered the epitome of femininity, beauty, and love, she's the patroness of water and music."

My fingers interlacing with Rafe's, I tugged his hand. "What's the connection between water and music?"

"They flow. *Benten's* the goddess of everything that flows." He gently squeezed her fingers. "As the story goes, a five-headed dragon—"

"You're finally getting to the dragon." Remembering the train station's red-and-white color scheme, I grinned as I jerked my chin toward him.

"As I was saying…" He faked a stern frown. "When a dragon terrorized a nearby village, *Benten* begged him to stop. But convincing him took so long that, in the process, she raised this island from the sea and built a home here."

"So where does a romantic legend fit into this tale?" A smile tugged my lips.

"She and the dragon fell in love. After they married and shared a long life, she died, and the dragon turned into that hill you see there, watching over her and *Enoshima*." He pointed to a prominence in the distance. "Even today, it's called Dragon Hill."

"Is that my imagination, or does it look like a sleeping dragon?"

"If you look long enough, maybe…" Turning toward me, he grinned. "Because of their love story, the island's become a romantic escape, as well as a popular wedding destination." He pointed in the opposite direction. "Several shrines are dedicated to *Benten*. Want to visit them?"

"Heck, yeah." The warm glow in his eyes touched me. "When else can I see where a five-headed dragon tied the knot with a goddess?"

A short cab ride took us to a steep stairway carved into the hillside.

"Why don't you take the lead?" Before we began the ascent, he stepped aside to let me pass. "If you stumble, I'll catch you."

"Thanks." Smiling at his thoughtfulness, I scaled the first set of steps easily, but the higher I climbed, the more hesitant I became. Stifling a groan, I kept my eyes on my footing, refusing to watch our progress. *I hate mountains and towers. Why am I constantly climbing them?*

"Are you all right?"

"Yeah." His words, coming from behind, startled me. "Why?"

"Thought I heard grumbling."

"Heights scare me." At the next landing, I turned toward him. "And all I've done in Japan is climb."

"They say exposure's the best way to overcome fear." He motioned toward a bench. "Have you tried visualization? Sit down and close your eyes."

Though leery, I followed his instructions. "Okay, now what?"

"Imagine climbing the next flight. In your mind's eye, look around and see how the scenery changes with each tier."

I peeked.

He grinned. "Keep both eyes closed. Now, one step at a time, picture yourself scaling the next flight and the next until you reach the top. Visualize success."

I envisioned the hike, until finally, with a satisfied sigh, I congratulated myself on the hypothetical climb. Then opening my eyes, I gave an affirming nod. "Let's do this."

"You lead—but go at your own pace." His cheek

dimpled. "This isn't a race, and we've got all evening."

"True." I glanced at the sun, low on the horizon. "But the path will be easier to see in the daylight." Anxious to put my visualization skills to the test, I grabbed his hand. "Come on."

At each level, I purposely stopped and looked behind at how far we'd climbed. Each tier's assessment got a little easier, and by the time I reached the top, I was chuckling.

"That wasn't bad, at all!" Thrilled at my accomplishment, I spun toward him. "In fact, that was exhilar—"A step above him, I gazed into his eyes, level with mine. My lips millimeters from his, I leaned toward him in an impulsive kiss.

His arms reached around me, drawing me close, and he returned my heat, joule for joule.

Gone was the two-year separation. With the kiss, I resumed the love I'd never lost—yet bitterly denied.

Then the voices of approaching people roused me, and I broke away as another couple came in sight. My cheeks burning, I ducked my head and stepped aside to let them pass.

When they were out of hearing, Rafe tugged my hand. "I didn't mean for that—"

"I don't know what came over—" I caught his gaze and started chuckling. "You go first."

"No, you."

Where do I begin? Glancing at the shrine in the distance, I squirmed. "Maybe the legend's true. Maybe *Enoshima* really does inspire romantic…inclinations."

"Tell yourself that if it makes you feel better." His mouth curving in a mischievous grin, he shook his head.

"Then what prompted that kiss?"

"Mutual attraction...even if *one of us* won't admit it."

I fidgeted beneath his irresistible gaze. *What is his hold on me? The past? He was my first love*—I swallowed the sudden lump in my throat—*my only.*

Then recalling the pain he'd caused, I stiffened. "When you walked out on me, I despised you. I never wanted to see you..." Caught in his gaze, I stopped.

"And now...?"

Torn between the attraction and the unhealed wounds, I bit my bottom lip.

"I let you down, and I'm so sorry." Pressing me to his chest, he drew a deep breath. "You're the only one I've ever loved. I was just too stupid to realize it until...events got out of hand." His eyes glistened. "If I could take back those two years, I would, but all I can do now is *try* to make up for it."

Though his words touched my heart, I shook my head. "But I'm leaving the day after tomorrow, and your life is here."

"Our timing's always been off." He paused. "Look, my contract ends in a month. If I don't renew it, and *if*..." He sighed in his throat. "If we *both* decide to give us another go, I'll relocate to the States. I'll do whatever it takes to be together again." His chin down, his gaze sought mine.

I opened my lips to say yes. Only my throat's constriction prevented me from blurting it out, but then I recalled his betrayal. *No, I won't fall for his empty promises again.* Clenching my hands, I broke free. "You pushed me away once. Part of me can't help but believe you'll do it again." Turning toward the stairway, I spoke over my shoulder. "And if we want to see the shrine before dark, we'd—"

He spun me toward him and, tipping back my head, kissed me in an embrace that left no question about his feelings.

When our lips finally parted, I grabbed hold of his shoulders to steady myself. My heart thumping from the adrenaline rush, I clung tight as the memories engulfed me. Then I returned the kiss, matching his intensity.

Moments later, he pulled back his head and searched my face. "Tell me you'll give me another chance."

Breathless, I was too light-headed to think. All I wanted was to nestle inside his arms.

"Will you?" He drew me closer.

His lips were so near, I felt his breath. Frustrated, I stood on my tiptoes, reaching toward him.

"Say you'll give us another chance."

More a groan than a verbal response, I threw my arms around his neck and met his lips in a kiss.

When we parted, he grinned. "That was a *yes*, right?"

My arms still clinched around his neck and my body pressed against his, I stifled a moan as my body fought my mind—hormones versus logic. Then I took a step back. "That was a 'let's see where we are a month from now' *option*." Then I tucked my hand in his. "Come on. Let's see the shrine."

Together, we climbed another flight of stairs and passed beneath an immense red *torii*. After scaling a final series of steps, we came to a large, woven-grass hoop suspended at the shrine's entrance. "Why are people queuing to walk through?"

"That's the *chinowa*. When you pass through the grass ring, your soul's ritually cleansed of all impurities—or so some say." His frown suggested he disagreed.

"How convenient."

"This shrine's about purification. Because Shintoists believe people are fundamentally good, and evil spirits cause wickedness, the *chinowa* symbolically cleanses your soul." Palm up, he reached for my hand.

Seeming like old times, I linked fingers with his. Then as our turn came to step over the green loop, I giggled and hopped instead.

"What's so funny?"

"The ring's made from grass, right?"

Squinting, he nodded. "Yeah...so?"

"Dried grass is straw, and brooms are made of straw..." My smile widened. "So, you *could* say we just jumped the broom."

Vertical wrinkles appearing between his brows, he turned toward me. "But as you've reminded me, I haven't proposed...so Ava West, may I have your hand—"

His serious tone made me uncomfortable. As the heat rose to my cheeks, I turned my palm up, joking. "Here ya' go. You said *hand*, not necessarily *hand in marriage*."

"True." The light faded from his eyes as we approached the open-air shop.

Hundreds of pink plaques dangled and swayed in the sea breeze. "What are those?"

"*Ema,* wooden prayer boards. Each holds a believer's prayer or wish. After being displayed, the boards are ritually burned, releasing the prayers. At *Inari* shrines, people pray for success in business."

Thoughts of Chase and *Fushimi Inari* crept into my

mind.

"But at *Enoshima*, people pray for luck in romance…"

Luck in romance. I spun my head to see Rafe's expression.

Pokerfaced, he pointed at the racks of fluttering pink plaques. "First, couples pray, then at Lovers' Hill, they take action." A smile played at his lips. "Interested?"

"Maybe…" Suspicious but intrigued, I struggled to suppress a smile. "But strictly from the perspective of researching my article."

"Of course." His tone was tongue in cheek. "This way." Tugging my hand, he turned onto a side trail lined with shops and stalls. "But first we need to make a quick stop."

He took me into one of the cramped stores displaying local handcrafts and snacks. Then he chose a heart-shaped tag and padlock.

"What are those for?" I cocked my head.

"You'll see." Smiling, he gave my fingers a reassuring squeeze. As we climbed a steep incline, he spread his arms, gesturing to the surrounding area. "This is Lovers' Hill."

An open-sided pavilion was perched on a cliff, overlooking the bay, and a stiff breeze carried the sound of a pealing bell—like a ship's bell striking the hours. Dong, dong. Dong, dong.

Wearing wide smiles, a couple stepped from the enclosure and attached something to the safety railing.

I stared, confused. "What are they doing?"

"Locking in their love, like at the *Pont des Arts* bridge in Paris. Couples bolt their love locks to that guardrail." He gestured toward the couple. "Then to ensure a lasting love, they toss the key in the bay."

"Unnecessary littering." Not committed to the idea, I curled my lip.

"In that case, why not keep the key as a souvenir?" His gaze homed in on me. "Add it to your collection...you already hold the key to my heart."

Though his earlier evasion had annoyed me, his directness now was unsettling. *Too much, too soon?* I turned away, searching for a new topic of conversation, and the pavilion came into view. "What's the point of ringing the bell?"

"That's the Dragon-love Bell. Legend holds that once a couple rings it, they're lucky in love." He wore a wistful, half-smile. "If you and I have any chance at a future together—especially with you leaving—we could use some luck. Are you game?"

Unsure how to answer, I chewed my nail, hedging for time. "I thought you weren't superstitious." Watching his reaction instead of the uneven path, I tripped.

He caught me in his arms, then bent his head toward me.

I hesitated, recalling the past, but yielded as much to my own frustrated needs as his. Greeting his kiss with two years' unrequited love, I felt whole again. The missing half was restored. *How I've missed...us.*

Then as approaching footsteps scraped the path, I broke away.

"Want to ring the bell?" He spoke in a gruff whisper. "While we have time..."

I glanced at the fast-approaching couple, nodded, and grabbed his hand as we stepped into the pavilion. Then placing my hand above his, I gripped the rope and pulled with all my might.

Dong, dong. Dong, dong.

"Lucky in love…it has a certain 'ring.' " I laughed while the bell pealed. But as we returned to the guardrail, the reverberations became a dull echo, and the joy faded. "This evening's been wonderful, but what does tomorrow hold?"

"I don't know, but let's seal our future with a kiss." Bringing his free arm around my waist, he grazed my lips. Then glancing at the nearing couple, he took the heart-shaped tag and a pen from his pocket. "Quick. Write our names while I open the lock."

Rafe and Ava. In a burst of whimsy, I drew a heart around the words before handing back the pen and tag.

He glanced at the hand-drawn heart, then looped our nametag onto the lock. After fastening it to the handrail, he held out his arm, inviting me to join him.

I put my arm around his waist, hanging my thumb in his beltloop as I admired our handiwork. His arm about my shoulders, I side glanced at his profile before staring out to sea. *How natural this feels…how right. But the day after tomorrow, I'll cross that ocean, and after that…?*

"What are you thinking?"

"We followed the superstitions—rang the bell and left a love lock, but—"

"Superstitions are nothing but mental suggestions."

I turned toward him. "But when my plane leaves, seven thousand miles will separate us. What are the odds of us *ever* seeing each other again?"

"The odds are bleak, but loving you has to increase them." His smile was sad. "There, I've said it. I love you. I've put my cards on the table. What happens next is up to you."

"Is it?" My chest aching, memories made the moment bittersweet. "You left me hanging once. How do I know you won't do it again?"

"Test me. If I don't live up to my promises this next month"—his Adam's apple bobbed—"tell me it's too late, and I'll stay in Japan. But if we stand a chance, call me, text me, write me, and I'll board the next flight—"

Dong, dong. Dong, dong.

Flinching as the bell pealed, I spun toward the couple responsible, their hands still gripping the rope. I recalled Chase's words: *Fate brings people together no matter how far apart they may be.* Then I turned back with a solemn sigh. "Guess we'll have to see what the future holds."

A grimace passing for a smile, he handed me the tiny gold key.

To his heart...

He glanced from his watch to the setting sun. "We have just enough time."

I followed his gaze, watching the fierce, crimson ball loom larger and larger as it plunged toward the horizon. *No wonder the Japanese chose the sun for their flag. How majestic.* "Time for what?"

"To catch the sunset from the Sea Candle."

Guessing at its meaning, I squinted as my imagination took flight. "Which is..."

"A combination lighthouse and observatory." Taking my hand in his, he tugged. "Come on."

I kept my eye on the late-day sun as we rushed to beat its plunge into the gold-tinged waves.

"The Sea Candle's lights are just coming on." He pointed to the beacon.

I spotted it rising above the treetops like a torch enflaming the darkening sky. Narrow at the bottom, the building widened as it climbed.

"Want to walk the staircase or take the elevator?"

More stairs. Déjà vu. I thought of the towers I'd scaled earlier with Chase and shuddered. But the setting sun's low-angled rays illuminated the lighthouse's spiral staircase, dispelling my fears. "It's bright as morning. Let's walk."

He grinned.

"What's so funny?"

"You." His grin broadened until his dimple appeared. "The visualization seemed to work."

"You're right...wow. Given the choice, I chose to walk. That *is* a switch." Chuckling at the irony, I hugged him. "I've been afraid of heights since I was three. Thank you."

"For what?"

"Helping me conquer my fear of heights."

"I didn't do anything."

"Your visualization technique worked. I'm not saying I'd scale Mount Everest, but thanks to you, I actually opted to climb these stairs." Using his arm as leverage, I stood on tiptoe to kiss his cheek. "Rafe Armstrong, you're a remarkable man."

Beaming, he pointed to the lighthouse's top tier, already lit in blue as the daylight waned. "If we want to see the sunset from the observation deck, we'd better hurry." Then grabbing my hand, he raced to the stairs.

I laughed as we climbed, hand in hand, with the sea breeze whooshing through the open-air stairs and the evening sky's crimson and gold tones changing into plum and amethyst. At the first tier's circular deck, I glanced at the elongated shadows stretching across the gardens below and tugged his hand, urging him faster. "Hurry."

By the sixth story, I was gulping air, but noting the ruddy blush of the sunset through the beams and girders, I found a second wind and pushed on to the observation deck.

Breathless, I gazed from the top tier as the wind whistled past my ears and swirled my hair into my eyes. Pinning back my hair with one hand, I forced myself to look at the breakers crashing on the rocks below. Dizziness overtook me for an instant, but I grabbed the metal railing and breathed deeply until the nausea passed.

"Are you okay?" Rafe stood behind me, his body a barrier against the windy gusts as his hands gripped the guardrail.

Nodding, I leaned back against his chest. "I'm all right"—I smiled over my shoulder—"now."

He brought his arms around my waist, spooning as he held me in a protective grip. "Look to your left, beyond the bay. That's Mount Fuji."

"It looks close enough to touch." I stretched out my hand as I would in a 3D movie, yearning to connect with its image. "And to think I'm climbing it tomorrow." My nonchalant, detached tone surprised me. "What did you do to me?"

"What do mean?" His grasp loosening, he turned me toward him.

"What magic did you weave?" I grinned. "Since your visualization exercise, heights don't send me into a panic."

"Don't give me the credit." Pulling me closer, his

hands around my back, he shook his head. "Change only comes by doing what scares the dickens out of you. You've climbed so much these past days, you've desensitized yourself. *You* overcame your fear, so take credit where it's due."

Rising on my toes, I reached my arms around his neck. "Maybe we make a good team, after all."

"Ya' think?" Bending his head, he met my lips in a stolen kiss, then glanced at the other visitors.

Becoming aware of our neighbors, I grinned, took my arms from his neck, and linked fingers with his. Then turning toward the west, I caught my breath.

The setting sun hovered above Mount Fuji's crater, igniting the sky with iridescent streaks of gold, polished brass, periwinkle, and lilac. Doubling the radiance, *Sagami* Bay reflected the shimmering heavens. Then for an instant, the sun expanded into a starburst, crowning the crater as its beams surrounded the peak like a glowing tiara.

He murmured something, but the wind swept away the sound.

"What?" Eyes on the horizon, I dared not turn my head for fear of missing the spectacle.

He leaned closer. "Diamond Fuji is what the Japanese call this moment, when the sun sets right over the mountain in a dazzling light display."

Breathing in the scene, I sighed. "I feel so insignificant compared to Fuji's grandeur."

"It's humbling." He gave my hand a gentle squeeze. "Nature puts our lives in perspective."

"How so?"

"The universe is so much bigger than BIG." He drew his free hand across the wide bay and sky. "Our lives may be in chaos." Again, he squeezed my fingers. "But one look at nature, and you *know*. If God could create this marvel, He can fix any part of our petty lives."

Even us?

The sun slipped from Mount Fuji's pinnacle and began its descent behind the mountain. As the sky's luminous glimmer faded from gold and periwinkle to deeper shades of plum and burgundy, the day's rosy glow gave way to the cold light of reason.

Remembering my deadline, I glanced at the time. *If we leave now, the ride back will take an hour. The article's due at eleven, and time's running out.* "I hate to say it, but I've got to go."

"So soon?" He turned toward me.

"This evening's been perfect…and seeing you again really has been great." I winced now that our time together was winding down. "But all good things must come to an end."

"You say that with such finality." A crease appeared between his eyes. "Are you talking about the end of the day or us?"

"I don't know." I bunched my lips. "Being here with you feels like old times." The afterglow of our kiss lingered. "But we have to be realistic. With me leaving the day after tomorrow, the likelihood of us seeing each other again is virtually nil."

"Matthew 19:26." He wore a gentle smile. " 'With God all things are possible.' "

"Yeah, but the *odds* of us sharing any future are astronomical." I leveled my gaze on his. "We have to be reasonable."

"Reason is nothing but a rationale for action. God doesn't need justification to act. With Him, *nothing* is impossible."

"Long-distance relationships are difficult under the best of circumstances." Taking a deep breath, I tried a different tack. "A positive outlook can't dismiss the miles between Tokyo and New York."

"Not positive thinking, what I'm saying is, God's power makes anything possible."

"You've become such an idealist." I stifled a long, slow sigh. "Just *try* to be practical, okay?"

"This isn't idealism or some inability to grasp reality. It's faith. It's a passion for what reason can't explain." He took my hands in his. "I believe—not in my power of positive thinking—but in God's ability to make the impossible possible. If it's His will, He'll find a way."

My chest tightening at the unlikelihood, I hunched my shoulders. *But are we meant to be together?*

Chapter 14—Tokyo

Thursday Night

I slowed my steps as we approached the apartment building. *Two hours 'til my deadline.* Wincing, I turned toward Rafe. "I'd love to ask you in for coffee, but I have to finish the article." I swallowed a sigh. "*And* I hate long goodbyes."

His fingers still entwined in mine, he slowly swung me to face him. He nodded, his mouth set in grim lines. "I know. It's late, and you've got a tight schedule."

"Wish I could slow time." I recalled the whirlwind weekend in Kyoto and the bustling days in Tokyo.

Chase came to mind unbidden. His face flashed through my thoughts, while scorching scenes from my dream flooded my psyche.

Where did that come from? I shook off the images, then looked at the man before me, and all other thoughts fled. "Tonight's zipped by."

"Time's a gift. The trick is to use it wisely." He gave me a dejected smile. "A lesson I'm still learning."

I considered the years we could have shared. *What would life be like if he hadn't married Ashley?* Resenting the lost time, I sulked. "Earlier you'd said if you could take back those two years, you would—that you'd try to make up the time."

He nodded.

"But making up time isn't possible because time's finite. If your timing's off, and you miss the opportunity, it's gone, once and for all." Resigned to our fate, I shrugged.

"*Tempus fugit.*"

"Yeah." I bunched my brow. "And I still have that article tonight…"

"I should let you go…" His words contradicting his actions, he pulled me closer in a sad embrace.

My hands limp at my sides, I hesitated. *Should I?* A shallow sigh escaped. *Why not? We're just old friends, hugging goodbye.* I slid my arms around him and lay my cheek against his chest, listening to his heartbeat.

His breathing jagged, his chest shook.

Is he crying? My own regrets were painful enough, but sensing his misery was unbearable. I stood on tiptoe, brushing my lips against his cheek to comfort him, but as I tasted his salty tears, an ache began in my chest. *The pain of separation.*

I remembered the pain when he had left me. Now, as I left him, the ache was just as agonizing. The lump in my throat too large to swallow, I tightened my grip as I silently said goodbye.

He crushed me to him in an inconsolable kiss.

The urgency of his mouth on mine triggered a moan, and I dug my fingers into his back, recalling the emotions I'd denied for two years.

"Excuse me…*Excuse me!*"

The words finally penetrated, and my eyelids flew open.

A scowling man stood with keycard in hand.

"Sorry." My cheeks burning, I broke the embrace and slunk away from the entry. Then taking Rafe's hand,

I pulled him aside.

"I really do have to finish that article by eleven."

He glanced at his watch. Then his gaze dejected, he took a business card from his vest pocket and pressed it in my hand. "Call, text, email me, will you? I promise…" His voice thick, he started to say more but instead stifled a sigh. "We're out of time, but please, Ava, please don't let tonight be the end."

Swallowing hard, I fished in my purse for the keycard and unlocked the door. "I hate long goodbyes." *I hate goodbyes. Period.* Turning my head, I bussed his cheek. "Take care." Then I hurried inside, brushing away my tears before he could see them. *I have no other choice, do I?*

****

Friday Early Morning

The ceiling lights flashed on, and the door slammed, waking me from a sound sleep.

"Ooops." Shushing herself, Mia burst into muffled giggles.

"Mia? Is that you?" I blinked at the bright overhead lights. Squinting and shading my eyes from the glare, I glanced at the time. *Three-thirty.*

The kitten jumped off my bed and scampered to the door.

"Yeah. I didn't wake you, did I?" Mia dimmed the lights and reached over to pet Ichiro.

"Well…" Swallowing a groan, I pulled on my robe. "Kind of…"

"Ooops. Sorry." Taking a bowl of azuki beans from the fridge and a spoon from the drawer, Mia set them on the breakfast bar. Then she started another round of giggles.

"What's so funny?"

"Nothing." Between snickers and chuckles, she poured a shot of sake as she stumbled onto a barstool. "Everything."

"Are you all right?"

"I'm great!" Mia lifted the shot glass to her lips and, with a practiced flick of her wrist, slammed down the sake. "In fact, tonight was a lot of laughs." Her shoulders shaking, she chuckled to herself as she gobbled the beans.

"Really?" I joined her at the bar.

Following her, the kitten hopped onto the third barstool and watched, its intensely blue eyes focused on the beans.

"Why? What was so funny?"

"Nothing…" Mia's glazed eyes opened wide, showing her dilated pupils, and she grinned. "Everything."

"What do you mean?"

"Atsuki had the bartender mix a 'special' for me." She grinned through clenched teeth and began giggling.

My ears perked at her emphasis. "What was in the drink?"

"Whatever it was, it was strong. At first, it gave me a headache, but it made the hours fly by."

"For you, too, huh?" Thoughts of Rafe reopened the raw wounds, and I swallowed hard.

"Huh?" Head tilted back, Mia gawked, wild-eyed, as if trying to focus. "What?"

"Nothing." Concerned for her, I shook off my own problems. "How much have you had to drink?"

"Just that drink and now this." Covering one eye,

she stared at me through the other as her shoulders shook with silent laughter. "That's better—just one of you now."

"This is only your second drink tonight?" I drew a deep breath. "You didn't take anything else, did you?"

"Nothing—oh, just a pill for my headache." Smiling brightly through gritted teeth, she lifted her hands, palms up, like a little girl. "All gone."

"What did you take?"

"I don't know." Mia shrugged. "Just a pill Atsuki gave me to feel better." She broke into a high-pitched bray. "And it worked. I. Am. On. Top. Of. The. World."

"What kind of pill?" Recalling Rafe's low opinion of Atsuki, I sucked in my breath.

"Who knows? But whatever it was, it did the trick!" Mia's eyes widened until the whites around her dilated pupils made her look like a Kabuki character.

"Can you describe the pill?"

She held up her hands, wiggling her manicured fingertips. "It was this pretty shade of pink—matched my nails perfectly. Oh, another thing." She raised her index finger. "It had a logo on it...some car manufacturer, I think."

"I'm not familiar with meds, but that pill sounds more like a party drug than a prescription." I made a mental note to look it up online.

"If Atsuki gave it to me, it's fine." Yawning, Mia worked her jaw back and forth. "Can we continue this conversation in the morning? I'm just a little sleepy..." Then she crossed her arms on the kitchen bar and lay down her head.

"Come on, sleepyhead, before you fall off that barstool." My arm around her shoulders, I helped her across the room. "Let's get you to bed."

Mia flopped on the bed, fully clothed, and didn't budge.

I glanced at her prone body as I put away the food. *What did Atsuki give her?*

****

Between listening to Mia snore, worrying about her lifestyle, and double guessing myself about Rafe, I barely dozed off before the alarm rang.

I stumbled into the kitchenette to make coffee and tripped over a dark form. Then muffling a scream as I struggled to see in the nightlight's dim glow, I flipped on the light switch and gasped.

Mia sat on the floor, legs sticking out straight, her back propped against the refrigerator, and her head lolling on her chest. Her mascara had smeared into dark circles, and she stared through zombie eyes as she drooled.

"What happened?" I knelt beside her and took her clammy hand in mine.

"Who're you?" Her jaw hanging loose, Mia slurred her speech. Then bracing her head against the fridge, she averted her eyes. Perspiration dripped from her face, and she shook uncontrollably.

"I'm Ava…" I gulped, afraid for her. "Remember?"

"Why're you here?" Her eyes wandered.

"To help you back to bed…" I tried to pull her to her feet, but Mia was dead weight. "Come on, get up. I can't lift you." I tugged her arm, managing to nudge her several inches, and when a narrow boning knife fell from the folds of her skirt onto the floor, I yelped. "What are you doing with a knife?"

Mia's eyes rolled back, the whites showing. Then

234

moaning, she rocked back and forth. A bloody cut on her wrist answered the question.

I yanked away the knife and tossed it in the cupboard, high out of reach.

Groping about, Mia opened her eyes and looked left and right. Finally, her dark sockets stared just above my head. "Where's my knife?" She tried rising but succeeded only in stumbling away from the fridge. Then she shrieked, "Give me my knife!"

I thought of calling for help. *What's the Japanese equivalent of 911?* But between my lack of Japanese and the need to act quickly, I scrapped that plan. Then I remembered her recent fondness for azuki beans.

Now that Mia no longer blocked the refrigerator door, I pulled out the bowl. Like cajoling a cat with kitty treats, I waved the azuki beans in front of Mia's nose, letting its aroma entice her. "Come to bed, and you can eat all you want…"

Rubbernecking, Mia grabbed at the bowl, but it was just beyond her grasp.

"Come on." I brandished the bowl closer. "I'll serve you breakfast in bed. Wouldn't that be nice?"

Inch by inch, half crawling and half knuckle-walking, Mia crossed the tiny apartment like a chimpanzee.

I helped her into bed and fluffed the pillows, so she could sit up.

Watching hungrily, Mia never took her raccoon eyes from the prize.

"Oh, I forgot a spoon. Or would you prefer a—"

Mia wrenched the bowl from me and, using her fingers, began wolfing down the beans.

"Don't you want a fork…?" As I listened to the

grunts, sniffs, and open-mouthed chewing sounds, I shook my head. *What is wrong with her?*

Ichiro rubbed against my calves, frantically meowing.

"It's almost as if you're trying to answer me." I gave a wry chuckle as I lifted the kitten and cuddled it against my chest. "But now what? I can't leave her alone..." Absently petting the cat, I glanced at the time. "And I leave for the train station in a half hour." I sighed. The unexpected answer came with a shout. "Rafe!"

Hissing, the kitten scrambled out of my arms, leaving behind a long scratch.

"Idiot cat! What's your problem?" I grabbed several tissues to blot the blood and called Rafe on my cell.

He answered on the third ring with a drowsy "Hello" and a yawn.

"Rafe, I'm sorry to wake you, but can you come to Mia's apartment right away?"

"Why?" His voice shrill, he rushed his words. "What's wrong?"

"Mia's..." I scratched my head. *How do I explain?* "I think Mia's having a reaction to some drug. A few hours ago, she was euphoric, but now she's in a stupor."

"You think she's overdosing? What'd she take?"

The facts sketchy, I shrugged. "All I know is Atsuki gave her a pill."

"I never trusted that guy..." He groaned in his throat. "What's she doing?"

"She's out of it—doesn't seem to recognize me. And she's cut herself. I'm afraid to leave her alone." I hesitated. *A few hours ago, I said goodbye and now I'm asking a favor.* "Can you please stay with her this morning...just until the drug wears off?"

"I have classes from nine to five." Mumbling, he stifled a sigh. "Can't you stay?"

"I can't. I'm catching a train to Mount Fuji in twenty-five minutes." I mentally groaned. *What awful timing.* "I don't know where else to turn, and today's my last chance to research my article."

"With Chase, right?"

His tone implied more.

"Yes…" *Why does Rafe make me feel I'm cheating on him?* "This isn't personal. It's just busin—"

Hissing, the cat whacked my arm, and I almost dropped the phone.

"Cat, what is *wrong* with you?" I pushed the kitten away. "It's just—"

"Business, I know…" He muttered under his breath. "Okay, I'll make some excuse at work. Give me a few minutes to get dressed and catch a cab."

"Rafe, thank you." A sigh escaped.

"Yeah, yeah…"

I cringed at the sarcastic tone, then glanced at Mia in bed. "This sounds off the wall, but her craving for azuki beans has developed into an obsession."

"What do you mean?"

"She couldn't even wait for a fork. She ate the cold beans with her hands, wiped the bowl with her fingers, and now she's licking them clean." Despite the situation, I had to chuckle. "She'd be funny if she weren't so frightening."

Crouching, Mia stared blankly through unfocused, zombie eyes, avoiding my gaze.

"I don't trust her like this." I shuddered, unsure if Mia was observing me or just spacing. "Not to sound melodramatic, but this *may be* a suicide watch."

"Be there as soon as I can—ten minutes if I'm lucky." His hurried words reflected the urgency.

"Thanks, Rafe. I really appreciate it." My shoulders slumped as I hung up. I felt guilty asking him to miss work, while I took a daytrip. Then I turned toward the cat. "And you. What's gotten into you?" With a frustrated huff, I locked him in his crate before glancing at Mia.

Her head lolling, she stared vacantly into the distance.

Hope she's safe while I shower and dress.

Twenty minutes later, the intercom rang. I buzzed Rafe in and waited at the front door.

"Got here as soon as I could. Rush hour." Fixing his gaze on mine, he paused before leaning over to buss my cheek.

Butterflies fluttered in my stomach, and I caught my breath. "Thanks again for coming on such short notice." Then shamed by his selflessness, I hid behind a tight smile.

The kitten yowled inside his cage, his cries like a baby screaming in pain.

"What's wrong with the cat?"

"Ichiro's being weird."

"I'll say." Rafe's shoulders dropped. "Sorry, but I can only get the morning off. The afternoon classes are part of my ministry."

"I understand." I glanced at Mia. "Hopefully, she'll sober by then and can manage on her own."

Mia stared blindly, her expressionless eyes shifting left to right.

Crap! I checked the time. "I hate to run, but…"

"I know." Crossing his arms, he took a wide stance.

"You have to meet Chase…"

His tone made me flinch. "I've got to research—"

"Right. It's just business…" He bunched his lips. "Don't worry. I'll hold down the fort."

"Rafe, thank you." My throat tightened in a combination of gratitude and guilt. *How can I ever repay him?*

****

I darted through the crowds and jay-walked at the intersections to arrive on time. Catching my breath, I scanned the station for Chase.

"You made it."

His voice from behind made me jump. "I didn't see you." About-facing, I flashed a smile as I focused on the day ahead. "Looks like a clear morning. Hopefully, we'll get some spectacular views from Mount Fuji."

"What happened?" His head cocked to the side.

"What do you mean?" *Could he possibly know about Rafe? About Mia?*

"You're actually looking forward to climbing a mountain?" Eyes like slits, he scrutinized me. "What's changed? Why doesn't the thought of heights frighten you?"

Not wanting to mention Rafe's assistance, I shrugged. "I tried a visualization technique, and, so far, it seems to work—knock on wood." I thumped my skull.

His face stony, he squinted through icy eyes.

Recalling how Chase had coaxed me up mountains and towers, I breathed a guilty sigh. *I appreciate his help, but I'm not attracted. So why do I feel like I'm cheating?*

Then Rafe's face came to mind, and I smiled inwardly as the circumstances resolved to black and white. *We went together all through school. We share a history. Seeing him again has rekindled those old feelings.*

Chase's sullen expression drew my attention. *I've known him only days. We went on a few excursions together, and I remind him of someone, but I don't feel anything...no chemistry...* Then recalling the dream, I squirmed, questioning the subtle nuances of gray.

Chase may have a certain animal magnetism, but the attraction is contrived. He triggers those emotions, and I simply react, right? I drew an uneasy breath. *He even called me an empath. Or* am *I attracted on some level?*

"He who runs after two hares catches neither."

"What?" His voice roused me from my reverie, and I snapped my head toward him. *Does he eavesdrop on my thoughts? He all but admits he can...* I felt naked with nowhere to hide. Then common sense took hold. *How ridiculous. He can't read my mind...can he?*

"Ava, you sadden me when you don't value my friendship..." He spoke slowly, as if ensuring his words registered. "Didn't I arrange this excursion to Mount Fuji?"

My chest tightened. "Yes—"

"Didn't I urge you to ask your publisher for an extension?"

Nodding, I bowed my head and stared at my shoes. "Yeah—"

"Haven't I shown you more sights and given you more insights for your articles than you ever...*dreamed*?"

My head snapped toward him at his choice of words, and I swallowed hard. *He's right. I never could've written the pieces without his help.*

Eyes widening, he spoke louder. "Haven't I?"

"Yes, *yes*."

"My time must mean nothing since you can't even do me the courtesy of being punctual."

I glanced at the busy train station's overhead clock. "I was here on time—"

"Barely." He harrumphed. "At least, you weren't an hour late like at *Arashiyama*. I guess I should be grateful for small favors…"

I cringed at the memory.

"You don't appreciate my friendship."

"I do—"

"Really? You don't show it when you're less than honest."

His words hung in the air as the train station's musical jingle sounded, followed by an announcement over the loudspeaker.

I swallowed the lump in my throat while swarms of commuters eddied and swirled past us.

"Ava, I can be a good friend. I can open doors for you…take you places you can only *dream of*." He shook his head. "Don't disappoint me…"

I chewed my lip. *It isn't like I'm cheating on Chase, so why do I feel so guilty?*

****

His wave gone unnoticed, Rafe groaned as he shut the apartment door. *Ava never looked back when she boarded the elevator. Why try to recapture what's gone…what I threw away? When she wanted me, I ran. Now that I want her, it's too late. She's moved on.*

Mia fidgeted on the bed, still staring wide-eyed as if in a trance.

What did Ava say about her obsession with azuki

beans? He pulled out his cell and searched online. Though skeptical at first, he choked as he read of the beans' connection to folktales and fox possession.

Mia's yelp roused him.

"Can I get you something?"

Fretting, she squirmed and wriggled as her eyes scanned the room.

"What can I get you?" He crossed to her bed. "Are you hungry? Can I make you something to eat?"

"Uh-huh." Averting her gaze, she nodded. "Azuki beans."

He searched the refrigerator but found only soy sauce, an open can of cat food, and a carton of expired milk. Checking her cupboards, he called, "Do you have any azuki beans?"

"Uh-huh." Walking as if in a dream, she crossed the room, sat on a kitchen stool, and pointed. "That cupboard."

Progress, at least. He found a pop-top can, dumped its contents in a bowl, and placed it in the microwave.

Mia's phone rang, and she answered on the first ring. "*Moshi-moshi.*" She nodded. "*Hai, Atsuki.*" Her agitation growing, she began breathing heavily. "Yeah." The whites of her eyes widening, she swallowed hard. "*Hai.*" She hung up, raced out of sight, and screeched at the top of her lungs. "He's gone."

"Who's gone?" His heart skipping a beat, Rafe ran after her.

"Ichiro." Pointing to the cat's empty crate, she sank to the floor and curled into a fetal position. "He's going to kill me."

"No one's going to kill you." He glanced at the crate's unlocked door. *I heard the cat just minutes ago.*

How did it get out? Helping Mia to her feet, he tried to ease her mind. "The kitten's somewhere in the apartment. Don't worry. I'll find it, okay?"

Sobbing, Mia rocked back and forth as she chanted over and over. "He's going to kill me."

"No one's…" He held onto her upper arms and peered into her eyes. *Wait a minute.* "*Who's* going to kill you?"

Stiffening, she refused to meet his gaze.

"Who are you afraid of?"

She squirmed from his grasp and tore about the tiny apartment, searching under the beds and behind draperies. "Here, kitty-kitty."

"Mia, try to calm—"

"You don't understand." In a frenzy, she screeched as she ripped pillows and sheets off the beds. "I've got to find him, or he'll kill me." Then she began opening every drawer and tipping out its contents. "Ichiro!"

The microwave dinged.

"Mia, stop worrying. No one's going to hurt you." He caught her by her shoulders and led her back to the breakfast bar. "Now, sit down and eat your azuki beans."

She went limp.

"Don't you want your azuki beans?"

Her eyes focusing on the microwave, she nodded.

"All right, then." Speaking in soothing tones, he helped her onto a stool. "Sit here, while I get you a fork, okay?"

Never taking her gaze from the microwave, she nodded.

He breathed a sigh as he placed the warm beans and a fork before her.

Staring through him, she mechanically fed herself.

Mia's non-response reminded him of Ashley. Recalling how small talk had pacified his troubled wife, he tried to make conversation. "Looks like a beautiful day outside—clear, the sun's shining. I bet you can see Mount Fuji from the *Tochō* today." He smiled. "You know, Ava went to Mount Fuji—"

"Mount Fuji?" Mia's spine straightened. "That's near…" Staring straight ahead as she stuffed azuki beans in her mouth, she mumbled incoherently.

He mentally replayed her garbled syllables and gasped. "Did you say *Aokigahara?*"

She reached for her purse on the bar. In a single motion, she popped a fuchsia pill and washed it down with a forkful of beans.

"What did you take?"

Her eyes glazing, she jumped off the stool and ran out the door, purse in hand.

"Mia, you're in no condition to go anywhere." He ran after her. "Mia…*don't* get on that elev—"

The doors shut.

I can't let her leave the building. He ran down the four flights of stairs. Gasping for air, he caught up just as she jumped in a cab.

No! He hailed another cab and, pointing out her taxi, told the driver to follow. "*Isoide!*"

Her cab stopped at the train station, where she blended with thousands of other commuters entering and leaving the building.

She can't get away. The similarity between Mia's behavior and Ashley's triggered unwelcome memories. Regrets about his marriage surfaced like bubbles in boiling water. *Why did I leave her alone that morning? Why did I go to work?* Work! *Do I have time to call? No.*

He trailed Mia until a troop of school children squeezed between them. Stifling a groan, he slowed to a crawl, helplessly watching as her blonde head disappeared around a corner.

On a hunch, he took the escalator to the Fuji Excursion Express train and, peering over the heads of the other travelers, spotted her at the ticket counter. By the time he reached her, she had moved out of sight, but following his instincts, he bought a ticket to *Kawaguchiko.*

He took the escalator to the train tracks and peered up and down the white-tiled platform, but he saw no sign of her blonde hair. *The train will be here any minute.* After texting work, he messaged Ava.

Rafe—*If my hunch is right, Mia's headed for* Aokigahara. *In case I can't stop her, catch her at the* Kawaguchiko *Station, the transfer point for Mount Fuji. Our train will arrive in an hour. Don't let her leave—*

Then he spotted a blonde head at the far end of the station, past the kiosk and beyond the boarding platform. Weighing the odds of missing the train versus finding Mia, he gambled she was the blonde and raced the length of the platform. "Mia!" He touched her arm.

"Can I help you?" A stranger turned toward him.

"Sorry." Out of breath, he gasped. "My mistake."

A seven-second, musical jingle sounded. Then a voice over the loudspeaker announced the approaching train.

He looked at the distance between him and the boarding area. *Will I make it?* The sensory triggers spurred him to action, and he sprinted back, arriving just as the silvery-white and blue express train whooshed into the station. Another jingle announced the doors were opening, and he joined the crush of waiting passengers jockeying for position.

Rafe craned his neck, peering above the stream of black-haired heads. When he saw no other blonde, he said a silent prayer. *Please help me find Mia. Whatever she's planning, if Atsuki's behind it, she's in danger.*

A bell like a ringing telephone and then a public broadcast announced the train was about to leave.

Just before the doors closed, he hopped aboard the last car, relying on blind faith. *If she's headed for Aokigahara, she's aboard...but is my hunch right?*

Chapter 15—Aokigahara

Friday

Just as the train pulled into the *Kawaguchiko* Station, my phone dinged with Rafe's text.

"Oh, no!"

"Something wrong?" Chase spun his head toward me.

A chime sounded. The doors opened, and the passengers raced toward the exits.

I tucked my phone in its holster. Then while we joined the debarking passengers, I synopsized Mia's situation.

"*Aokigahara*...Suicide Forest." His eyes widening, he pulled me behind the kiosk, out of pedestrian traffic. "If she's involved with Atsuki, she *is* in trouble."

"Why—"

"Because Atsuki isn't what he appears."

"He isn't *Yakuza*?" I recalled Rafe's objections to his underworld connections. "But I saw his tattoos."

"They're nothing but illusions." His grimace passed for a wry smile. "He's not *Yakuza*. He's an old adversary—a *nogitsune*."

"A dark *kitsune*, right...?" I squinted as I recalled the definition, then ducked my head, hiding a smile at his superstitions.

"This is no laughing matter." His jaw clenching, he

locked his gaze on mine. "Atsuki creates conflict, then feeds off his victim's pain."

"How?"

"*Kitsunetsuki*—"

"*Kitsune what?*"

"Fox possession. Like clinical lycanthropy in the West, where people think they transform into wolves or werewolves, with *kitsunetsuki,* people believe they morph into—"

"Foxes…" I caught my breath. Put into my Western perspective, his superstitions sounded improbable *yet* almost rational. Then his earlier conversation about the similarity of human and fox DNA came to mind. If it's 'as close as science proves, why couldn't these beings shapeshift?' *People might imagine they're animals, but foxes impersonate people?* I shook my head. *Not possible.* "No."

"Don't dismiss—"

A loud chime sounded, followed by a public broadcast that drowned out his words.

I held my hands to my ears and mouthed the words. *Can't hear.*

Last-minute passengers jostled past us to squeeze aboard the departing train. The doors closed, and the train whooshed from the platform.

When the noise subsided, Chase continued. "Similar to skinwalkers, a *nogitsune* can assume a person's shape—even mimic his or her voice, mannerisms, and personality."

Irritated with his tall tales, I stifled a sigh. "What've these myths got to do with Mia?"

"*Nogitsune* aren't imaginary boogeymen." His gaze caught mine. "They exist."

"Do you mean…" I struggled to remain rational. "Are you *implying*—"

"I'm *telling* you. They exist."

"So, by extension"—dreading the answer, I had to ask—"*kitsune* exist?"

His chin high and his neck exposed, he gave a curt nod.

My shoulders slumped, and my purse slipped from my arm. Unnerved, I avoided his gaze as I bent to retrieve it. "You're saying these legends—"

"Are real."

I rubbed my bottom lip as I digested his words. *He said his great-great-great-grandmother was kitsune and passed for human—according to a family legend.* A grin playing at my lips, I studied him, unsure how to separate fact from fiction. Then I burst out laughing. "Oh, you! You're just pulling my leg…again."

His gaze unwavering, his stormy blue eyes leveled with mine.

Reminded of an overcast sky just before a gale, I swallowed hard, and my laughter died in my throat. "You're serious?"

"Dead serious." His voice was devoid of any emotion. "For over a thousand years, Japanese medical practitioners considered *kitsunetsuki* a disease. Even into the twentieth century, psychologists believed fox possession caused mental illness."

"But not anymore…" Crossing my arms, I hugged myself, seeking reassurance. "Right?"

"Today, therapists consider *kitsunetsuki* a psychosis or a culture-bound syndrome. Although"—he shrugged—"its symptoms can extend to people familiar with the Japanese culture."

"Symptoms?" I squinted. "Like what?"

"Like craving azuki beans or refusing to make eye contact."

I recalled Mia's recent obsession. "I don't buy your story about fox possession, but my friend has developed a sudden fondness for azuki beans." *And she wouldn't look me in the eye this morning.*

"You said she's working on her dissertation in Japanese Studies?"

"Yeah."

"So, she's familiar with the culture. Believing in *kitsunetsuki* might not be fashionable in this age of supercomputers and artificial intelligence, but stories still circulate in the tabloids and mass media."

"For example?"

"In 2019, a doomsday cult member rammed his car into pedestrians on *Takeshita* Street, then pled not guilty on the grounds that the cult was fox possessed. And as recently as 2022, the *Sessho-seki* split in two."

Skeptical, I squinted. "The *what* did *what?*"

"The killing stone…according to legend, it imprisoned an evil *nogitsune* vixen. Her spirit escaped when it split in half and began spewing sulfur fumes, killing anyone that approached."

"You're wasting time." I glanced at the clock overhead. "What have these folktales to do with Mia?"

"You asked for examples. Your friend's in trouble. If she's on her way to *Aokigahara,* it's because Atsuki masterminded it through *kitsune* seduction."

"Seduction?" The hairs rising on the back of my neck, I about-faced.

"Mind control. A dark *kitsune* seduces through mental manipulation. By establishing and maintaining the target's gaze, a *nogitsune*—"

"Or a *kitsune*?" Recalling the times I'd fallen under the spell of his mesmerizing gaze, I shook off a chill.

"Or a *kitsune*."

The strange attraction began to make sense. *How often has he triggered my emotions—or shaped my dreams?*

"A *nogitsune* can control its victim's mind—even bend time or go back in time." His chin dipping, he grimaced. "The *nogitsune* removes his prey from reality by contriving everything they see, think, or feel."

"So, you admit you're—"

A musical jingle sounded, followed by an announcement over the loudspeaker. Then a train roared into the station obliterating all conversation.

Chase pointed to the level above and gestured to follow him up the escalator.

While the moving staircase carried me away from the platform's din, I studied his face: Finely chiseled chin, upturned nose, and pointed, foxlike ears. As I stepped off the escalator, I caught his arm. "You once told me your great-great-great-grandmother was *kitsune*—"

"So say family legends." He turned toward me, his eyes boring into mine.

"Wouldn't that…make…make you…" His trenchant, sapphire eyes distracted me. Stumbling over my words, I forgot what I wanted to say. Confused, I blinked. "What was I saying?"

"You said you wanted to wait for your friend's train." The corners of his narrowed eyes crinkled in a quasi-smile.

I did? I tried to recall but drew a blank.

"If Mia's going to *Aokigahara*, she'll take the Retro Bus." He glanced about the large complex. "Finding her inside this station would be difficult, at best, but if we wait outside by the bus stop, we can't miss her."

This time, he smiled a toothy grin, exposing strong, white teeth. As he walked beneath the station's glaring, overhead lights, the shadows played tricks on my eyes.

I stared at his gaunt cheeks, long chin, and pointy nose. *He looks like a fox.* Covering my mouth, I gasped.

"What?" Then sunlight streamed through the station's windows, illuminating his face, and Chase's attractive features reemerged.

"Sorry." A nervous laugh escaped my lips. "I'm just a little jumpy."

"Understandably." He gestured toward a snack counter. "Let's get a hot cup of *matcha* and wait outside."

Ten minutes later, I exited the station, cup in hand, and froze in my tracks. The view was breathtaking. Gaping, I inhaled the majesty of the scene.

Mount Fuji loomed before me, looking just as I'd seen in hundreds of pictures, its snow-topped peak and symmetrical mound rising regally. *But it fills the entire horizon.* Panning slowly from left to right, I drank in the scene, awestruck. *It's immense.* "Wow…"

"*Fuji-san* is spectacular, isn't it?" He chuckled like a teacher delighted at his student's enthusiasm. "Especially, the first time you see it." Then the corners of his mouth sagging, his gaze met mine. "Viewed through your perspective, I delight in life. Every time I introduce you to something, you breathe new life into it. You make every day an adventure, even if vicarious. Through you, I'm young again."

What do I say? His sad expression nagged at my conscience. "You've made these past days unforgettable, and I owe you such a debt of gratitude—"

"I don't want your gratitude…" Pausing, he homed in on my eyes. "I want you to stay with me. *Stay!* We can tour Japan…Asia…the world, for that matter. You wouldn't have to work as a journalist. I have money enough for ten lifetimes, but I have no one to share life with—no partner."

He grabbed my shoulders and spun me toward him. His eyes danced like blue flames as his enthusiasm animated his features.

A sped-up, streaming video of panoramic vistas and exotic locations bombarded my mind in rapid-fire succession: Beachcombing in the Maldives, snorkeling in Galapagos, sailing in Ko Phi Phi. The colossal rate of imagery feeding into my mind left no time to absorb it. Spellbound, I peered into his face as cinematic vignettes blitzed me at lightning speed.

Though shell-shocked from the barrage of information, I found it intoxicating. *I've heard of information overload…infoxication. Does it have anything to do with foxes?*

The intensity of the data transfer exhausted me, yet I could not break his gaze. Instead, I became absorbed in his flashing eyes—a mesmerizing kaleidoscope of twinkling lights and wild blue yonders. I became disoriented, then adrift. After several moments, I quit struggling and merely gazed into their depths.

"Come with me. Say you'll come."

Over and over, he urged me as he held me in his gaze.

"I…" Distracted, I could not recall what I was about

to say. Fragments of scenes whizzed through my mind: Dubai, Riyadh, Jerusalem, Addis Ababa, Marrakesh, Cairo, Saint Petersburg, Brussels, Venice, Athens, Barcelona…

"We'll travel the world. Say you'll come."

Like flickering strobe lights, the fast-paced visuals, along with his whispered chant and piercing stare, made me dizzy. My concentration faltered, and my thoughts scattered. His repeated mantra penetrated my mind until my goals were one with his…*travel. I love to travel…love…*

A vague concept tugged at my soul. *What is it? I can't think.* Then the nagging became needling jabs, prodding my psyche to remember. *Love…*

Rafe.

I blinked, bewildered. As if Chase had snapped his fingers, I woke from a hypnotic trance and took a deep breath to collect my bearings. *Where am I?*

Mount Fuji filled my field of vision, and the sight helped ground me. *We were talking of its beauty when…what? What happened?*

"*Fuji-san* isn't only beautiful. It's holy." Chase's gaze sought and captured mine. "But unlike many sacred mountains, scaling it isn't sacrilegious. Just the opposite. Climbing it is a pilgrimage with its Shinto shrines, *torii* gates, and Buddhist temples. For many, it's the experience of a lifetime."

Trying to make sense of the disconnect, I glanced at the mountain before turning toward him. "Have you ever hiked it?"

"Many times." His eyes shimmered in the morning sun. "Life holds few journeys I haven't taken." The corners of his mouth drooped. "But only you renew life's fresh scent—like wet grass after a spring shower or the aroma of freshly whisked *matcha* or a brisk whiff of salt air…"

Salt air. Rafe came to mind. I smiled, remembering our evening stroll along the beach.

"Well, *do* you?"

"Sorry." Waking from my reverie, I flinched. "Could you repeat that?"

"I asked." His eyes like crackled cobalt glass, he stared. "Do you like your *matcha* tea?"

I glanced at the forgotten cup in my hand. Unsure if it was still too hot to drink, I took a tentative sip. It was cold, but despite the temperature, I forced a wan smile. "It's fine." *How long have we been talking?*

"Your friend's train should be here in thirty minutes." His mouth curled into a sly half-smile.

Is he reading my thoughts? I tilted my head.

"Like I was saying, you rejuvenate me." His gaze sought mine. "Each time I show you a different sight, you bring it to life."

"And you've made Japan come alive for me." I groaned inwardly. *How do I respond truthfully without hurting his feelings?* "Traveling with you has been wonderful. You've introduced me to experiences I never would have found on my own."

"And I can introduce you to so many more if you'll just let me…" Like twin bonfires, his eyes snapped and crackled. "I *know* you like to travel. Come with me. Together, life will be an endless voyage. We'll sail the world, stopping in every port as long as we like." His stare intensified.

Gazing into his eyes—deep azure pools—I envisioned white-sand beaches along cerulean seas.

Scene after scene of exotic locations bombarded my mind, and the longer I fixed my gaze on his, the better his idea seemed.

"Say you'll come with me." Over and over, he urged. "Come with me. Say you'll come away."

Come away...Between the tantalizing imagery and intoned whispers, I could think of nothing else.

"We'll navigate the globe—travel the seven seas. Our lives together will be one continuous escapade."

Our lives together...I always thought someday Rafe...I awoke with a jolt. Blinking as I emerged from my trance, I tried to focus.

"You can't hide it."

"Hide what?" Shoulders hunching, I flinched.

"Neither a cough nor love can be hidden." The lines around his eyes seemed deeper. The corners of his mouth sagged.

"What do you mean?"

"Don't play dumb." His lip curled. "It doesn't become you."

I shook my head. "I honestly don't know—"

"Don't pretend." Then he held back his head, stared, and gave a mirthless laugh. "Irony of ironies, you *don't* know, do you?"

"Know what?" His intellectual dance frustrated me. "What are you talk—"

"I exploited your weakness—wanderlust. I flooded your mind with images of the exotic lands we'd visit— the amazing life we'd lead. You *were* tempted." With a deliberate lift to his brow, he tilted his head. "But you love another, and your attachment is stronger than any psychological seduction."

Seduction...? I snapped to attention. "What?"

"Distant horizons and unlimited vistas lured you, but your *addiction* is uncompromising. Your stubborn regard for—"

"Rafe?" I blinked as his words took hold. "No, I'm *scarcely* attracted."

"Deny it all you want." His laugh was dry. "The Japanese believe the most extreme form of love is secret love, and in your case, so secret, that even you don't know…or you won't admit it, even to yourself."

"No." Scowling, I shook my head, but the memory of Rafe's lips on mine made my cheeks burn.

"You remind me so much of *Yua*"—his gaze was unfocused, as if glimpsing a memory—"several hundred years ago."

I leaned forward. "Several *years* ago…?"

"Several *hundred* years ago." Shaking his silvery head, he focused on my face. "Seven hundred and fifty to be exact…I was twenty-two—"

"Stop it! I'm in no mood for your tales." Exasperated, I pulled back. "I'm worried sick about Mia, and here you are telling juvenile jokes."

"I'm telling you the truth." He clenched his jaw. "And I'm telling you for Mia's sake, so you'll understand."

"So I'll understand *what*?" I cocked one brow.

"Everything I've told you about *kitsune*s and *nogitsune*s is true—"

"Just peppered with several half-truths, right?" Beating him at his own game, I sneered.

"Everything I've told you is true…" He bit his lower lip, pausing.

"You're joking." Chin dipping, I tipped my eyes to peek. "Aren't you?"

He shook his head.

Details he had mentioned in earlier conversations flooded my mind. "You're seven hundred and seventy-two?"

"Next winter." His gaze earnest, he nodded.

"And your great-great-great-grandmother was *kitsune* but passed for human?"

"So they say." He nodded.

"So 'they' say…?" Suspecting another put-on, I squinted.

"That's the truth."

"What are you going to say next?" Curling my lips, I snickered. "*So help me,* Inari*?*"

His brows shot up. "I don't insult your religion, so don't mock mine."

Religion? I shrank back. "Are you saying, you actually *believe* this hogwa"—one glance at his reddening face, and I chose another word—"superstition?"

"Creed." A vein pulsed in his neck. "I believe the word you want is *creed*, and as a devotee of *Inari*, I'm a sworn guardian."

His steady eye contact made me blink. *He looks sincere, yet he just tried to seduce me.* I couldn't hold back a snicker. *He's no guardian angel, that's for—*

"No, I'm no angel."

My jaw dropped. "You *did* read my mind. You've been reading it all along, haven't you?"

"Read your mind? Yes. A guardian? Yes, but an *angel*…?" His lips rose in a sly smile. "I'm also a male with physical needs." The smile faded. "I'm lonely without a woman's company. I yearn for a woman's touch." The corners of his mouth drooped, and he spoke in a flat monotone. "Which brings us full circle to where this conversation began. You remind me of a woman I almost married—"

"Seven hundred and fifty years ago…" Sarcasm dripping, I rolled my eyes. "Right?"

"Please. I asked you once not to mock." His back straightened as he lifted his chin. "The sting of separation and grief is just as sharp as if I'd lost her yesterday, and I'd appreciate your dropping the cynicism."

My cheeks burning, I ducked my chin in a penitent nod.

"Atsuki also was attracted to *Yua*, but she chose me." Scowling, Chase curled his lip. "Rather than accept rejection, he shapeshifted as me, using *kitsunetsuki* to lure her to his bed."

"*Yua* was your fiancée?"

He nodded. "Her name meant binding love and affection." He grimaced. "When she woke from the trance and realized what she'd done, she threw herself off *Ichinomine*."

Threw herself off… A shudder slid down my back at thoughts of Rafe's wife jumping to her death and Mia racing to Suicide Forest. Then recalling Chase's dejection when they visited the peak, I smacked my forehead. "I'm so sorry. When you said she left you, I thought she broke up with you. I had no idea…"

"You couldn't have known." He shook his head. "But finding you at *Inariyama*, catching you at the very moment you slipped…" He took a deep breath. "You renewed my spirit, my *joie de vivre*."

"Why do you say that?"

"When I saved you, I regained my self-respect." Staring at nothing, he seemed to gaze inwardly. "I failed to protect *Yua*, but by helping you, I redeemed myself."

"What a coincidence meeting at Mount Inari." Questioning the idea, I made a face. "But I don't believe in coincidences…"

"Nor do I." As if my words roused him from his reverie, he turned toward me. "And the timing…Why did you come to Japan this week?"

"Like I mentioned, I was recently promoted—"

"And this was your *first* international assignment, right?" His ears perked.

I nodded, recalling the whirlwind preparations to expedite my passport. "The promotion was last-minute, leaving me barely enough time to—"

"What's the name of your magazine?"

"Globetrotting Getaways, but we just merged with Sunrise Empirical Publications."

Sucking in his breath, Chase came to attention. "When?"

"The day I landed my promotion and assignment." I tilted my head. "Why?"

"Sunrise Empirical Publications is one of the *Yakuza's* money-laundering companies."

"*Yakuza*." The idea sounded too far-fetched to consider, yet I had to ask. "Do you think Atsuki has anything to do with this?"

"I wouldn't be surprised." Chase sighed. "He's despised me since *Yua*…" He stared into the distance, mumbling. "And he knows I visit *Inariyama* every year for the lantern festival…"

"Are you saying he arranged our meeting?"

"What are the odds of you being assigned to cover the *Fushimi Inari* Shrine on the same day Sunrise Empirical Publications takes over your magazine?"

Arching his brow, he challenged me.

"So, my promotion was a setup…" Disillusioned, I sniffed at my hollow victory before remembering my friend's vulnerability. "But what's Mia's connection with all this?"

"Good question…" He turned toward me as if to speak. Then he stopped and stared.

"What?" Distrustful, I squirmed.

"You look so much like *Yua*." Wearing a radiant smile, his face relaxed into an abstraction of love. "You could be her twin. What a shame you didn't share her…" He caught his breath, and the nostalgic smile disappeared behind a wary frown. "Why would you stay with a friend instead of checking into a hotel if you were on a business trip?"

"Everything happened so quickly…" I squinted as I recalled the sequence of events. "Mia called out of the blue…said she'd been thinking of me."

"When was this?"

"The night I got the promotion and assignment—"

"Coincidence?" His brow shot up.

Shaking my head, I made the connection. "Now that you mention it, hardly. When I told Mia about the upcoming trip, she said, 'Why not stay with me? It'll be like old times—one long pajama party.' "

"So, you two are old friends?"

"We've known each other since college."

"Does she have any pictures of you?"

"Probably dozens…but at least one…" I rummaged through my phone's photo collections. "This one." I handed him the phone. "Mia and I were buddies."

He glanced at the photo's composition. "Did you edit someone out of the picture?"

261

"Yeah"—I frowned—"Rafe."

Chase's pupils contracted into tiny pellets. "Has Atsuki seen this photo?"

"Not this one, but Mia has an unedited version that includes Rafe." I recalled Atsuki's words the night we met. "He said I looked like the picture with Mia."

"So, he knew you looked like *Yua* and that you, Mia, and *your friend*"—he sneered—"had a history…"

"What are you thinking?"

"Atsuki masterminded this whole scenario." His jaw line hard, Chase ground his teeth. "You three and I are all pawns in his little *dorama.*"

"*Dorama?*"

"*Terebi dorama*—television melodrama." Nostrils flaring, he gave a sarcastic sniff. "Atsuki has no empathy, no conscience. He couldn't care less what happens to you, Mia, or *your friend.* He has one goal."

"What's that?"

"Revenge. Atsuki may have possessed *Yua's* body, but he didn't win her heart. To his way of thinking, he lost, and I won. His only way to even the score is to beat me at my own 'game.' "

"I don't understand." I squinted, trying to follow.

"Had you felt for me what I feel for you, he would've used *kitsunetsuki* on you."

Imagining Atsuki's hands groping me made my skin crawl.

"He truly is evil." Chase's chest rose in a silent sigh. "But since you're obsessed with"—his lip curled—"*someone else*, his plans backfired."

"What'll he do to Mia?"

"Life means nothing to Atsuki. He's incapable of remorse." He sucked air between his teeth, making a hissing sound. "Mia's expendable."

"No, not if we find her first. Can you help?" The words were out before I thought.

He groaned as if in pain. "*Karuma.* Karma." His laugh was derisive. "The irony."

"What?" I shrank back. "What's wrong?"

"You asked me to help."

"Yeah…" I puckered my brow. "So?"

"You don't understand." Giving a resigned sigh, his body slumped. "When asked, I have no choice. As a guardian, I'm obligated to help."

"You're serious?" I wrinkled my nose at the idea. *He's no more supernatural than I am…*

"You still question who I am…*what* I am…" Turning, he faced the train station's window behind him. "Look. What do you see?"

The sunlight shining on the window acted as a mirror. His reflected image showed close-set eyes, high cheekbones, a narrow, furry chin, and…

A snout! I covered my mouth with both hands, muffling my scream to a yelp.

His reflection vanished as a passing cloud blocked the sun. When he turned back, his attractive, youthful face leered.

My adrenaline spiking, I grabbed my purse and darted inside the crowded station. *Am I losing my mind? Shapeshifters don't exist, yet I can't unsee his image.* I ducked behind a column.

I've got to escape…take the next train back to Tokyo. Searching for the ticket counter, I peeked around the pillar. Then I remembered Rafe's text. *I can't leave Mia if she's on her way.* I checked the time. *If my train arrived an hour ago, hers should be here any—*

Chime tones rang, and an announcement came over the PA system.

Is that her train? Guessing was pointless. Unable to understand Japanese, I debated where best to wait for her...just in case. *Outside by the bus depot?*

No, Chase is there. Loath to face him, I stood just inside the station by its bank of doors. *I can't miss her here.*

Like worker ants emerging from their colony, the newly arrived passengers surfaced on four escalators. Inundating the terminal, they surged through the station's dozen exits.

The crowd's impetus forced me to the side, limiting my view to only the nearest doors and obscuring the rest. *Chase was right. The bus stop would've had a better view.* Frustrated, I joined the exiting masses, hoping to see a larger area outside the station.

But as the crowds thinned, my spirits drooped. *Did she slip past me?* Peeking from behind a tour group, I glanced at the bus stop but saw neither Mia, nor Chase.

Then I spotted her at the corner. Sprinting, I dashed past the couples hauling suitcases and the families towing small children. "Mia!" I cupped my hands and shouted at the top of my lungs.

Never hesitating or acknowledging me, Mia stepped inside the waiting, fire-engine red convertible.

How couldn't she hear me? Is she deaf? Dazed?

Slipping down his sunglasses, the driver peered over the rims and met my gaze.

Atsuki!

He twisted his lip in a snarl, then gunned the engine. The car roared to life, careening as it burned rubber.

Only then did I see Chase board a taxi. He waved

his cell phone before slamming the door, and the cab dashed after the sports car. My phone buzzed.

Chase—*Take the Retro bus to the Lake Sai Bat Cave and meet me at* Aokigahara—

Despite my running off, would Chase still help...? His words came to mind: "When asked, I have no choice. As a guardian, I'm obligated to help." *Could he possibly be a—*

"Mia's kept a step ahead of me since she left the apartment."

Rafe? Tearing my gaze from my phone to the familiar voice, I did a double take. My pulse spiked as I recalled Chase's words: "...the most extreme form of love is secret love, and in your case, *so* secret, that even you don't know...or you won't admit it, even to yourself."

Is it true? I recalled the last two years of turned-down dates and lonely nights, and the reason suddenly became clear. *I couldn't move on because Rafe's the only man I've ever loved. No matter how often I denied it, I've never stopped loving him. Even Chase's dreams and mental manipulation couldn't break that bond.*

Weak-kneed from admitting to my feelings, I took a deep, centering breath. *Get a grip. Finding Mia is all that's important now. Time enough to think of Rafe on the flight back tomorrow.*

"That's the last taxi." Rafe glimpsed Chase's fast-retreating cab, peered up and down the street, then pointed to an old-fashioned, canary-yellow bus. "Looks like that bus is our best bet."

"And its doors are closing. Run!" No time for explanations, I sprinted across the street and hammered on the glass doors until they opened with a hydraulic whoosh. "Lake *Sai* Bat Cave?"

Nodding, the driver tapped the meter and pointed to the fare chart.

"I've got it." Rafe fished in his pocket for his wallet, then spoke with the driver as he paid our fares.

While the bus pulled into traffic, I grabbed the last two seats in the rear and took a deep breath, grounding myself. *Stay focused.*

Rafe navigated the center aisle, swaying and gripping the backs of the seats to brace himself against the bus's pitch and roll. "I'm getting my sea legs." Wearing a self-effacing smile, he sat close, his arm grazing mine.

A shiver ran up my spine. *Keep it together.* I scooted over and pressed against the window. "What'd you ask the driver?"

"Directions." Rafe's voice had a harsh ring. "The woodlands' trailhead begins near Bat Cave, and he warned not to go off-path for *any* reason."

His tone chilled my blood. "I didn't plan on today's hike becoming a search party…"

"*Aokigahara* is big—roughly fourteen square miles." His gaze leveled with mine.

"That's a lot of ground to cover…"

A smile flickered in his eyes. "Locating Mia may be like finding an honest politician in Congress."

"I forgot your quirky sense of humor." Despite the grim task ahead, I snickered at his morbid humor. "Just hope this bus ride isn't a wild-goose chase."

"What other choice do we have?"

My shoulders sagged. "If it weren't for Chase's advice, I'd think taking this bus was a hopeless waste of time."

"What do you mean *Chase's advice?*"

"You saw his text, didn't you?"

He shook his head.

"Then why did you recommend taking this bus?"

He pointed to the destination sign above the windshield.

Though the sign appeared in reverse from inside the bus, I could still read *Saiko & Aokigahara Shuyu.* I rubbed my forehead, kicking myself for walking out on Mia this morning. *Fourteen square miles...* "Are we chasing rainbows?"

"Don't confuse this search with tilting at windmills. We're doing all we can."

"Just hope it's enough. Mia was acting weird before I left but not desperate. What sent her over the edge?"

"Ichiro escaping."

"I'm sure I locked his crate before I left." *Didn't I?* Second-guessing myself, I glanced out the window.

The woodland's densely packed foliage lived up to its name—Sea of Trees.

Then its other nickname came to mind—Suicide Forest—reminding me of the situation's urgency. "Why should a missing cat send her into a panic?"

"Who knows what drugs Atsuki gave her or what he said on the phone?"

"Or what hold he has over her..." Sick with worry, I shared Chase's tales of fox possession.

Rafe sat back, blinking. "No matter how farfetched those ideas sound, they almost make sense in light of Mia's actions, especially if Atsuki planted suicidal thoughts in her head when she was drugged."

Suicidal? I grabbed his arm. "I caught her with a knife this morning, but what makes *you* suspect she's desperate?"

"As she left the train, she dropped this flyer." His jaw clenching, he pulled a brochure from his pocket.

I recognized Mia's scrawl beneath a picture captioned *Aokigahara* Lookout Tower—*One step and it's done—*

An image of Mia leaping from the tower flashed through my mind. I jammed my hands into my armpits to keep them from trembling. "At least, this narrows the search."

The corners of his mouth turning down, he gave a terse nod. "The driver said three kinds of people visit that forest: Hikers for the scenery, thrill-seekers hoping to find a corpse, and the walking wounded seeking escape."

"Seeking escape..." I sucked air between my teeth.

"I've never been to *Aokigahara*, but one of my students swears *yūrei*—faint souls, what we'd call ghosts—prowl about." His nose wrinkled. "Supposedly, it's haunted by those left there to die."

The hairs rising on the back of my neck, I recalled Chase's description of *oyasute*. "Sounds like the forest has a long association with spirits." My gaze met his. "Can we find Mia before she joins them?"

Chapter 16—Aokigahara

Friday Afternoon

When the bus stopped at the Tourist Information Center, I inquired inside.

"The trail begins behind the parking lot. At the crossroads, turn left and follow the path to *Nenbahama*, where you can catch the bus back to *Kawaguchiko* Station." The clerk pointed out the route on a brochure's map. Then his smile faded. "Don't wander off-trail. Not everyone who goes missing in *Aokigahara* commits suicide. Some simply get lost and die of thirst."

A chill slid down my spine, and I reached for Rafe's hand.

Thanking the clerk, we hurried to the trailhead. A few feet into the route, we came to the crossroads and turned left.

Flinching, Rafe stopped.

"What's wrong?"

"Do you hear that?" His ears perked.

I listened and shook my head. "Hear what?"

"Doesn't that sound like Mia?"

I listened again and shrugged. "All I heard was a bird."

"Must be my imagination." He snickered.

Three minutes later, he craned his neck and peered into the forest's tangled mass of tree limbs, roots, vines, and vegetation. "You *had* to have heard that."

"Nope, only a bird." I shook off another chill. "You're making me nervous."

"I don't blame you." His laugh was dry. "Now, I'm hearing voices—*a* voice, anyway—but I'd swear it's Mia." Sighing, he rubbed his hand across his stubbled chin.

The sound was like sandpaper on wood, contrasting with the forest's oppressive stillness. No breeze penetrated the thick foliage. No leaves moved. Nothing flew above the canopy. Nothing scurried beneath the leaf litter. Except for my mind's nervous chatter, the only noise was the rasp of his five o'clock shadow and, occasionally, one lone bird.

The farther we walked, the darker it became as the trees swallowed us, sound and all.

Two minutes later, he snapped his head toward the thick undergrowth alongside the trail, listening. "That *is* Mia. I have to check it out."

"Don't go off-path." I grabbed his arm. Though our goal was to find her, I didn't want him taking any unnecessary risks.

"I'll be careful. I promise." He pointed to a symbol on the flyer's map. "Here's the tower—about halfway to *Nenbahama*." Then he traced the trail with his finger. "Just follow your nose. If I don't catch up with you in a few minutes, I'll meet you at the tower—but do as I say, not as I do." He gave a dry laugh as he handed me the map. "Stay on the trail." Leaning over, he drew me toward him in a kiss.

The familiar scent of his lime aftershave surrounded me as my lips met his. Emotions I'd denied merged with fear in a sensual cocktail, and I threw my arms around his neck, crushing his body against mine. *What if I never see him again?*

****

"Rafe!" Mia's cry was urgent. "Rafe…over *here*…"

Caught up in Ava's kiss, he opened one eye, peeking. Through the web of interlacing branches, he saw movement. *Mia?*

Slipping from Ava's embrace, he took her hands in his. "I hate to leave you alone, but I swear I hear Mia calling."

Though her shoulders tightened, Ava nodded.

His lips grazed her cheeks in a parting kiss, and he ducked into the thicket. Within four steps, he lost sight of everything except knotty tree trunks, gnarled boughs, and moss-covered rocks.

"Rafe…this way…over here…" The sound didn't originate from any one point. Instead, it seemed to emanate from the air, drifting from place to place.

"Keep talking, so I can follow your voice."

"Over here."

Correcting his course, he veered left, penetrating deeper into the woods. After several minutes of silent trekking, he recognized a broken tree limb. *Am I going in circles?* "Mia, where are you? Keep talking, so I can find you."

"You're almost here."

"Keep talking." Climbing over fallen logs and dodging low-hung branches, he peered through the thick foliage and spotted her blonde hair. "Okay, I see you."

"Hurry…"

When he reached the spot, he found only yellow wildflowers.

A faint voice called in the distance, "Over here…"

Again, he followed the voice, tripping over vines twisted with tree roots and stumbling over raised clumps of mossy ferns.

"Here…"

He searched in every direction but saw no landmarks, distinctions, or any differentiations. Without so much as a rabbit trail for a clue, everywhere—everything—looked the same.

"Rafe…please…" Mia's call was muffled.

"I'm coming. Keep talking." After half an hour, he recognized the broken tree limb again. *This is insane. I'm going in circles.*

"Hurry…over here…"

Am I imagining her voice? He tried the GPS navigation app on his phone, but it showed a generic map of *Yamanashi* Prefecture—no specifics. *A lot of help this is.* He dialed Ava's number, but his phone could not get a signal, and the call dropped. *Now what?*

Glancing at the broken tree limb, he struggled to get his bearings. *I headed north when I left the trail, so to find it, I need to head south and retrace my steps.* He started on a path and winced. *This is south…isn't it?*

****

The farther I hiked, the spookier the forest became. No birds sang. No wind rustled through the trees. No gravel crunched beneath my feet. The packed-dirt path absorbed even the sound of my footsteps. Hearing only my heart pounding, I whistled Tchaikovsky's 1812 Overture to drown out my fears.

Five minutes went by—ten. *Where is he?* Worried, I peered into the trees. Beyond a foot or two, visibility disappeared in a tangled mat of branches and undergrowth.

Fifteen minutes passed, twenty. Moldering memories crept into my thoughts. I checked my cell. No messages—radio silence. Anger began replacing fear. *He abandoned me once. Would he do it again? Here?*

No. Recalling his thoughtfulness over the past days restored my faith in him. *But what if he's lost? And what about Mia? And even if I find her, will I be too late?* Sweating from the stress, as well as the humidity, I wiped my brow. *No breeze. The air's stifling.* Panicking, I reverted to an outgrown habit: Chewing my nails.

A snapped twig startled me, and I screamed as a leg emerged from the undergrowth. Then I recognized the shoe, pants, shirt, and face. "Rafe!" Gasping with relief, I raced into his arms. "Thank God you're safe."

His clothes were stiff and dry to the touch. I glanced at his starched shirt, comparing it to my own soggy blouse. "You must've adapted to these temperatures." I dropped my arms to my sides as I stepped back. "I don't want to get you sticky."

"That doesn't matter." He opened his arms wide. "Let me hold you."

Cuddling him, I nuzzled his neck, breathing in his scent. *Ginger?* Squinting, I blinked and sniffed again, recalling his lime aftershave. *Ginger?* I backed away.

"What's wrong?"

"Nothing." Turning aside, I shrank from him as I tucked my hair behind an ear.

"Something's bothering you." His smile disappeared. "What?"

I shrugged. Suspecting was one thing, but voicing my concerns was another. *I'd sound ridiculous.*

"Hey, this is me you're talking to." Turning me toward him, Rafe gently held my shoulders. "What's bothering you?"

"I'll sound silly." I forced a nervous laugh.

"Try me." His smile returned.

I took a deep breath—like preparing to jump off the high board. "You don't smell the same."

He burst out laughing. "Sorry." Then his cheekbones rising as if smothering a laugh, he bit his lip. "What's different?"

"You smell like ginger, and—"

"Ginger grows wild here. I literally stumbled into a patch of it." Chuckling, he sniffed his hands. "Guess I do smell like ginger. Anything else"

I glanced at his shirt's stiff neckline and his crisply pleated pants. "And your clothes feel different."

"How so?" He tilted his head to the side.

I hunched my shoulders, feeling like a dunce. "Your shirt is starched, not wilted like mine." Fidgeting, I grimaced.

"That's because it's non-iron, one-hundred-percent cotton with a wrinkle-resistant finish that withstands humidity." He spoke by rote as if reading a magazine ad.

"Okay, I've succeeded in making an idiot of myself." I shook my head at myself. "Now that *that* nonsense is behind me, did you see any sign of Mia?"

"No." His chest rose in a suppressed sigh. "I must've imagined hearing her."

"Understandable." I cringed, recalling my own bizarre suspicions. *Ginger…starched shirt…what was I thinking?* "Imaginations can run rampant in these woods."

"Either that, or Mia outfoxed me, but my detour cost us time. We've got to find her before dark." He tightened his grip on my shoulders. "After sunset, she isn't safe on these paths. Even if *yūrei* don't haunt this forest, Asian black bears and wild boar prowl at night, not to mention desperate people, contemplating suicide."

"Hey, have you tried calling her—"

"Cell phones don't work out here. The signal can't penetrate the forest."

"Could you track her through GPS?"

He shook his head. "Even if her cell phone's GPS-enabled, the soil's high iron content would interfere with radio-signals." He tugged at the keychain compass dangling from my purse zipper. "See what I mean?"

The compass needle spun round and round.

"What's it doing?"

"Aligning with the rock's natural magnetism." He spread his arms wide, encompassing the whole area. "This entire forest stands on an old lava flow."

"Lava?" I looked about, but thick foliage hid the rocky soil.

"From Mount Fuji's last eruption."

I stared, amazed. "How do you know all this stuff?"

"I've been here before." His smile was lopsided.

Confused, I did a double take.

"Not to commit suicide if that's what you're thinking." His laugh had an ironic ring.

Frowning, I recalled his earlier words. "I thought you'd never—"

"What I meant was…" Peering hard into my eyes, he smiled. "I've read about this area…heard about it so often, it's *as if* I've been here."

The longer I stared into his eyes, the more plausible his words seemed, yet a nagging suspicion made me break his gaze.

He held out his hand, palm up. "Come on. Let's find

Mia."

"Yeah, we'd better hurry." Pretending to misunderstand, I handed him the map and sprinted past. "Like you said. We've wasted enough time."

The trail was deserted, and with the trees converging on both sides, nothing was visible above or beyond their overarching boughs. I felt trapped—vulnerable. *How must Mia feel?* Worried for her, I chewed my nails as I rushed toward the tower.

Then from the dense forest's silence came a man's voice.

"Hear that?" Unsure if I imagined it, I glanced at Rafe to confirm it.

"Yeah." He nodded. "It's Atsuki. According to the map, the tower should be around the next bend."

My adrenaline pumping, I sprinted ahead. A steel-frame fire tower rose above the treetops, where another path intersected ours in a small clearing. Tilting back my head, I counted seven flights of stairs.

Mia straddled the top platform's safety railing, dangling one leg over the side while she sobbed hysterically.

I screamed at the top of my lungs. "Hold on!"

Oblivious to the shouting below, Mia cringed at Atsuki's every jeering taunt.

Rafe beside me, I rushed to the tower and scrambled up the first flight. The open stairway wobbled, its weather-worn stairs creaking and bouncing with each step. As my old fears returned, I grabbed the railing with sweating palms and psyched myself. *No time to visualize. Keep climbing. I've got to help Mia.*

I pounded up the second tier, then the third. Gasping, I stopped to catch my breath.

"Ava…" He paused as mottled sunlight glimmered through the trees, casting more shadow than light.

"What?" I glanced at Rafe's long chin and pointy nose. *He looks like a fox. No, he looks like Chase.* A scream died in my throat as my legs buckled. *That can't be…*

"I always keep my promises. I have no option." He sprinted up the stairs.

His words echoed Chase's reassurance at *Arashiyama* and again in Tokyo. *Am I seeing things?* Wobbly, I glanced after the retreating figure. Then I sat on the steps, put my head between my knees, and breathed deeply until the dizziness passed.

As his footsteps bounded across the overhead platform and started up the next stairway, I martialed my strength and followed as fast as my shaky knees would carry me. But by the time I reached the next platform, his footsteps resonated from two stories above.

The higher I climbed, the louder Mia's sobbing became, but I no longer heard Atsuki's heckling. When I reached the tower's platform, he was gone. *Atsuki didn't pass me on the stairs. Where is he?* I looked about the open scaffold.

Mia straddled the safety railing, one leg in and one leg outside the barrier. Her eyes fixed on the ground, she leaned forward at a precarious angle.

Rafe stood several feet from her, talking quietly.

I choked back a scream. "Mia, don't jump!"

Rafe shook his head and held up his palm, motioning me to stay put. Then he turned back to Mia. "Talk to me." He took a step closer. "Tell me what's wrong. This is me…Rafe. You can tell me."

"No." Peering down and leaning farther over the

edge, she lifted her inside leg, poised to leap. "It's useless."

"What's useless?" Stepping closer, he barked the words.

Mia's head whipped toward his commanding tone. Her unfocused eyes wandered. "What?"

"Tell me what's useless." He inched closer. "Tell me your story."

"Story?" As her eyes rolled back in her head, she teetered. "What story?"

"Tell me how you got here." He silently crept closer. "I'm listening."

Mia's vacant eyes gazed into the distance. "What?"

"How did you get here?" He glided toward her.

Her glassy eyes growing wider, she stared at a steel girder as if hypnotized. "What?"

"How did you get here?" His feet moving imperceptibly, Rafe edged closer.

"Ask someone who knows." The air shimmered. The steel girder shifted and flexed as Atsuki appeared from the shadows.

Letting out a strangled scream, I glanced about the open platform. *He couldn't have hidden behind that narrow girder...Did he shapeshift?*

Rafe grabbed Mia's wrist. Wrenching her from the railing, he flung her toward me while he confronted Atsuki. "So, it's finally come to this."

"This way." I edged Mia toward the stairs. "Come on."

The men shouted in Japanese, their tones belligerent.

Mia turned toward me, wild-eyed. "Where are you taking me?"

"Downstairs." I grabbed her with one hand as I gripped the railing with my other. "You're safe now. Just keep walking."

"Where am I?" Her eyes wide and vacant, Mia cringed as she glanced about. "What am I doing here?"

"You really don't know?"

"No, I can't remember." Sobbing, she leaned against me as we slowly descended.

A shouting match echoed from the platform above.

"What's happening?" Mia stopped to listen.

"I don't understand Japanese, but I'd guess Rafe's reading Atsuki the riot act." *At least, I think it's Rafe.*

Heavy footsteps and creaking boards overhead signaled a scuffle.

When we reached the fourth tier, I glanced above, but the platform blocked my view.

A loud thump on the steel girders reverberated throughout the steel structure, then another. *What are they doing? Having a shoving match?*

A clanging sounded—metal striking metal. The shouting intensified, and the tower shook from the men's skirmish.

"Hurry." I rushed Mia down the open stairway to the third tier.

Making a whistling sound as it fell from above, something clattered to the tower's cement base.

I peered over the side and saw disjointed pieces of a railing. *The safety barrier must've given way.*

The tower vibrated as footsteps pounded overhead like two Sumo wrestlers grappling.

Worried for Rafe, I leaned backwards over the handrail and craned my neck to see above.

The two men teetered on the platform's edge, their

arms locked as they struggled against the railing. The barrier protested with a metallic squawk, metal grating against metal.

Roaring like a wounded bear, Atsuki head-butted Rafe, forcing him backwards, until he teetered at the platform's edge.

Rafe shouted in Japanese as he grabbed Atsuki's throat, choking him—pulling him.

The metal railing creaked and whined as it bowed and, with a clanging groan, broke loose.

I pulled back as pieces of railing whistled past my head.

"Ava…" Rafe's voice echoed as he fell.

Closing my eyes, I winced as one sickening thud sounded after another. I yanked Mia's hand, screaming, "Hurry!"

"No, leave me alone!" Her eyes fearful, Mia pulled away and retraced her steps up the open stairway.

First cajoling, then pleading, and finally bullying, I talked her down, one tier at a time. Coaxing Mia from the tower kept my mind off the sight I dreaded, but the battle of wills only delayed the inevitable.

When I finally stepped off the stairway, I listened for clues but heard no moans or cries for help…*Rafe's dead.* Choking back tears, I forced myself to approach the two crumpled bodies on the ground.

But instead of two men, two foxes lay lifeless. One a red fox, the other was silver-gray, and beside it lay the kitten's collar.

What? Doubting my eyes and sanity, I blinked.

Chase's shapeshifting tales zipped through my mind. *Could they possibly be true?*

I caressed the silver fox's head. *Who were you?*

Rafe? Chase? Chase posing as Rafe? I recalled his words when he'd gained Mia's confidence. 'This is me...Rafe. You can tell me.' I replayed Chase's response after asking him for help. "I have no other choice. As a guardian of *Inari*, I must help when asked." *Did Chase sacrifice himself to save Mia?*

"Ava, where are you?"

"Stay where you are, Mia! Don't come any closer." *How could I explain Ichiro's collar?* Acting before I thought, I tucked the choker in my purse, then stroked the silver fox's silken fur. *What were you—half human, half fox?* "Goodbye—"

A bloodcurdling shriek shook the forest's silence.

"What happened to these poor foxes?" Kneeling, Mia joined me.

Now that she's here, the less I say, the better. Maybe she won't remember any of this nightmare. "Why do any male animals fight?"

"Females?"

"That or territory." I caressed the lifeless gray fur a last time. *Maybe in Chase's case...honor?*

"Where are we?" Mia looked about, confused, as if peering through fog.

"*Aokigahara.*"

"Where?" She squinted.

"Suicide Forest." I stood and brushed off my knees.

"Why am I—"

"I'll explain later, but right now we have to follow this trail to *Nenbahama.*"

"Why?"

"So, we can catch the bus to *Kawaguchiko* Station and take the train back to Tokyo."

"Didn't I see Rafe?" Wearing a dazed expression,

Mia frowned as she glanced at the tower. "Where'd he go?" She stepped off the path, into the woods, and the green branches closed around her.

"Mia, stay on the trail." I caught her hand, yanked with all my strength, and pulled her back on the path.

"Where's Rafe?"

"He's de...I don't know." *I can't think about him now. First things first. I've got to get Mia home.* Though sick with worry, I had to focus on the immediate danger. I grabbed a pen and scrap of paper from my purse.

"What are you doing?"

"Leaving Rafe a message." *If he's still alive...* After tucking the note in the handrail, I took Mia's hand and started left, then turned right, unsure which trail headed toward *Nenbahama. Is* this *the right trail—the right direction? What if we get lost in the dark and can't find our way out?* I took a deep breath, guessing which path to take.

Recalling the park attendant's warning, I wiped the perspiration from my forehead. *All four paths look alike. Why didn't I pay more attention?*

A faint sound carried through the still air. I stopped and held my breath. "Did you hear that?"

"Hear what?" Mia squirmed away, her feet scuffing the soil.

"Shush." I grabbed her hand. "Hold still. Listen." Again, an indistinct noise sounded in the distance. "That...did you hear it?"

Mia shook her head.

Am I *hearing things now?*

A muffled voice called from the thicket's green tangle. Then a leg emerged from the undergrowth. "Ava!"

"Rafe?" I recognized the voice but doubted the sight. "Is that *really* you?"

"A scratched and bruised facsimile." His wry smile appeared behind his smudged face and five-o'clock shadow.

I recognized his offbeat sense of humor and ran toward him, stopping a heartbeat short to sniff his neck. "Lime." Breathing deeply, I smiled as I placed a tentative hand on his crumpled shirt. "It *is* you!" Then I threw my arms around his neck.

"What was that about?" He held me close until Mia's shoe scraped the gritty path. Then he pulled away, letting his arms fall to his sides. "Mia, thank God you're safe."

Slack jawed, she stared blankly.

He caught my gaze. "What happened?"

"I'll fill you in later but look at this." Dragging Mia with me, I led him to the two lifeless foxes.

"What—"

"Honestly, I have no logical explanation." I pressed my finger to my lips, then nodded toward her as I retrieved the note. "I'll tell you my suspicions later, but first we have to find our way out of this forest."

"Don't worry." He pointed. "This is north, so this is the trail to *Nenbahama*."

"This isn't the path I'd have picked." Looking up one trail and down the other, I hesitated. "How do you know it's north?"

"Because I gauged it by the sun."

"But the trees blot out the sky." I glanced at the impenetrable canopy above. "How do you *know*?"

"Because it's the same method I used to catch up with you. When I came to a clearing and saw the sun's position, I got my east and west bearings. From there, I reckoned north and south." He flashed a confident smile as he pointed. "This way."

Head tilted, I stared at the other trail.

His smile dimmed. "You still don't trust me, do you?"

****

I described the events while Mia slept on the train ride back to Tokyo. "What I *think* happened doesn't make sense. Chase looked and sounded just like you."

"What made you suspicious?" He gave me a crooked grin.

"He smelled like ginger—not lime—and his shirt was starched and pressed. Except for those details, he *was* you." Fidgeting, I fingered the kitten's collar. "*And*…I found this collar beside him. Bizarre as this sounds, I'd swear the kitten spied on me when Chase wasn't around. I can't help but think he—"

"Shapeshifted?" Rafe's raised brow challenged me.

"It's too farfetched to consider, yet…" I held up the collar. "How else would this get from Mia's apartment to the middle of a forest?"

"How do you know it's the same collar?" He studied it. "I've seen dozens like it."

"Good point." I scratched my head. "But Chase told me legends where *kitsune* charmed people into believing any scenes they created."

"Fox magic?" A cynical smile fluttered at his lips.

"I'm serious." Processing the day's events, I chewed my nail. "And you were right about Atsuki…at least, partially." I glanced at his eyes, trying to read his thoughts. "Do you remember the night I met him, when he said I looked like the picture with Mia."

"Yeah." Rafe nodded. "So?"

"So…" I brought up the photo on my phone.

"You edited me out." His voice sounded hollow as he fingered the cropped photo.

"Mia's copy shows the three of us." Embarrassed, I snatched the phone from his hands. "So Atsuki knew we had a history…"

"What are you thinking?"

"That he hatched this whole plot with you, Mia, and me. He gambled with our lives like we were mahjong chips." I grimaced. "According to Chase, he and Atsuki were old adversaries. Everything that happened this week was staged to even an old score—even my assignment."

"No." Rafe scowled. "I can understand Atsuki taking advantage of Mia, but anything beyond that's a stretch."

"It's true. At least, I believe so." Making strong eye contact, I leaned toward him. "The same day Globetrotting Getaways merged with Sunrise Empirical Publications, I was assigned to Japan. That night, Mia called me unexpectedly and invited me to stay with her."

"That *is* coincidental." Rafe took a deep breath.

"Not really…" I shook my head. "According to Chase, Atsuki had one goal—to beat him at his own game."

"What kind of game?" He peered into my eyes.

"I don't know…" Hoping he believed me, I chewed my thumbnail.

"You're biting your nails." He gently pushed my hand away from my lips. "What aren't you telling me?"

"Apparently, I resemble someone they both knew"—I swallowed—"a *long* time ago."

"I always suspected Chase's interest was more than altruistic." He pressed his lips into a fine, white line.

"You were right. He made that clear today."

"And what about you?" His gaze homed in on mine. "How did you feel about him?"

Ducking my head, I squirmed as I remembered the dream. "He was persuasive, and I *was* tempted, but aside from reacting to his manipulation, I never shared his feelings." I tossed my chin, meeting his gaze. "Although, Atsuki's interest was farther-reaching."

"What do you mean?"

"According to Chase, Atsuki could bend time—possibly even *go back in time* to alter events."

"So?"

"*So*…maybe Ashley didn't act on her own." I arched my brow. "If Atsuki knew we had a history—"

"Which, apparently, he did."

"He could've planted that whole pregnancy obsession in Ashley's head—"

"*And* the idea to commit suicide…" Rafe trailed off as he stared out the window. When he turned back, his eyes were moist. "I remember the night she 'gave birth' to her 'little kit' with its 'cute, pointy nose…' "

"Kit?" My ears perked. "Pointy nose…?"

"Knowing what I know *now* and looking back"—his chest rose in a silent sigh—"I wonder what other vile thoughts Atsuki planted in Ashley's mind."

I glanced at Mia. "Or hers…"

****

I let them into Mia's apartment.

"I didn't even take my keycard." Mia shook her head. "Guess I didn't plan to come back. If it weren't for you two…" She swallowed hard.

"What are friends for?" I gave her arm a friendly squeeze, then handed over my keycard. "Might as well return this since I'm leaving on an early flight."

"I'll miss you." Mia clasped me in a warm embrace, then letting go, hugged Rafe. "You were right about Atsuki."

"None of us realized just how dangerous he was."

"I never want to see him again." She curled her lip in disgust.

"Something tells me you won't." I arranged my features into a smile. "What are your plans now? Will you still work as a hostess?"

"No, I don't want any connection with that life…not anymore." She shook her head as her gaze swept the apartment. "Neighbors always said this 2LDK was unlucky. I'll move as soon as I find another place."

"I *may* know of an apartment opening up soon." His gaze silent but eloquent, Rafe turned toward me.

What's he thinking? Eyes narrowing, I crooked my neck.

He turned back to Mia. "I'll let you know what I hear."

"Hope the place allows pets. Which reminds me." Mia's eyes opened wide. "I couldn't find Ichiro this morning. Hope he didn't get out." She started searching behind the draperies and under the beds. She looked beneath the rumpled pillows and sheets, then checked the bathroom.

Moment of truth. "Mia, I have to tell—"

"Ichiro?" She called from the other room as she banged cabinet doors and opened and slammed drawers.

I fingered the cat's collar in my purse. Then debating how much information to share, I caught Rafe's gaze. At his nod, I decided to come clean. "Mia—"

"Oh, *here* you are, you little rascal." Cooing to the kitten while she carried it to the kitchenette, Mia scratched behind its ears and set it on the bar. "Are you hungry, Ichiro?"

The cat turned toward me, meowing as its mesmerizing blue eyes stared into mine.

Chase? I dropped my purse, its contents scattering across the floor. As it fell, the collar rolled toward Mia.

"How'd you lose your collar, you naughty kitten?" Retrieving it, she fastened it around the cat's neck and stepped back to admire the effect. "There. Aren't you a handsome tommy?" She crossed to the cabinet and held up a can of cat food in each hand. "Tuna or mackerel?"

Meowing, Ichiro jumped off the counter and rubbed against her leg.

"Tuna?" Mia glanced our way. "I'll just be a sec while I feed him."

I waved Rafe toward the window. "You know where I found the collar. What do you think?"

"Maybe cats *do* have nine lives." He chuckled.

"Be serious." I scowled. "How could a cat's collar get from Mia's apartment to the middle of a forest?"

"It can't." He met my gaze.

"I don't know. I'd hate to think I brought her something…supernatural." I rubbed my hand across my lips. "You don't think this cat could be Chase, do you?"

Meowing, the kitten crossed to me and head-butted my calves.

"Are you *just* a kitty?" Whispering, I stooped to pet it. "Or more?"

The cat rubbed its soft, silky head against my hands as its fluffy tail wrapped my wrist in a caress. Then with a parting meow, it padded back to Mia, purring.

"Aww." Mia bent over to pet it. "What a sweet tommy. I'm so glad he's here." She caught my gaze. "He'll be good company after you leave. Somehow, he makes me feel safe."

The cat's China-blue eyes opened wide as it stared directly at me.

Chase's words replayed in my mind. "As a guardian of *Inari*, I must help when asked."

For an instant, the feline's pussycat nose seemed to lengthen. Its eyes slanted, and the face resembled a fox more than a cat.

I yelped.

"What's wrong?" Rafe grazed my arm.

"Would you look at the time?!" Covering with a nervous laugh, I glanced at the clock. "Going to bed is pointless. I might as well catch the next train to the airport. I've got to arrive three hours before my early-morning flight to clear immigration and customs, *plus* the express train takes another hour—"

"How long will it take to pack?"

"Why?" With my mind running a mile a minute, I was unprepared for his question.

"Unless you have any objections, I'd like to see you to the airport, but first, I need something from my apartment."

"Should take me about an hour to shower and pack. Is that enough time to run home and back?" I studied his expression. *What's he thinking?*

Chapter 17—Tokyo

Saturday

Lulled by the train's gentle rocking, I rested my head on Rafe's shoulder and drifted off.

The kitten entered my dream on stealthy, pussy-willow paws.

"Ichiro?"

The cat swelled and grew until its nose, legs, and tail resembled a fox, not a feline. As its legs lengthened, it stood upright and strode toward me. Then its front paws and claws developed into arms with hands, and its silvery fur became a gray silk suit.

Chase! Suspicions confirmed, I froze, my scream dying in my throat.

But his serene blue eyes dispelled my fear like a balmy Mediterranean breeze. Images of Caribbean beaches entered my mind, the ocean gently lapping their shores and washing away my concerns.

Relaxing, I tentatively touched the vision's arm. "You're alive?"

"This wasn't my time."

"Why are you here?"

"You asked for my help." He shrugged. "You leave me no choice but to watch over Mia."

"No, *here*." I gestured to the space around me. "Why are you in my dream?"

"To wish you safe journeys, high climbs, and new peaks."

"High climbs and new peaks…what a laugh!" With a dismissive sniff, I jerked my chin. "Last week, those words would've petrified me, not cheered me on."

"And now?"

"Thanks to the recent climbs—and partly to you—heights don't hold the same terror." Mildly surprised, I smiled. "Now, your words inspire me."

The train's chime tones sounded, and Chase devolved from man to fox to cat, until only his blue eyes remained.

As I woke, I blinked, focusing. Instead of two eyes, two blue LED lamps on a gated railway crossing glowed through the train's window. *Was it a dream…or more?*

"Wake up, sleepyhead." Rafe smiled as he gathered my bags from the overhead bin. "Next stop is the Narita International Airport."

"Already?" I covered a yawn. "Sorry, I didn't mean to doze when you were nice enough to see me off."

"It's still 'yesterday.' " His smile was sympathetic. "You've had a long day."

"And it's not over yet." I gave a dry laugh. "I still have to write the last article, but that's the 'good' thing about long flights. I'll have plenty of time."

"Speaking of time…" His smile bitter-sweet, he reached for my hand.

I lacked the emotional energy to resist, letting my fingers lay limp in his.

"I've been thinking—"

Another train chime sounded, and as the doors opened, the passengers clambered toward the exits.

Unprepared for an emotional farewell, I welcomed

the reprieve.

After handing me the carry-ons, Rafe collected my suitcase from the oversized rack and glanced at his watch. "We're a few minutes early. Want to grab a cup of coffee?"

"Sounds good." Then I held up my index finger. "On second thought, let's make it *matcha*."

He did a double take. "When did you develop a taste for *matcha*?"

"The last few days." Thoughts of Chase brought a half-smile to my lips.

Minutes later, I sank into an upholstered booth. The tearoom's carpeted floors and acoustic ceiling tiles muted the airport's chimes and announcements.

As the air terminal's hubbub faded, I inhaled the tea, its grassy aroma bringing back memories of *Fushimi Inari's* ethereal beauty. The steaming brew reminded me of the mountain's foggy mist, reviving me.

Then I felt Rafe's gaze. I took another sip, mustering the mental energy to face him. "Yes…?"

"If I could take back the last two years, believe me, I would." His shoulders slumped. "But they're gone. All I can do now is make up for the time I wasted."

His eyes' warm glow tempted me, but cradling the cup in my hands, I shook my head. "If we had months instead of minutes, maybe, but when I finish this tea, I'm leaving." I smiled to soften the rejection. "Besides, you've made a life here. You have a job, commitments—"

"My contract ends in a month…I wouldn't renew it if I thought…" Fumbling in his pocket, he started over. "If you'd *consider* giving us another try, I'd leave here in a heartbeat."

He slipped a ring on my finger. "Give me a month. If you even suspect we have a chance, say the word. I'll leave my job and follow you to Manhattan."

Setting down my cup, I swiveled my hand, letting the marquis diamond shimmer beneath the overhead lights. *Something's familiar*...Forgotten memories rushed in, and I blinked back sudden tears. "This ring was your mother's, wasn't it?"

His lips bunching, he gave a curt nod.

His expression held hurt mixed with hope—yet beneath it, the look of love. "You're giving me her engagement ring when I'm...when I have to..." I broke off, not wanting to voice the inevitable.

His Adam's apple bobbing, he swallowed. "Then don't think of this as an engagement ring." He lifted his shoulders. "Consider it 'earnest money.' " His lips curled in a half-smile. "At least, I'm earnest."

Was Rafe always this sensitive? Swallowing the lump in my throat, I recalled the night I'd waited and waited. *No, not always, but how much was due to immaturity?* I pressed my lips together. *And how much was Atsuki's doing?*

The airport's chimes sounded, followed by an announcement.

I glanced at my watch. *Between the three-hour boarding window, thirteen-hour trans-Pacific flight, LA stopover, connecting flight, and cab ride from the airport, it'll be twenty-four hours before I get home...to my empty walk-up apartment...*

I thought of the busy weeks ahead with my new job description. *But if Atsuki arranged my promotion, will I even have a job?* I sighed, too tired to think that far ahead.

Then I remembered the solitary nights in New York, comparing them to my recent evenings in Tokyo. I looked into Rafe's glistening eyes. *Are those tears or just the reflection of the overhead track lights?*

"Flight 2654 now boarding for New York at gate G 47."

The loudspeaker's nasal voice sliced through my thoughts, and I flinched.

"That can't be your flight."

"No." I shook my head as I again glanced at the time. "But it reminds me. I've got to go through security, customs, immigration—"

"Stay…" He placed a light hand on mine.

"I can't." *I won't slide down this slippery slope.* Steeling myself, I drained the cup. "I've got to go." The diamond flashed under the lights, capturing my attention. *How I'd dreamt of this moment, but that was two years ago.* I handed back the ring.

"No, keep it." Again, Rafe's hand covered mine. "At least for a month, then if you don't want it, send it back. I'll understand but give us a chance. Give *me* a chance…"

The attraction was strong. Magnetized, I couldn't pull away.

"A month." He lightly closed my fingertips around the ring. "That's all I ask."

I glanced from our hands to his warm, hazel eyes. A calmness entered my chest, as if my heart knew better than my mind, and I breathed deeply, savoring the moment.

"Flight 2654 now boarding for New York at gate G 47."

But reminded of time, I shook my head. "It's too

late." Pulling free, I set the ring on the table and used my hand as leverage to stand.

Again, he slid the ring on my finger. "A month…that's all I ask."

"I'll…" My shoulders slumping, I sighed, then glimpsed the tearoom, burning its image into my memory. *Where he proposed*…"I'll think about it." On a whim, I took out my phone and snapped a picture of Rafe with the tea shop in the background.

My feet dragging, I dawdled as we approached the security line. *What am I going back* to? *A lonely apartment…an uncertain job*…Wincing, I glanced at the long, switchback queue.

A sign announced, *Ticketed Passengers Only Beyond This Point.*

"Guess this is it." I juggled my phone's boarding pass, passport, and luggage to hug him one last time.

"Stay." He crushed me against him.

As I breathed in his subtle lime scent, the tickle of his breath on my neck gave me goosebumps. "*Honestly*, I wish I could, but it's too late." I spoke before I thought—before the filters kicked in—surprised that my words rang true. I squeezed him, leaned in for a chaste peck, then broke away. "Gotta' go."

In line, I turned once to wave. Then facing forward, I looked to the future.

By the time the security line wound around the cordoned maze, he had disappeared into the crowd.

My eyes burned, and the rest of the queue was a blur. *What am I doing? Maybe it's* not *too late. Is he still in the terminal?* I glanced behind me, craning my neck to see, but Rafe was nowhere in sight.

He's gone…Fear gripped me as a bleak emptiness

gnawed at my chest.

"Next." The agent beckoned me with a crooked finger.

As I approached him, I wiped my cheeks. Dropping my passport, I fumbled with the mobile boarding pass. "Sorry. I'm just a little"—I gulped—"nervous." I took a deep breath, centering myself, and forced a wan smile.

He returned my documents and waved over the next person.

After clearing immigration and customs, I found a seat at my gate and glanced at the time. *More than two hours to second guess myself*...I opened my phone's photo app and scrolled to the recent picture of Rafe. Smiling, I trailed my fingers along his digitized face. *If only*...I sighed. *But it's too late.*

Listless, I swiped through the album until I came across my selfie. Recalling Chase's assurance that the grotto was a "spiritual power spot," I chuckled. *But right after that, my publisher* did *agree to extend my stay...Was that a coincidence? A twist of fate?*

Then something in the photo caught my eye. *Is that? No...it can't be. Can it?* Squinting, I enlarged the picture. In the background, stood a silver fox. I gasped as I recalled asking Chase how to recognize disguised fox spirits. *Apparently* kitsunes *do show their true colors digitally. So, Chase's stories were true...which means my feelings toward him were nothing more than manipulated reactions.*

And my feelings for Rafe? Were those real? I looked at the ring, turning my hand left and right to catch the light. *How can the diamond dance and flash while I feel so numb?* Drawing hope from its irrepressible sparkle, I texted him.

Ava—*Are you still here? I've been thinking...maybe we can make video calls over the Internet...or maybe you could visit...or—*

Or what? I made a quick bet with myself. *If he's still here...I'll stay in Tokyo.*

Ava—*Maybe it's* not *too late—*

I hit send and crossed my fingers. But as the minutes ticked into an hour, reality set in. *He's left the airport and is probably on the train.* My chest caving, I thought of Chase's words: "Grab opportunities when you find them." *She who hesitates...*I finished the adage with a disgusted snort. *I sure know how to fix things.*

Demoralized but lacking any other options, I checked my messages.

Low battery.

Eight percent? Oh, crap! I forgot to charge it. I dug in my purse for the charge cable. Then scowling as the phone died, I squeezed my eyes shut. *Darn it!* I left the cord plugged into Mia's nightstand. *What an idiot! Now, I won't know if he got this message or texted back until it's too late. Crap!*

The two hours crept by slower than a sloth. Bored, I walked the length of the terminal twice, first to buy a magazine and then to get a cup of coffee and bagel.

"Flight 2731 now boarding for New York at gate G 45."

*Finally...*But as I grabbed my carry-on and joined the boarding line, the consequences hit home. *I have nothing in New York. Why go back?*

I found my window seat and, out of habit, started to put my phone in airplane mode. *A lot of good that'll do.* Then I stared at the ring, losing myself in its sparkle. *Did Rafe get my text before the battery died?* Annoyed with myself for leaving the charge cable—leaving Tokyo—leaving Rafe—I lifted the window screen for a last look at Japan.

The morning sky was still as black as *Shinjuku's* crows.

It should be light by now.

A raindrop hit the window, then another and another.

Great. On top of everything else, we'll have a turbulent takeoff.

The sky let loose as a downpour pelted the plane from stem to stern. Resonating inside the cabin like hail on a tin roof, the cloudburst was deafening.

This storm's a sign. I flipped through the magazine but was unable to concentrate. *I should've stayed.*

"Ladies and gentlemen, this is the captain. For your safety, the tower's advised us to wait out the current conditions."

What next? Engine trouble?

****

Still on the tarmac two hours later, I peeked through the porthole. The rain drove sideways in horizontal sheets, blasting against the windows. As crosswinds buffeted the wobbling plane, the roiling clouds mirrored my mood.

"Ladies and gentlemen, this is the captain again. The winds are gusting at forty knots. For your safety, the tower's ordered us to deplane."

The coach class erupted in a cacophony of groans and protests.

I queued to exit, too sapped to care what happened next. After four hours of reproaching myself for leaving Rafe and Tokyo, I was resigned to yet another delay.

As I crossed the skybridge, faint strains of a familiar oldies tune wafted through the passageway, and when I entered the waiting room, the music swelled.

No! I froze in my tracks, forcing the last remaining passengers to step around me.

Rafe held an iPad, playing "our" eighties' rock video, and when the band belted, "Let's give it a shot," he sang along. After setting the tablet on his suitcase, he lifted me off my feet and twirled me in the air. Then cradling my head in his hand, he gripped me in a bone-crushing embrace as he tilted me backwards in a kiss.

Laughing and crying, I struggled to catch my breath. "What are you doing here?"

"I read between the lines."

"What?" He made no sense, but I grinned, elated to see him.

"I got your text—"

"You did?"

"When you didn't answer my messages, I checked the airline tracker app and saw your flight was delayed—"

"So, *what* are you doing here?"

"I'm getting to that." He chuckled. "Mia's taking over my apartment *and* my teaching contract…"

I blinked, afraid to ask. "Does that mean—"

"I'm moving back to the States." He brandished his boarding pass. Then his entire face a question, he stiffened, as if bracing. "Ava, will you mar—"

"Yes!"

Recipes

Cherry Blossom Cookies

Celebrate Spring with these buttery cookies topped with honest-to-goodness cherry blossoms.

Ingredients

*1 (30 grams or 1.06 ounces) pack salt-pickled cherry blossoms (about 35 pieces)
1 cup flour
pinch salt
1 stick unsalted butter, softened
1/2 cup confectioners' sugar
1 large egg yolk
White sparkling sugar
*Note: Salt-pickled cherry blossoms are available online.

Instructions

Separate the intact cherry blossoms from the damaged. Soak both groups separately in water for 1/2 hour. Squeeze the excess water from the damaged blossoms, pat completely dry, chop finely, and set aside. Lift each intact blossom from the water, gently shaping its petals onto a paper towel. Cover with another paper towel, pat dry, and set aside.

Combine the flour and salt and set aside. Beat the softened butter until creamy, gradually blending in confectioners' sugar. Mix in the egg yolk. Stir in the flour mixture until smooth. Fold in the minced blossoms and shape the dough into a roll or tube. Cover it with plastic wrap and refrigerate for an hour or more.

Preheat the oven to 350 degrees. Sprinkle white sparkling sugar into a rimmed cookie sheet. Remove the plastic wrap from the dough. Roll the dough in the sugar granules. Set aside the dough and unused sugar.

Line a cookie sheet with parchment or a silicone baking mat. Using a sharp knife, slice the dough into 1/3-inch-thick rounds. Place them on the cookie sheet, leaving an inch between the cookies. Arrange the intact cherry blossoms on top, lightly pressing into the dough. If desired, dust the tops lightly with the remaining white sparkling sugar.

Bake at 350 degrees for about 15 minutes or until the cookies' edges start to brown. Cool for five minutes on the cookie sheet. Then carefully transfer the cookies to a rack to cool completely. Yield: 12-15 cookies.

Matcha Mochi

Like matcha tea? You'll love these springy treats!

Ingredients

1 1/2 cups sweet (aka glutinous) rice flour
1 cup sugar
1/2 teaspoon baking powder
1 1/2 teaspoons matcha (green tea) powder
1 cup water
3/4 cup coconut milk
3/4 teaspoon vanilla
*3 tablespoons confectioners' sugar
*Note: Rice flour may be substituted for confectioners' sugar.

Instructions

Preheat oven to 275 degrees. Grease an 8-inch square glass pan. Combine the rice flour, granular sugar, baking powder, and matcha powder. Set aside. Mix the water, coconut milk, and vanilla in a separate bowl. Gradually stir the wet ingredients into the dry ingredients, mixing until smooth. Pour the batter into a well-greased glass pan, cover tightly with foil, and bake for 60-75 minutes, or until the top is soft and gelatinous, yet holds its shape when touched. Remove the foil and set aside until it cools. Then recover with foil and allow to set overnight at room temperature.

Turn the *mochi* onto a confectioners' sugar-dusted cutting board. Wrap a sharp knife in plastic wrap and cut the *mochi* into small cubes. Generously dust all sides of the cubes with confectioners' sugar. Yield: 2 cups.

A word about the author...

Dr. Karen Hulene Bartell is a best-selling author, motivational keynote speaker, wife, and all-around pilgrim of life. She writes mainstream fantasy steeped in the supernatural, frontier romance, and multicultural, offbeat love stories that lift the spirit.

Dr. Bartell lives in the Piney Woods of East Texas with her husband Peter and her 'mews' - three rescued cats and a rescued CATahoula Leopard dog.

http://www.karenhulenebartell.com/